**THE PLENUM
CHRONICLES**

THE
DATACENTER

K.S. ALLRED

This book is dedicated to the survivors;
those holding it together,
the ones falling apart,
and the friends we lost.

1

After

I'M SWIMMING IN A sea of antipsychotics. I want to answer the question, but opening my mouth is like moving a train with my bare hands. My hands lay limp in my lap. My dirty, broken nails with chipped nail polish, my hands with bruises and the scabs of wounds that haven't healed.

"Danielle," the doctor says. "How're you feeling?"

He doesn't have the doctor vibe; no white coat. My head moves to track something in my peripheral vision, but there's nothing there. The room is barren, an exam room with chairs, locked cabinets, and a counter he's using as a desk. He's watching me.

"Danielle?"

I'm fascinated that my name is a question. His name is a question too. If he told me it, I've already forgotten. So much of what's going on is a question and it's impossible to separate if it's the drugs or something else. "Danni," I correct him.

"Okay, Danni. How do you feel?"

I feel like an inhuman thing, that deep in my core, I'm flawed beyond repair. All eyes are on me, and not just his insistent eye boring into my consciousness. Every hole in the wall and ceiling is an eye, an unblinking eye. The floor is covered in cheap off-white linoleum. I look at it. It stares back.

"Can you look at me?" he asks. His voice is kind, but his eyes are probing in a way that makes me shift in my seat.

The request initiates movement; I can't move unless there is impetus. I have no momentum of my own. I turn to him.

"What are you seeing?" he asks.

"The walls have eyes." I think I say it to be ironic, but I have no way of knowing. I'm disconnected from reason.

"Do you feel like you're being watched?"

I shrug in my first voluntary movement of the session. He's about fifty. I'm less than half his age. But I feel infinite, as if I've existed in this room for a thousand years, and at the same time like a single-celled organism that lives for a day before breaking down and disappearing as if it never existed. He leans in, placing his elbows on the counter and his head in his hands. His brow wrinkles. This must be his concerned face.

"Can you answer my first question? Do you remember what it was?" He examines me under the microscope of his preconceived notions of reality.

"How do I feel?" I ask myself the question. He nods and rolls his hand, bidding me to continue. "I'm a puppeteer inside a marionette." The absolute silence of the room soaks into my ears and for the first time, I notice the smell: antiseptic. This place feels sterile. It's antithetical to who I am.

"Can you tell me what that feels like?"

I slump in the chair. "I'm grasping for strings to move my dead limbs. It's like the nerves that make my muscles move are severed, or maybe they're floating around me, outside my body."

"Are you floating outside your body?"

"If I say yes, will you change the drugs?" My head rolls and my eyes find his penetrating stare.

"Are you sleeping?"

"I need to leave." I'm unable to get up and open the heavy wooden door to find my way out.

"Danni, I think it's important that you're here," he says.

"Can I leave?" The question has so many meanings. *Am I allowed to leave? Am I capable of leaving?*

"Not right now," he says. He exhales and rubs his forehead.

"But I can?" I wonder if the door is locked. And if it isn't, would the next one be?

"Your evaluation hold is up today. Staying will be up to you."

I register mild surprise that I've been here three days. "So I can leave?"

"Are you sleeping?"

It's only been three days since it happened. Maybe I can still get my life back. If I can get out of here.

"I don't know if you'd call it sleep. I'm unconscious for twelve to fourteen hours a day." *And a zombie for the rest of the time.*

"No more nightmares?"

When I close my eyes at night, the things I've seen are seared onto the backs of my eyelids. Sleep is the enemy. "I don't remember them."

"Why don't we start at the beginning and see where we should go from there." He tilts his head. "Do you remember what brought you here?"

I spit laughter, a soulless bark.

"Is it funny?"

"I don't have the luxury of forgetting."

"Why do you call it a luxury?" He's so nonchalant. I squint at him.

"Is that a serious question?" I'm not trying to hide how ridiculous I think it is. The things I've seen are burned into my brain in such stark contrast that it's like looking at an old monitor with screen burn. I still see it when I close my eyes. I'll always see it. I close my eyes tight and shake my head as if it will dislodge the thought.

"Yes." He nods for emphasis, to assure me of his sincerity. I sigh out of exhaustion, not ready to abandon my defenses.

"If I could forget, I wouldn't be here. I'd still have a job. Maybe not, but I could look for a job. I'll just write down *Contosa Mental Health* as my mailing address and see how many calls I get. Wait, I don't have a phone. I need to get out of here."

My teeth chatter from clenching my jaw too long. The tension of being awake for a day and a half straight is ratcheting up my spine. But I had slept. Or had I? Maybe they just strung the days together with artificial light and woke me as soon as I fell asleep.

3

"Why is not having a job the first thing that comes to mind?" Now he leans back, uninterested in his own question. He must get many interesting cases. I'm boring him. The girl who went crazy wanting to keep a job. If I minimize the trauma, maybe it'll be manageable. I can convince myself to be okay long enough to fake it until it is okay. But that's not how this works. A squirming feeling in my chest reminds me, a feeling I don't yet have a word for.

"Oh, silly reasons. I like to eat. I have a certain predilection for indoor plumbing." I'm unable to emote, but my sarcasm is fully intact. No facial expression needed.

"Do you feel those things are in jeopardy?"

"They were pretty fucking precarious before all this shit." A twinge of pain ripples through my chest. My breath hitches in my throat.

"You okay?" Nodding, I wave him off. He continues, "Let's start there."

The cloud of medication is thick like soup; cream of Risperdal or Seroquel. I can't remember. "Start where?"

Water soaks into my soft-soled shoes, seeping into my socks. Flinching in surprise, I pull my knees to my chest. Nothing indicates he sees what I see. I look at him to confirm my reality. He doesn't. I lower my feet back down and swing my foot, splashing two to three inches of standing water. The water isn't coming from anywhere: The doorway is dry, the faucet is off, and the walls aren't weeping. I'm an island in the world's tiniest lake. But after what I've seen, this is pretty tame. A faint, high-pitched buzzing noise permeates the room, like cicadas but two octaves higher.

"As you said, 'before all this shit' and when things were 'fucking precarious.'" He smiles like he's in on a joke.

I tap my foot against the surface tension of the water, daring him to notice. He looks at me, giving no sign that he sees what I see. I'm afraid to look, afraid it's real and terrified it's not.

"Fine. Let's talk." My hands clench in my lap. I'm trying to keep from scratching an itch that I'll never be able to reach. I check the water level again. Maybe it's best if I don't tell him everything.

2

Before

BEFORE MY FIRST TECH interview, Carlos gave me a book to read. That's how I fell in love with technology. Specifically, it was learning about binary. A bit, a contraction of *binary digit*, is either on (1) or off (0). A bit is either on or off, zero moral ambiguity, zero doubt. It was simple and elegant. It represented order and predictability in a world where I had none. My life was a complicated and confusing mess consisting of a checkered past, a trail of bad relationships, and many, many questionable choices. I was whatever the opposite of binary was. And I was running late for work, again.

"Little bitch," I snapped at the ball of fur and teeth. She lunged forward, pulling the leash taut. Carlos's apartment door was a few steps from mine, and I'd managed to drop my purse, the dog treats, and lunch bag. The 15-pound furball bit me as I tried to wrestle the treats away from her. I picked up everything, huffing as I slung the heavy purse over my shoulder.

As I lifted my hand to knock, my purse slipped off my shoulder again. I gave it a withering look and instead of knocking just opened the door and threw my bags down inside. Without looking behind him, Carlos waved with his left hand, as his right was furiously clicking his computer mouse. His long, curly hair was pulled into a low ponytail.

"That's what you get for fucking with me," he said, laughing.

"I can see you're fully caffeinated. Up early or still up?" I asked, pushing my things far enough inside so I could close the door and drop the leash.

"My guild had a thing last night," he said, stroking his short, sparse beard.

I nodded in understanding even though he hadn't turned around. "I hate this dog." I examined my hands where she had chomped down but didn't break the skin.

He spun in his computer chair. "No you don't. Otherwise, you'd let your roommate leave her alone for fourteen hours a day."

"It's so she doesn't shit on the carpet. I have a deposit to think about."

"Whatever you say, my evil little sister." He nodded. He didn't believe me, which was fine; I didn't believe me either. Carlos wasn't my brother; we'd been friends since high school. He had bestowed the title on me, not little sister but evil little sister. It suited me just fine. Although Carlos doled out wisdom more like a grandpa than a brother.

Carlos's apartment was less apartment and more of a place to sleep between gaming sessions. It was always dark, smoky, and everything had a finely cultivated layer of dust. The fridge held soda and little else. The kitchen was for making coffee and nuking triangle pizza nuggets that passed for food. In the space designated as a dining room were two computer desks, one for Carlos and another for guests since the last roommate abandoned it. When he had a job, this is what he called *living the dream.* All he needed in life was caffeine, a fast internet connection, and a place to sleep.

"How's things with the roomie?" he asked, putting his ankle on his opposite knee.

"Dreaming about me apparently." I threw my hands up to illustrate the ridiculousness of it.

"Like *dreaming about you* dreaming?" Carlos raised an eyebrow.

"Yes, which is stupid. It was like this whole thing when we decided to become roommates where she was worried I was going to hit on her. Seriously, no chance of that. But now she seems disappointed that I haven't. Then she tells me this shit and it's super uncomfortable."

"Could be worse." He shrugged.

"Could it, really?"

"Remember when she thought you slept with her ex-boyfriend?" Carlos couldn't keep himself from laughing about it.

"Oh my god, don't remind me. She cried, yelled, and then when I finally convinced her I was joking, she didn't talk to me for a month. That was a great month." I sighed. "Now look at me. We live in a world where Kurt Cobain is dead and I'm taking care of her dog, who she named after Britney Spears. If that's not a commentary on this post-dot-com-bubble world we live in, I don't know what is." I took a twenty dollar bill out of my right pocket and set it on the counter. "For helping with Britters this week."

"Thanks." Carlos wouldn't take money from me unless he'd done something to earn it. I couldn't give him much, but he walked her and picked up her crap. "Cobain's been dead for years; maybe you should get new heroes. And what do you have against Britney?"

"It's more about the pop culture landscape in general." In truth, I wasn't ready to move on from the '90s. The world was moving on from the decade where I finally got to be cool. Well, relatively cool. I had still been the poor kid at an upper-middle class high school trying to fit in. But for the first time in my life, it was cool to shop at thrift stores. I wore ripped, hand-me-down jeans that were two sizes too big, and people no longer stared or giggled. The '90s were a time where authenticity was revered and selling out was bad. Those were things my soul needed, and I wasn't ready to give them up just because it wasn't fashionable.

Carlos shrugged. "Just saying, maybe it's time to move on from grunge."

"Said the man smoking cloves and wearing Doc Martens. How's the job hunt?"

"It's industrial, not grunge, and it's shitty. Severance ran out two weeks ago, the unemployment check is a little help, but it won't be coming forever, and word is there are three to five hundred applicants for every tech job. I can't even get a help desk gig. I'm competing against guys with computer science degrees with management experience for a low-paying call center job." He lit another clove cigarette and took a deep inhale.

"Sorry to hear that," I said.

"That's the world we live in." He spun back around in his chair. "What do they say? *What doesn't kill you makes you want to die?*"

"I don't think that's it." I set the dog treats and leash on the counter next to the twenty-dollar bill.

"I'm sure it's something like that. Come on, Britters. Time for a nap?" He patted his lap and Britters jumped up, wagging her tail, tongue lolling out to the side as he scratched her behind the ears. I checked the time on my flip phone.

"Shit. I'm going to be late."

"Aren't you always late?" he asked.

"Like five minutes. I'm in I.T. It shouldn't even count. 'Danni.'" I deepened my voice and tried to make every word sound as awkward as possible in an imitation of my boss. "'It's important that we have a presence in the building at eight, when people begin working. Information Technology is customer focused. If we're not here to serve the customer, we aren't serving our purpose.'"

"He seriously said that?" Carlos frowned.

"Basically."

"Well, better to have a job," he offered, and I felt a moment of guilt for complaining about my job, but I kept going.

"Oh, I didn't tell you the best part. They also started having us log what we're spending our time on. We have to fill out a spreadsheet and try to remember what we did every hour of every week. We're an IT team of four with the bureaucracy of a four-hundred-person team."

Carlos raised an eyebrow at that and shook his head.

"What?" I asked.

"Nothing," he said. His tone said it was something. He knocked the ash off his cigarette into the ashtray.

"Don't mess with me; I haven't had my coffee yet."

"They're capacity planning. It could be good. Maybe they have a project coming down the pipe," he said.

"Or?" I pushed.

"Or they're looking to right-size the organization." He looked at Britters in his lap.

"You mean fire people?" I was familiar with the term corporate leadership liked to use to sanitize the act of laying people off.

"Maybe, but you'll be fine," he said. "You're smart and you have more experience than your coworkers."

"And seniority." I nodded. He was right. All good points. "Well, I better get my ass to work so I can do stuff I can log. Five minutes: got coffee. Twenty minutes: read email." I winked and hunched over as I slung the laptop bag and my purse over my shoulder before grabbing my lunch bag. Carlos was right: Better to have a job; especially one with a little job security.

3

Before

IT WAS A SLOW Friday morning at the office. No one was around to notice or care that I walked in the door seven minutes late.

I leisurely made myself a cup of coffee: one packet of hot chocolate powder and piping hot coffee mixed in a Styrofoam cup. It was my poor man's café mocha. My desk was a graveyard of computer parts, a cup of various screws, tools, and paperwork I never bothered to look at or deal with. To me, it was perfect, a collection of trophies and the spoils of battle.

A good desktop tech's desk is never clean or organized. If it was, it would mean I didn't have enough work to do. Something about being surrounded by the odds and ends of the job made me feel at home. I'd adopted this as my identity: coffee-guzzling computer geek, helpful to their faces but sailor-mouthed and otherwise surly. And when the inevitable happened, some wayward soul would walk up looking for assistance, they'd look over my cubicle wall and find me surrounded by computer guts and they'd ask me: "Is there someone around that can help me with my computer?" Or my personal favorite, "Are you, like, an IT girl?" It's like walking into an operating room and asking the person in scrubs with the scalpel if they're a surgeon. I'm sure they'd want to say "No. I just cut people open for fun. You wanna hop up and let me give it a try?"

I wondered where the other technician was. He was probably in the back already, hard at work. Some people had to work hard at it to get the same amount of work done that came naturally to the rest of us. He'd had a big year, recently promoted to the Desktop Support team, meaning that we were now a team of two; he'd gotten married; and last weekend, he moved into his new house. Everything was coming up roses for him.

My year had not been so hot. Recently dumped, my roommate was either hostile or absent, my rent was about to go up, and I was trying to figure out how to ask about getting a raise the following week when I hit my two-year anniversary.

As I sipped my coffee, I gave a side-eyed glance at the open computer on my desk. I had worked on it yesterday. A woman from upstairs poked her head in, interrupting my thoughts.

"Danielle, can you come with me?" she asked.

I tried to remember her name. It was Kathy or Christina.

"Sure." I locked my computer and followed her, still trying to remember her name when I remembered she was in human resources. What I thought was someone asking for help on a computer problem was me being escorted to HR. My mind raced. Usually if there were layoffs, IT was notified the day before or the morning of. I wasn't notified, which meant only one thing. As we got to her office, I'd put the pieces together. She closed the door behind me and sat next to me in front of the desk. I sat and clasped my hands in my lap. *Don't cry.*

"Danielle," she began. I didn't correct her. Before she started, I was already calculating my next move. "I'm afraid we're going to have to let you go. As you know, the company has been affected by the current economy and we've had to make some difficult decisions. It's never easy to do this. You'll be receiving a week of severance."

"One week?" It took the wind out of me. I needed more than a week to find a job. *What can I sell?* I was always planning for things that might never happen. What would happen if my apartment burned down? What would happen if my engine exploded and I had to buy a new car? What would happen if I won a million dollars, and what kind of computer would I buy? That last one was not relevant, but some what-ifs are more fun than others.

"It's corporate policy. One week of severance per year of service." She pursed her lips.

"It would be two years next week." Maybe I wanted her to feel bad, worse than she already did. It was funny. One week was going to cost me one week of pay.

"We'll honor that and make it two weeks." She made a note.

I had to bite my tongue not to sarcastically thank her for throwing a few more nickels my way because I desperately needed those nickels. If I was lucky, I'd be able to pay my half of next month's rent and then be tapped out. Everything else she said flew around me like flies at a picnic. In my head, I was already packing my desk, making a list of people to call and things I needed to do to make sure I would still have money for food after I paid my rent.

"Review these documents. Not now; take your time. Once you sign them, we'll release your severance check," she said, handing me a folder. I took it. It took it all sitting down. My stomach twisted in knots. Her words sounded distant, as if she was far away. How did this happen to me? Did they lay off the entire desktop team? I could do this job in my sleep, and sometimes I did. But why was it me?

"That's it?" I asked.

She nodded. "You can take your time and clean out your desk. We'll pay you through the end of the day, but you can leave as soon as you've collected your things." It didn't sound like a suggestion. The door closed behind me.

I packed up a few things and left a mess of computer parts and papers. On the way out, I saw my boss out of the corner of my eye. I wanted to say goodbye, but he hurried down the hall. I couldn't blame him for not wanting to see my face, even if that made him a coward.

My coworker, the recently-married-and-just-bought-a-house coworker, was nowhere to be seen. It dawned on me why it was me and not him. I had more seniority, more experience, and was better at the job (aside from a slight tardiness issue), but they picked the guy with a new wife and a new house. I didn't have anyone counting on me. But I also had no one to count on but me.

Carlos's door was unlocked. I didn't bother knocking and went straight to the kitchen and grabbed a beer from the fridge. It was ten in the morning, but what did I care? I didn't have a job.

Britters barked and scratched at the inside of Carlos's bedroom door. "Hold on," he said. The door opened and she ran out to me. I slid down the wall to the floor with my beer. She jumped into my lap.

"Aw, fuck. It's you."

"Love you too," I said.

"You know what I mean. You being here means…" He trailed off, not wanting to say what was obvious.

"That I hate you for being right," I said.

"How much did you get?"

"Two weeks after I sign something that says I won't sue them." I tossed the folder on the floor. Britters licked my face and I scratched her behind the ears.

"Sorry; that's brutal." He shook his head.

"What was that about how stuff that doesn't kill me just makes me want to die?" I took a swig of the beer.

"Well, I think it really goes, *What doesn't kill you makes you want to die, then eventually you learn an important life lesson and get a better job making more money.*"

"Nice try." I gave him a cheesy grin and a thumbs-up.

"Well, at least you have something to fall back on." He shrugged.

He was trying to make me feel better, but it had the opposite effect. I squinted at him from the floor and shook my head.

"You could do a few nights a week, just enough to get through this. I'm not saying you should give up and go back to dancing full-time…"

"I can't do that again. It'd be going backwards. And you were the one who told me I could do something else. You said, I believe the words were, 'Why don't you go into computers? You're smart enough. You should totally do that.'"

"Shit was different four years ago. We were living in the land of milk and honey, with high-paying tech jobs on every corner. I couldn't have foreseen that we'd be wandering in the desert for forty years." Carlos sat on the floor next to me.

"We live in the desert, so technically we're always wandering in the desert."

"All I'm saying is that at least you have something you can do if you need money."

"That's not who I am anymore," I said. But what was the saying? You could take the girl out of the club, but you can't take the club out of the girl.

"Hey, it was a thing you did. It was never who you were." He pointed at me to drive home his point.

13

"Thanks, Carlos."

"And sometimes you have to take a step back in order to move forward. It doesn't mean anything other than you like electricity, food, and sleeping inside."

"You know I went from a gentleman's club to the boy's club. It's basically the same thing. In both places I'm a just a girl that no one takes seriously." I shook my head.

"You're the bravest person I know."

I rolled my eyes at him. "I don't feel brave. I feel like a disaster on soggy toast." I took another drink. "Every inch of me is exhausted and spent."

"Bravery isn't how you feel. It's what you do when you feel like soggy toast. You're going to lick your wounds, update your resume, and hit the ground running. You'll have something soon."

"How did you get so wise, old man?" I winked at him.

"It comes with the gray hair."

I took another drink. "How is this my life?"

"Stop that," he said with mock severity.

"Feeling sorry for myself? Can I have an hour or something and then I'll pick myself up again?"

"No, stop. You're drinking my 401(k)."

I laughed and offered him the bottle. He took a sip and handed it back to me. It felt so good to smile and laugh. Britters nuzzled up against my neck. "I should cash out my 401(k). That'll buy me...a month? Maybe? Good idea, Carlos."

He shook his head. "'Good idea' isn't the right phrase. It's called survival mode. You do things contrary to your long-term survival to get through what's in front of you at the moment. It's why being poor sucks so much."

Britters hopped off my lap and went to take her place on the couch. Carlos's words rang in my head. I grew up poor and it drilled into me the desire to never be hungry, to never have a cashier give me a look of pity as I counted my change and put food back. Girls like me don't go to college. Girls like me don't get out. I shook my ass for a dollar. Big deal. Other people have done worse to feed themselves. I did it till Carlos showed me a way out, showed me that a different life was possible. It worked for a while, too. I felt stupid that I ever believed it could be real.

14

"It's going to be okay, Brits," I assured the dog even though she was already asleep. "I'm going to make a few phone calls. You should get some rest. I'll take her back home with me."

"Okay. Let me know if you need anything," Carlos said, scratching his head and yawning.

4

Before

EVERY CONVERSATION FOR THE next hour was a rehash of the same words and phrases. *Hey, long time no talk. Yeah, it's rough out there. I'm wondering if you know of anyone hiring.* Rinse, repeat, about fifteen times. I called every person I knew from my last job who got laid off at the same time to see if they had any leads. One guy had started a new job the week before, went to lunch on Wednesday, and came back to find the building locked. The company had gone under with no notice aside from a sign on the door. I promised him if I heard of anyone hiring, I'd let him know.

My phone sat idle on the counter. I watched it, willing it to ring. The perfect job that I hadn't yet applied to was going to call. But the more stories I heard from people, the harder it was to be positive. I was already doing poverty math: *If I skip paying my car insurance, then I can pay electricity and eat. If I can find a sale on ramen, I can stock up and have food for a while.*

I paced the floor and shook the mouse to wake my computer. After an hour of swearing and tapping at the keys, I had an updated resume that I felt pretty good about. The name line stood out. My name in 28-point font screaming that I was a girl, *Danni.* I placed the cursor behind my name and changed it to read *Danny.* It took so little to get thrown off the pile when the pile of resumes is in the hundreds. A wall of text: too long, didn't read, toss. 10-point font and narrow margins, toss. They can be picky, and they want someone who "fits in with the team." They don't think of it as gender discrimination, they think of it as "team dynamic." Girls get offended and don't laugh at *innocent* jokes. And

I'm sure just as many managers don't want to tell their wives they hired a young woman and deal with the insecurities or accusations. I entertained the idea of a slight deception to increase my chances of getting my foot in the door. Then I backspaced again and changed my name back to Danni. It was always better to lead with the truth.

The phone hadn't rung once, but I stared at it, hoping for something to keep me from making the next call. The call I didn't want to make and also struggled with not making every day. Steve, the ex-boyfriend, if I could call him that. It'd been a few months, if you didn't count that one—okay, two—lapses in judgement. Maybe I should email him. Although that sounded like a slippery slope into another lapse in judgement. Or was a phone call worse? *He's probably at work,* I reasoned. *I'll just leave a voicemail; he probably won't even call me back.*

Ring.

"Hello," he said.

Fuck.

"Hi. How are you doing?" I felt uneasy and wished I'd thought this through. I didn't even know what I was going to say.

"I'm good. What's up? I'm at work," he said, a cheerful tone in his voice. I imagined the broad grin spreading across his face as he spoke.

"Yeah, I mean no. I got laid off today," I held it in this time. *This guy wasn't going to get to see my tears.*

"I'm sorry; that's awful. Common right now," he said.

"Yeah. I know you know a lot of people. I thought maybe you might know of an open position somewhere." It sounded impossible as it left my lips. I cringed, waiting for yet another rejection from him. I hated the rejections, but the yeses were so sweet.

"I don't know of anything, but I can make some phone calls," he offered.

"No, you don't have to go out of your way. I just thought you might know of something. You're good at that whole networking thing, people and computers," I said.

"It's no trouble." The words hung in the air. I didn't know what to say.

"Yeah, that would be helpful. Just let me know if you hear anything. I'll just be here, doing nothing, waiting by the phone," I joked and shook my head as soon as it came out of my mouth. "I'm not picky. I just need something that will pay the bills." *Way to sound desperate.*

"Sure. I'll let you know," he said.

"Yeah, thanks. I'll talk to you later."

"Later," he said and hung up before I did.

I snapped the flip phone closed and cranked back my arm like I was going to throw it into the wall, instead tossing it on the couch. Having done everything there was to do, all I was left with was either staring at the walls or watching TV. The conversation was stiff, like talking to an acquaintance, not the man who'd seen me naked and knew my secrets. This is what we'd become, lovers to strangers, ships in the same ocean that no longer pass in the night. Maybe that's all we did, pass in the night. Here I was, meaning to disconnect myself from him and still doing things that kept me connected. Maybe there would always be this invisible string that tied us together, a tenuous, fragile thing. But I couldn't snip it.

The day had taken a toll on me, and after a quick lunch, I found my way to my bed for a nap. My sleep was so deep that when the phone rang, it took several rings before I stirred.

"Hello." I turned on my side, twisting a strand of my hair in the fingers of my free hand.

"Are you asleep?" Steve asked.

"I was. You wanna come over and wake me up?" I asked, my inhibitions wiped away by the depth of my sleep. His voice was probably a dream, a dream that was about to get a whole lot better. He said nothing, but he was smiling. I heard it in his breathing. I knew the words and what they did to him, and I threw them around with abandon, something he both loved and hated about me. I made no apologies.

"I made a few phone calls. There's a help desk job opening. It's graveyard," he said.

I opened my eyes wide as I struggled to wake up. I buried my head into the pillow. Why was I flirting when what I needed was a job and not Steve in my bed? "Wow, that was fast."

"I talked to the hiring manager. They're doing interviews next week. Send me your resume and I'll forward it on to him. I'm not going to lie; he's received over four hundred applications for a graveyard help desk shift."

"I mean, it's not my first choice. No one likes doing help desk. But I've been a night owl before. I'm sure I can do it again."

"Yeah, well, the job isn't yours yet. But I can get you a foot in the door and at least off the pile," he said.

I sat up in bed. "Yeah, of course. Thanks for making the call. Even if I end up getting something else, it'll be good to get some interview practice, right?"

"Absolutely. I'm sure you have some other irons in the fire already."

"Yeah, the first thing I did when I got home was call everyone I know and update my resume." As if that needed to be said.

"Well, send over your resume and I'll get it over to him. Hopefully you'll get a call soon."

"Thanks, Steve. I really appreciate the help." It was pathetic to call him. It was more pathetic that he was my best choice.

"Yeah, of course. You know I care," he lied.

It was something he had to say because all he had were those words, because his actions said something entirely different. Our year-long relationship wasn't a relationship. He broke up with me without explanation and without fully breaking it off. I was still licking my wounds months later. I'd lost my pride, and maybe I was waiting for him to give it back to me.

"I know you do," I lied. "I'm sending it over right now."

We said our goodbyes and I pulled myself out of bed and to the computer to send the email. I hovered the cursor over the send button. *Ugh, help desk.* The graveyard shift didn't have me jumping up and down either. It was just an interview. I hit send.

My optimism faded with every passing day. The phone hadn't rung for a single interview, not even the job that Steve referred me to. The only email responses I received were automated confirmation receipts. I broke down and cashed out my 401(k) to make ends meet. They money still hadn't arrived, and I checked my back account five times a day.

My cell phone rang on the bed behind me. I jumped up and dove for it, then paused to take a breath before answering, "Hello."

"This is David Darlington with the Fabricom Group. I'm contacting you regarding the Computer Operator position you applied for to see if you were available to come in for an interview."

"Hi, David." I put on my best professional phone voice. "Thank you for calling. Yes, I'm available."

"Great. Does Thursday at three p.m. work for you?"

"Yes, that's perfect." I would have met him in a dark alley at three in the morning if it meant a steady paycheck.

He gave me the address and directions, then he hesitated. "We're on the third floor, but when you drive up to the building, you'll see a single-story building. But you're still in the right place."

I tilted my head into the phone, trying to parse his words to figure out the meaning behind them. "I'm sorry?"

"It's a little odd. The other floors are underground."

"Oh," I said. "Okay. I'll see you Thursday at three."

I snapped the phone closed and jumped up and down. Britters barked at me and jumped around my feet. Even the idea of working in a basement couldn't get me down. I'm a computer geek. I don't need things like light and fresh air anyhow.

5

Before

THE SINGLE-STORY BUILDING HAD an elevator where the only button was a down button. In the elevator, I brushed specks of something off my arm and tried to slough off the stink of desperation. I wore a white button-up shirt and black slacks. I rolled my eyes; I looked like a waiter. The buttons puckered open at my breasts and I pulled at the shirt, smoothing it. It didn't help. I dipped my hand into my shirt and adjusted my breasts. The buttons laid flat again and I sighed in relief.

I got off the elevator at the third floor onto a walkway that was open to the elements. Below the walkway was a courtyard on the ground floor, the *underground floor*. A faraway high-pitched buzz hummed all around me. It was disorienting but I didn't have time, so I brushed it off and hurried to the office where David was waiting for me at the reception desk. The office itself was empty. I took a step backward toward the door. David smiled.

"Danielle Porter?" he asked, reaching out his hand to shake mine.

I nodded, wondering if I should run. My eyes adjusted to the dim lights of the office.

"I wanted to be sure to meet you here since there's no receptionist and it'd be easy to get lost. We've had some downsizing and most of our staff works out of other locations. But the datacenter is here, so we have a bit of a skeleton crew, if you will." He chuckled as if this were funny.

"You'll be meeting with the hiring manager, Joe Powel. It's this way," he motioned down a dark hallway.

I supposed it didn't occur to them, with the male applicants, that this was weird. They seemed completely oblivious to how creepy it was, meeting a strange man in an empty building who leads the unsuspecting woman down a dark hallway. I followed him; what was I going to do, leave? We reached an empty office at the end of the hall. No pictures, no stapler, just a cup with a few pens in it. Joe nodded brusquely, stood, and extended a hand. I shook it, certain to make my handshake firm, trying to communicate my resolve and dependability in one gesture.

"Thank you, David," he said, sitting back down.

"Thanks," I echoed to David as he closed the door behind him and disappeared down the dark hallway.

Joe didn't look up at me. He was in his mid-fifties. The scowl etched on his brow and the lines on his forehead suggested he hadn't smiled since it was an involuntary response to passing gas as an infant. The hair on his head receded from his unpleasant face.

"How are you?" he asked in a clipped tone.

"Fine, thank you. And you?"

"Fine. What do you know about the position?" he asked.

"It's a Computer Operator position, working third shift. You're looking for a candidate with a few years' experience, comfort providing phone support, and experience dealing with the backup jobs."

He rocked back in the chair.

"I have four years' experience providing support on the phone and in a corporate environment. I—"

"I've seen your resume." He waved me off. Being shushed in an interview was a new experience for me. "You're not working currently?"

"No, sir." My shoulders curved forward. I'd been through this experience before, when the interviewer has made up their mind about you before you walked in. In cases like that, HR often had a hand in the screening process.

"Why did you leave your last position?" His eyes narrowed at me.

"I was laid off. It was a luxury industry that was hit particularly hard by the recession."

He scrunched his nose as if this were a detestable topic. I stopped talking.

"Steve recommended you. I don't think a lot of him. But I owe him one," he said. Maybe it was a lie and Steve had something on him. The idea he'd call in a favor for me brought a faint smile to my face. I furrowed my brow and tried to focus on what Joe was saying. "I have to interview you and because David is here, I have to make that look good. I don't want there to be any mistake about this. I am not thrilled. But you will be on time, correct?"

"Yes," I answered.

"And you will complete the tasks assigned to you?"

"Yes." At this point, I was going to say yes to just about anything he asked me.

"Because while Steve called in a favor, the favor does not include the company being taken advantage of. I still need someone who can do the job."

His candor was jarring. I picked my jaw up off the floor and gritted my teeth. It was clear that he didn't like me or the position he had been put in. The feeling was mutual.

"I understand. I assure you that I am a good employee. I am very capable and fit well into any team."

He was clearly a dick and I questioned whether I should take the job even if he offered it to me.

"Can you pass a background check?" He lowered his gaze with a look that said he questioned the likelihood.

"Yes," I said, trying not to sound offended.

"I need someone who isn't a fuckup."

"I am not a fuckup." It felt like a lie. I'm usually five minutes late everywhere I go. I had no job. It was hard not to think I was a fuckup. I also didn't swear in interviews, but apparently there's an exception for everything.

"The shift is Tuesday through Saturday from 10 at night to 6:30 the next morning. The other guy on third shift works Sunday through Thursday, so you'll be alone two nights a week. Any issues with that?"

"No."

"Be on time. Do the work. Don't make waves. Don't cause trouble. Don't complain," he said, looking at me only to gauge if I was lying to him. "Understood?"

I nodded. My throat was dry and uncomfortable.

"Good. I can't officially extend an offer till the background check clears. We need to stay in here long enough so there aren't questions."

"I'm sorry?" I said, unsure of his meaning.

"If you go walk out of this office now and I tell David that we've found the right candidate, it's suspicious. We'll sit here for"—he checked his watch—"twenty-seven minutes."

I looked at the door and then back at him. This had to be a joke. What kind of workplace was this? He turned in his chair toward the wall and buried his head in his laptop. I twisted my hands in my lap, pausing to examine my nails, then returned to fidgeting. Rinse/repeat for the most awkward thirty minutes of my life.

***

I went straight to Carlos's, knocking and opening the door at the same time. He was on his computer, where he always is if he's awake.

"Hey," I said.

"S'up," he said. "How was your interview?"

"I don't know how to answer that question. I'm just going to vent at you for the next five minutes—minimum." He punched some keys on the keyboard, pausing his game, and spun his chair toward me.

"Go," he said and lit a clove cigarette.

"This is the interview that Steve set me up with," I said.

He nodded.

"I thought he'd put in a good word for me and then I'd knock it out of the park with the interview. Get an offer in a few days and start my new adventure as a graveyard help desk chick." I took a deep breath.

"I take it that's not what happened?"

I paced the floor, gesturing for emphasis. "No. It was the weirdest fucking thing I've ever been through in my life."

"Surely not the weirdest." He gave me a look that said he knew where the bodies are buried. Which he did. Carlos probably had a better mental inventory of the skeletons in my closet than I did.

"Okay, not the absolute weirdest, but pretty fucking weird. He says Steve called in a favor and he's not happy about it but if I can promise I'm not a fuckup, then I have the job. But because there's an HR guy there, we have to sit in silence in an office while he reads email and I stare at the wall."

"Bizarre," he said.

"Thank you! I know, right?"

"You're still going to take it?" he asked.

"He's an asshole." I turned to him.

"But they pay money, right?" He took a drag off his cigarette.

"Well yeah, but—"

"Is it enough to pay your rent?" he asked.

"Yeah. I just—"

"Then what's the problem?"

"Did you hear anything I said?" I looked at him with wide eyes to punctuate my intensity.

"You know what else I hear? Your stomach. When was the last time you ate something other than ramen?" he asked.

I pursed my lips and looked away. The tightening in my stomach wasn't hunger. I didn't want him to be right. How is this my only option? What had the world come to that working night shifts for the asshole of the century was my best career move?

"It's easier to find a job when you have a job. You can keep looking. No one is saying this is forever. It's just for now. But you need to suck it up and be a big girl," he said.

"Being a grownup is hard." I threw my hands up like a child.

"So hard," he said.

25

"That's what she said." I winked at him.

"Ha ha. Dirty slut. Speaking of which, the imaginary boyfriend called in a favor for you? Is that going to cost you a blow job?"

"Gross. And no. Not saying that it's off the table, just that there was no quid for his pro quo," I said.

"That's the real reason not to accept though," he said.

"What? You just gave me this whole thing about how I should take it. Now you're telling me there's a reason not to take it?" I folded my arms over my chest.

"I'm just saying that the further you get away from that guy, the better."

"He's not a bad guy."

"God, you're such a girl. Defending the douchebag who broke your heart." He shook his head, then turned back to his computer screen.

"Fuck you," I said. But I didn't really mean it. He had a point, even if I didn't want to hear it.

"It's not good to feel like you owe him anything." He lit another cigarette and pointed it at me.

"It really did sound more like extortion than him calling in a favor. That's nice, though, right? Not every guy would extort someone for me." I smiled.

"That's true. It's very nice that, on your behalf, he'll have low morals that don't involve dropping his pants." Carlos took another drag and tapped at his keyboard.

"Take it? Don't take it? I need the money. I have to take it," I said.

It all made my head spin. Nothing about this was going to be easy. If I passed up this job, it might be another six months till the next opportunity came along. It wasn't uncommon in this job market. And what would I do? Sleep on Carlos's couch? And the big question hanging over everything: Is this really the life I want? Because Carlos did have a point: Dancing was an option. The gap in my resume could be explained by the job market, although I didn't relish the idea of that conversation in interviews. As much as the market sucks, people expect you not to have holes in your job history. And then there was the on again, off again struggle to disconnect with Steve and our relationship completely. This was another tie, another reminder of him in my life.

Carlos was typing away on his computer in his game. "Yeah..." he said, his voice trailing off. "You could always get out of IT. That's what I want to do."

I walked to the kitchen and opened the fridge, just to have something to move. "Why?"

"I took a hobby and made it a job. I used to love this stuff and now I hate it."

"What would you do?" The contents of the fridge were two beers, soda, and a bottle of ketchup.

"I dream of being a truck driver, or working on an assembly line. Anything that doesn't involve talking to the public."

"Are you joking right now? You're the one that talked it up and said it was such a great career path. You're the one that got me into this field."

"You don't have to do what I do." He shrugged.

"You're my Obi-wan. What would happen to Luke if Obi-wan hated being a Jedi?" I closed the fridge and opened a cabinet.

"Maybe I could be a developer? I already live off caffeine and nicotine. And I thrive in dark environments. Those are the qualifications, right?"

"What do you eat?" I asked.

"I don't. It's too expensive," Carlos said.

"Good call." I nodded and shut the cabinet door.

6

After

THE FORM IN FRONT of me demands answers. The woman in scrubs nods with a head tilt. She feels sorry for me, and I hate her for it. The paper asks my name, age, and address. *Will I still have an address after this?* I worry that everything in my life has been wiped away for reasons I don't understand. I'm holding a pen in my injured hand. I don't remember picking it up. It's a cheap ballpoint pen with a fake sunflower taped to it—a cheery detail in a dreary place. My hand throbs and I can't decide if I should pick at my chipped nail polish or the freshly scabbed-over wound on my hand. I poke at the wound. It reopens.

"Do I have to sign this?" I ask. I look around for someone to answer, but no one looks at me. Can they hear me? Can they see me? *Am I really here?*

At the top of the form, bold capital letters scream at me: CONSENT FOR VOLUNTARY INPATIENT TREATMENT.

"I have commitment issues." My voice sounds apologetic. Maybe that's the real reason the woman in scrubs feels sorry for me: I'm not funny.

"You don't *have* to." Her tone suggests it's in my best interest.

"But *should* I?" I hide my now-bleeding hand behind my back, afraid of what she'll say or write in my medical records if she sees it.

"The fact that you're asking someone you met five minutes ago says something about the place you're in." Her weak, forced smile makes me think she's trying to come across as compassionate. Her badge says her name is Darla. I used to have a badge with my name on it. "The doctor recommended that you continue treatment on an inpatient basis."

I try to read it again. The words are bouncing around, refusing to form sentences. Nothing makes sense. I scan the room for answers but the only things I see are white walls, linoleum, and heavy wooden doors that require a badge to get through...just like my job.

"Can you read it to me?"

She smiles, pointing at the first section, but her eyes are lifeless and dim. I stiffen and jerk back when she reaches toward me. "It says you've read your Patient's Bill of Rights, that you consent to treatment, and you've been informed about the types of medication, examination, and procedures that might entail. It also states that to be released you'll need to be discharged or provide seventy-two years' notice."

"I'm sorry?"

"Three days." My eyes follow her finger as it finds the spot on the page. She said 72 years. I heard it.

"I provide you notice?" That *sounded* voluntary.

"Yes. Notify the staff." Her smile wraps around her face.

Nothing about this feels voluntary. The woman's mouth widens, baring rows of teeth like a shark until it takes up her entire face. I chuckle because she's quite literally all smiles. I step back, faltering before regaining my footing. I rub my arm. It's like feeling a hair on my arm only to discover it's a black widow. I have a constant feeling that something is crawling on me, but instead of it being on my skin, it's in my chest.

A young woman in scrubs, with short dark hair and glasses, flashes me a smile as she walks by. My eyes snap back to Darla, whose smile is closer to a sneer, but at least it's in proportion to the rest of her face this time.

"I can't tell you what to do. Either you decide to get better, or you don't. But wouldn't it be nice not to have to live like this, Danielle?"

She puts the pen in my hand, a soft gesture that feels like she's twisting my arm. There's a lullaby in her words: *How wonderful it would be not to feel like this*. To be in a place where someone can take care of me.

"My name is Danni." I sign.

"Ivy, can you take her to the third floor and get her settled in?" The young woman with short dark hair and glasses turns around and comes back toward me.

The floor begins to shake. Someone is screaming. A man in scrubs hurries over and then slows, approaching me like I am a wounded feral animal.

It's me. I'm screaming. My heart beats in a stuttered rhythm.

I pivot and run the other direction; the ground shakes with more intensity at every footstep, moving toward and away from my feet in an unpredictable rhythm like a clatter bridge on a playground. Falling to the floor, I claw it for purchase but find none. My blood smears the floor as the wound widens. My entire body quakes in time with the ground. Dozens of small shadows are cast across the room, giving the impression that the lights are flickering. I squeeze my eyes closed, refusing to believe the lies they are telling me.

7

Before

MY FIRST DAY ON the job, I showed up at two in the afternoon. I checked and rechecked my notes from the call. Yes, I wrote 2 p.m. Showing up in the afternoon made it feel like I was already late. I anxiously checked the time again and the printed directions. I pressed the down button, entered the elevator, and traveled down into the earth. This time, I had a few minutes to take in the courtyard. The building was like a zero on a digital clock, hollow in the middle, with fake grass at the bottom. Planters, with real plants, dotted the perimeter of the courtyard. The office was on the third floor, which was the second floor if you counted from the bottom floor up, which would have been the normal way to do it. The building seemed inverted, with all the windows facing toward the inner courtyard instead of the street like a normal building.

I'd wasted enough time taking in my surroundings, so I headed to the office with the reception desk with no receptionist. The door was locked and I didn't have a badge.

In a few minutes, I'd be officially late for my first day. The elevator dinged, followed by quick footfalls and a shuffling sound. A guy about my age was jogging while shouldering a red backpack on one side. It clattered like broken pieces in a box as he ran. He had brown hair, was six-foot flat, and while not exactly overweight, he was broad. I hoped that he was going to let me in. I know a geek on sight, and this was a geek, one of my people. So I smiled. He got to the door, went around me, and swiped his badge; the door beeped to allow him in.

"Hi," I said.

"Hey," he said, but it was more of a question.

"I'm the new girl," I said motioning toward the door.

"The new guy is a girl?" he asked.

"Last I checked," I said.

"Dan?"

"Danni," I corrected. "It's short for Danielle, but everyone calls me Danni."

"Well okay, Danni Dan." He swung the door open for me, gesturing me through. I tried not to roll my eyes. He scrunched his forehead, so maybe my annoyance wasn't as well hidden as I thought.

"Thanks," I said.

"Are you a casualty of the economy?" he asked.

"You mean is that why I'm working the graveyard shift on a help desk?"

"Pretty much."

"I got laid off a month ago." The hallway was a dark tunnel without a light at the end of it. My eyes adjusted to the darkness of the office. As we moved down the hallway, a faint glow appeared and my shoulders relaxed half an inch. "That's what happens when you work for a golf company and business goes in the shitter."

It was my habit to swear often when I first started a new job. My first technical job, I was the only girl on a team of almost thirty guys. Unbeknownst to me, they had been warned to be on their best behavior. After a few hours working with them, I realized it was eerily quiet and not a single one swore or cracked a joke. It was like someone had died and they were in mourning. I said *fuck* every other word until they relaxed and it no longer sounded like I was working in a library. As the girl, I needed to set the tone and give them the heads-up that I was just one of the guys.

He raised an eyebrow and then nodded as if he understood. "I've been here for five years. But it's a good gig. We lease the bottom two floors. They used to be full. They moved some of the operation offshore, but it's too expensive to break the lease and they can't find anyone to sublet it to. Lots of office space available these days."

"Yeah." We reached our destination deep in the back corner of the building. The hallway curved to the right as we walked up to a counter; the help desk area was open to the hallway. Off to the side there was a large wall, in a track that went in front of the counter.

"It's a wall. It slides and closes off the room. Not that we close it very often. Oh, this is Jason. And I didn't introduce myself. I'm Rudder."

Jason squinted at me.

"Dan is a Danni." Rudder motioned at me with a thumb.

"Huh, I wonder why he didn't mention that?" Jason said. "All we were told was that Dan was starting today. But we're second shift; some stuff doesn't filter down to us the same as it does for first shift. Right?" he asked Rudder.

Rudder shrugged in reply.

"You good if I give her the tour?" Rudder asked.

Jason gave a thumbs-up as he dropped into his chair and turned to his computer monitor. The next ten minutes were a whirlwind tour of the eighty-to-ninety-percent empty floor. During that time, I got the whole history of Fabricam Semiconductors, or at least the last five years of it. How the help desk and datacenter used to be in a Fab off McDowell and business was booming so they expanded into another building, but then the semiconductor business started to wane. They moved some stuff offshore to save money and they ended up reducing headcount and closing the Fab entirely.

Rudder talked fast and walked even faster. We exited the main office entrance, back to the walkway that was open to the outside. "Now for the tour of the fourth floor. It's mostly storage."

He pressed the down button on the elevator. "There are two stairwells on opposite sides. But I'm lazy."

It brought us to the bottom floor, also called the fourth floor. Like hearing the alphabet backward, it sounded weird and wrong. "There's not much to see, but you should still know what's here. There are rounds we do, just to check on everything. You'll walk through everything once, and the second check is just the datacenter. It's pretty much the furthest point from the stairs, another good reason to take the elevator."

"All four floors?" I asked. That would be a lot of walking.

"Just the bottom two. The top two floors are either empty or occupied by different tenants."

He badged in at the reader; it beeped and clicked. He pushed the door open and I was hit by a blast of cool air. It had a temperature differential of at least forty degrees and a pressure differential too; the room practically sighed when the door opened. The lights were low; the fans and the air conditioning unit created a constant shushing noise.

Rudder flipped a switch and fluorescent lights flooded the room. I shielded my eyes. Even though we'd come in from outside, it was very bright. Rows of servers were housed in tall black racks, narrower than a refrigerator but taller, and lit from top to bottom with small green LED lights. The room was the size of a basketball court.

"And here is the real reason we're all still in this building: the datacenter." His voice conveyed both annoyance and awe at the same time. "When they got estimates for relocating, it was north of one million dollars and seeing as rent is less than that and causes no down time, here we stay. They pay rent on an empty building and try unsuccessfully to sublet the space we aren't using."

I had no words. I followed him through row after row of server cabinets. He grabbed a clipboard from a hook on the wall. "This is the checklist. Tasks are separated by shift. Yours are at the bottom."

He walked me through all the checks, which mostly consisted of checking the lights on every server, which sounded worse than it was. If everything was green, move on. Scan for glowing amber lights and listen for beeping. Simple.

"Oh, and don't move the floor tiles."

"Huh? Why would I do that?" Redecorating was not on my agenda.

"Sometimes people move them around and it screws up airflow in the plenum."

I squinted at him, hoping there was more explanation.

"You've worked in a datacenter before, right?" There was genuine surprise in his voice that it might not be true.

"Two years call center and two years desktop support. They didn't let the desktop monkeys do much in the server room at my last job. And it was a smaller company, so the server room was more of a closet than a datacenter."

"No datacenter experience? Huh." He shrugged.

"I know my shit and I learn quickly."

"Sorry; just wasn't expecting that. Joe didn't tell us much about you. I just assumed he'd get someone with datacenter experience." He shook his head.

"I had a personal reference." My face was hot. This happened to me sometimes. People assumed a lot about me based on appearances. There would always be guys that assumed I got somewhere because of my tits, because of who had seen them or wanted to.

"Sometimes it's all about who you know." He smiled.

I exhaled a sigh of relief and halted construction on the invisible wall I'd started to build. It was possible I misread him. Rudder's lack of sarcasm caught me off guard. Typically, I spent way too much time trying to decipher people's inner dialogue based on subtle glances and tiny movements.

"Great. What was the word you used?"

"Oh, right. The plenum. I love that word," he said.

"What is it?"

"Depends on the context. It means a few different things, but in this context, it's the airspace below the floor used for cooling and for the lazy network admins to abandon network cables in. The HVAC unit next to the entrance outputs directly under the floor. Also, it's an assembly of the members of a council."

"That's...interesting," I said, unsure of what I thought about it or his regurgitating definitions at me. But I committed all of it to memory. I wanted to prove myself and master the ins and outs of the server room to show I deserved to be here just as much as anyone else, even more so. He was affable and nerdy; I could work with that.

"I love it when a word means multiple things, or sometimes just the sound of words. We didn't have a TV when I was a kid, so I read a lot. I like words. Anyhow, so here the HVAC pumps cold air directly into the plenum, the space between the raised floor and the subfloor. There are hot rows and cold rows." Rudder started walking to the back of the room, yelling over the hundreds of fans. He pointed down a row. "This is a cold row. See, the floor tiles here are perforated; the cold air comes up through the floor. The server pulls the cool air in through the front vents," he said as he took a few more steps, "then expels hot air out the back into the hot row. The heat rises, then gets pulled back into the HVAC, which is then cooled and pumped back into the floor." He grinned as if this were the coolest thing ever.

"So why do people move the tiles?"

He shrugged. "Because they're lazy? They get cold in the cold row, so they move things around while they're working and don't put them back."

"Right. Assholes," I agreed.

"Exactly." He nodded and smiled. "Speaking of putting things back, the tile puller is over here." He pointed to a large handle with two large suction cups on it that was hanging from the wall. He picked it up and slammed it onto the floor. It made a loud thud. "Pull up here and the suction cups hold the tile." He strained, lifting it to show how it worked. "Then to release, pull this and..." The tile released and thudded back into place. "Always put it back."

"Cool. Thanks."

He hung it back on the wall. He paused and then tilted his head side to side as if he were weighing something. "Something I should mention that the other guys won't..." He looked at me and back at the rack of servers. The air conditioning unit shut off and the room creaked and cracked in relief. The noise lowered a few decibels.

"What's that?" I asked.

"Well, the building can be a little creepy. We're three floors down. When this building was designed, it was going to be a four-story building." He spoke in a volume that was just below yelling so he could be heard over the hum of the datacenter.

I nodded, unsure of where he was going with this little history lesson.

"But after they bought the land and the building plans, there was an ordinance passed for this part of Phoenix. The residents didn't want a high rise, not that four floors are a lot. But you'll notice the billboards are the height of the building. It's because in this part of town, you can't have anything over a two-story building. Anyhow, they had the plans. They'd paid an architect so when they approached him with their dilemma, he decided they'd just dig down instead of building up. Then they could say it's energy efficient or something like that. So that's how we have this odd little building. I heard after it was built, the architect climbed on the roof and did a swan dive to his death in the courtyard."

I paused, squinting at him.

"Kidding, but the rest is true. It's a joke they tell all the newbies. But they don't usually tell them it's a joke."

I exhaled and rolled my eyes.

"But the thing is, the building wasn't designed to be below ground and it's open in the middle, so there were some unintended side effects," he said.

"Like?" I was expecting more *screw with the new girl* type ghost stories.

"Well, have you heard of infrasound?"

"No," I said, crinkling my brow.

"It's sound below what the human ear can hear. But even if we can't hear it, we can still sense it. It's the thing that makes the hair on the back of your neck stand on end and makes you feel like someone is watching you."

"I don't get it," I said.

"The building has infrasound. It's like sound you feel instead of hear. Like the odd feeling you get if you stand too close to the speakers at a club. Ghosts aren't real, infrasound is, and it can make you feel like you're being watched or like there's something there that isn't. I'm just giving you a heads-up because I know it can be creepy to work third shift and if you get spooked and leave, then I have to work twelve-hour shifts two days a week. So just don't get freaked out, okay? I have a second job, and it can make scheduling difficult."

"Got it. Ghosts aren't real, the building isn't haunted by the ghost of the architect that didn't kill himself, and the weird vibes I feel are just the vibrations of sounds I can't hear. So you're saying *don't be a girl* about it?"

"Well, those aren't the words I would have chosen. But sure. Don't be a girl about it," he said and smiled like he was in on the joke. "And do the checks on time."

37

"If you don't believe in ghosts, why are you warning me?" I asked.

"I've had to cover the night shift a few times. Even though rationally I know it's nothing, it's creepy. But it helps to know the scientific reasons behind it. It helps me keep my head on straight." He walked toward the back of the room.

"And?" I asked, following after him.

"And what?" He didn't look at me.

"There's more to this story," I said.

"What makes you say that?"

"Well, you just met me and you're giving me this whole speech about how I shouldn't be scared. Either you think girls scare easily, or something happened and you're worried I'll get scared and leave, meaning you'd have to cover the night shift," I said.

He looked back and raised an eyebrow before sighing, "Yeah, the position is open because the last guy couldn't handle it."

"And the truth comes out. Couldn't handle what?" I walked backward around him so I could see his face.

"He got freaked out; he tripped on a few stairs and said the building was trying to kill him. It got bad and he wasn't doing the checks or the turnover report. Anyhow, he walked off in the middle of his shift on a night where he was the only one working. You're here. I'm going to show you the backup tapes."

At the back of the room were six enormous red tanks, one after another in a single line across the wall, each one only a few inches shorter than me and too wide for me to wrap my arms around. The metal shone like polished blood under the artificial lighting. Mounted on the wall next to them was a handheld fire extinguisher with a bright red handle and black metal nozzle tip. I stopped, pointing at the large red tanks, trying to remember something Carlos had once told me.

"That's the fire suppression system. It's halon, so if it goes off, get out. Hold your breath and run. It sucks all the oxygen out of the room."

"I thought that was bullshit," I replied.

"Which part? You don't want to be in here when it goes off."

"No, I mean the 'suck all the oxygen out' part," I said.

Rudder grimaced. His eyes went up and then looked back at me. "It's not good. It goes off. Get out. Maybe it's just something they tell you to scare you enough to do what you need to do if it ever happens. They're going to replace them eventually, but not because they're bad for people. It's because they're bad for the environment.

"So, the backups are a little complicated, but there's a clipboard to help with what tapes to rotate on which days," he continued, I mostly listened to the rest of what he had to say, but I left with more questions than I started with. My expression must have given me away.

"If you have problems on a night you're alone, you can call me. If I can't answer, I'll call you back when I can talk."

"I hate calling people when they're off work."

"I'm still working, just not here, and sometimes it's slow. It's not a problem."

"Why would you do that?" I asked, hoping I didn't sound ungrateful.

"The smoother that second and third shift run, the less scrutiny we get and the more they leave us alone to do our work. The last thing you want is the boss checking in on us."

"Does he?" I frowned in disgust.

"No, not really. But we look out for each other and cover for each other when we need to."

The words made sense, but I resolved to never need to call. In my experience, no one likes being called during off hours. The admins sign up for it; they get paid more than we do, and they generally still get bitchy about being called at night. The thought of calling for help from someone not at work made me more uneasy than the joke about the architect jumping off the roof. He smiled.

"Cool, thanks," I said, not meaning a word of it.

8

Before

On Saturday, my second night working by myself, it only took a few hours before I was crawling the walls. I'd twice opened a new email to Steve and deleted the draft without sending it. First, I'd try to sound breezy, like I was just catching him up on the new job and thanking him for the reference. Then I'd cut to the chase and bring up the memories that would hit his buttons.

It was hit or miss if he'd shoot me down. The chance of that increases if he has all day to think about why he shouldn't come over. But sometimes he likes the distraction. No matter what I do, it's a roll of the dice. Unless I just walk away, but I hadn't figured out how to do that yet. I was pathetic. It's not like I didn't have other options. I cleaned up okay.

He'd never fully shut me out, even after we broke up. Okay, after he broke up with me. He still answered his phone, he still came over, still said yes about as much as he said no. The only time I knew what he was thinking was when he said yes, and then he was an open book. To him, I was a book he kept picking up and putting down, not enough to keep his interest but just enough to keep coming back.

He was like a brainteaser that I couldn't let go of. A problem I rolled around in my brain over and over until I figured it out, only I never did. Carlos called Steve my invisible boyfriend, which was fair. Our relationship was invisible. He never involved me in his life. I'd give him deadlines in my head. If he doesn't introduce me to his friends in a few months, I'll break up with him. All the deadlines flew by as I fell deeper in. I was addicted to his attention and the way he made me feel. One time he said he had love for me but wasn't in love with me. That was the biggest crock of shit I've been fed in my life. What he had was a need to alleviate his guilt about the nature of our relationship. What I needed was to solve the puzzle: Why was I desirable but unlovable?

I rolled my chair backward and spun in front of the bank of monitors to check the backup jobs were finished. A few were still running. No point going down until all the jobs were done. I rolled back to my computer. The third floor was silent except for the sound of my computer and the hum of the refrigerator in the break room across the hall. I thought about closing off the room by pushing the sliding wall closed, but I shuddered at the thought of closing off the only exit from the room. It was designed as a shipping desk, so they could close after shipping was done for the day. Most places had roll-down locking shutters for that; we had a rolling wall.

My eyes were weighted with sandbags, my neck was a Slinky, and I struggled to keep my head up. The time inched by as the post-lunch stupor set in. Even my meal had been pathetic. With the last of my money, I'd bought ramen noodles. I'd bring a packet, a bowl, and a fork and nuke it in the microwave. I walked across the hall and poured myself a cup of coffee from the same pot I made at the start of my shift, and followed it with a large pour of sugar and powdered creamer. I stirred the angry burnt concoction as I yawned and returned to my desk, determined to stay awake for the entire shift.

Heat from the coffee radiated through my body like being wrapped in a cozy blanket. It was a race to see if the caffeine kicked in before I fell asleep. I picked up the clipboard and ran down the list of checks to be done once the backups were complete. I walked though it in my head, tracing the steps I'd take... walk into the hall, turn left instead of right, walk to the end, walk back to the other end of the office. *It'll be dark*, I thought. *Maybe I'll take a flashlight.*

I saw it in my head so clearly: the empty desk and abandoned office supplies, spare keyboards and phones. Everything was the same but in my mind's eye, the pale light cast a malevolent shadow.

I exited through the double doors. Outside on the walkway, I held the clip-board with one hand and dragged my other hand across the railing. I made my

41

way down through the stairwell and out into the courtyard. It was so vivid in my mind. The night air brushed across my skin, like the touch of a lover, and a light breeze tousled my hair. The courtyard was the same, concrete planters with blooming flowers dotted along the perimeter of the fake grass, a few park benches and nothing but stars above me. Across the courtyard was a door. The door was solid, just like the ones leading to the stairwell. Solid with a glowing red sign above it. I was devoid of conscious thought, unable to look away. I moved toward it as if on a conveyor.

The wind carried whispers of unfamiliar words, but a knowing came over me as if in a dream. Answers existed behind this door. Answers that were meant for me. I reached for the handle; it was cold in my hand. A large, inhuman figure in a giant dark cloak appeared on the walkway two floors above me. The figure turned. Its features were obscured; it appeared as a dark shadow, larger than a man, without a discernible head or neck. The same knowing came to me again: The figure is death, or maybe just a type of death. *Change is a type of death*, the wind whispered. This creature would change me, kill me, or perhaps both. And just like in a dream, things that don't make sense coexisted. The figure was on the second-floor walkway and I was in the courtyard, but also, it was standing at the opening of a large canyon and I was at the bottom of a great crevasse. We watched each other, waiting for the other to make a choice.

I turned the handle and pulled the door open an inch. A piercing scream tore through the courtyard. I released the handle to cover my ears. The door slammed shut; the dark figure rose over the railing and descended into the courtyard.

Pain exploded in my head and shoulder as I hit the ground. I was awake. It was a dream. *Wasn't it?* I rubbed my head where it had landed on the concrete sidewalk. The courtyard was unchanged: no door, no shadowy figure. I'd fallen asleep on the park bench near the door to the datacenter. The air conditioning unit in the datacenter kicked on and the window rattled. In the middle of the courtyard, three floors below ground, I looked up at the peaceful sky. It was like standing in a pit, or a grave, but surrounded by an office building. Waking up in the courtyard was disorienting. If I didn't know, I'd swear I was on the ground level or a regular building. I patted my pockets and looked around. I didn't have my phone or the clipboard. *But I was just upstairs.* I pushed the thought away. I must have come down to use the bathroom, and maybe I fell asleep. *Did I sleepwalk?* The question seemed ridiculous. I had no memory of leaving the help desk, but here I was. I shuddered in an attempt to shake it off. *Infrasound. That's what Rudder said. It's nothing.* I repeated this to myself over and over, adopting it as my new mantra. The screech of the creature from my dream reverberated through my head as a faint, high-pitched buzzing noise.

9

After

I'm DROOLING ON MYSELF and pain throbs through my body every time I move, like I've been hit by a truck. The light streaming through the window is an assault on my senses, one that feels cruel and inhumane.

I pull the blanket over my head. Rolling over on my side, I wince. My arm is sore. I try to put a name to this place; the word that comes to my mind first is asylum. Do people still use that word? I like it; asylum, like sanctuary. It's a place of relief. *Why don't I feel relieved?*

My eyes adjust to the light and I pull the blanket down enough to see the bare room. It's my second night in this room. I take inventory of my surroundings: two beds, two doors, two small dressers, and one window. A door leads into the hallway and another to a bathroom. The walls are a soft beige; the color suggests a state of mind. They want me to feel beige. It's the color of neutrality. A color whose purpose is to blend into the background and go unnoticed. I'm here. How long have I been lying in bed, looking at these walls? Time is like cornstarch and water; the viscosity depends on how much force it encounters. Time has never had less meaning and yet there is tension from every second lost being here.

There's a tap at the door as it opens. It's the young woman in scrubs with short dark hair and glasses who was asked to take me to the third floor.

"Hey, Danni. How are you?" She smiles, walking in with an armful of linens.

I sit up in bed and run my hand through my hair, feeling my scalp as I go, unsure of how to answer the question. An uneasiness comes over me and a tightness starts in my chest. I want to crawl under the blankets. I cross my arms over my chest.

"It's seven a.m. Breakfast is at eight. Group is at ten."

"What's your name again? Sorry; I'm terrible with names. And faces. Basically, I'm just bad with people in general."

"Ivy." She unfurls the sheet across the length of the unoccupied bed.

"I'm sorry about before. I..." I trail off, unsure how to finish the sentence. How do I explain panic that has no logic behind it? There are no words for it; it came on like a freight train.

"Before?" She looks at me, confused.

Instead of assuaging my shame, it intensifies it because now I have to explain, and live longer in this moment. I search for the words.

"Oh, downstairs? Don't worry about it." Her easy smile puts me at ease.

"Thanks." I swing my feet out from under the blanket and onto the floor. "Am I getting a roommate?"

"Yes, sometime today. Beds don't stay empty long."

"Do you know anything about her?"

"Nope. You have some time to shower if you want," she suggests hopefully as she finishes tucking in the blanket.

"A shower?"

"A shower can do wonders for your mental health."

"Maybe." I pause. The idea of getting undressed, washing myself, and getting dressed again sounds exhausting. Something I do every day, but today it is a gargantuan effort and overwhelming.

"Great. You need anything?"

I shake my head. She lingers and for a moment, I wonder if she said something that I missed.

"I shouldn't say anything," she says in a hushed tone. She scans the room as if to check that we're really alone in the room. "Yesterday, you had a bit of an outburst and they had to sedate you."

I rub my sore arm.

"You want to not do that often, if you can help it. I know sometimes people can't. I'm just saying, if you can find a way to calm yourself, it's better for you."

"I'm not good with subtlety on a normal day," I say.

45

She gnaws her bottom lip, "There's another ward in the hospital, the violent ward. You don't want to end up there. So, if you feel it happening, try to slow your breathing. Breathe in, to the count of four." She inhales as she counts out four seconds on her fingers. "Hold for four, and exhale to a count of eight." She exhales slowly. "Your rate of breath will change your heart rate and if you can slow your heartbeat a little, you can reduce the effects of an anxiety attack."

"Do they teach you that here?"

"No. I have anxiety and it's something I read about. It helps. It's not a substitute for medication and therapy. But hey, it's free and it's better than nothing."

"Thanks," I say, looking down at my hands.

"All right, I'm off to do my checks. Be back in twenty," Ivy says and then disappears out the door. Standing takes all my energy and focus. Any coordination I once had is gone. I used to be able to spin in five-inch heels and now I'm a frail sack of potatoes. My hospital-issued slippers make sandpaper noises as they brush across the linoleum.

The water pressure is pitiful, but the water is hot. Showering in an unfamiliar place is like a complicated math equation that takes all my focus and time to solve. *Get it together.* After my shower, I'm standing in the bathroom, wrapped in a towel and realizing that I didn't bring clean clothes into the bathroom with me. The towel isn't big enough to cover me completely. I can't remember if Ivy shut the door behind her. I stare at the dirty clothes on the floor, contemplating. The possibility of being seen nude isn't the issue; God knows enough people have seen it already.

I don't know what to do in this situation. Not everyone wants to see all of this. I don't want to put on dirty clothes, but I also don't want to walk naked into the room if the door is open or right when Ivy comes back to do her checks.

I finally decide to make the towel work. The towel is so small it barely covers my breasts, and opens up exposing my thigh. I pick up my clothes in my free hand, the towel coming untucked and almost falling to the floor.

"Fuck." I secure the towel around me, opening the door with the hand holding my dirty clothes. The heavy bathroom door slams shut behind me. I nearly jump out of my skin, then the door from the hall opens.

Darla enters with a woman who's close to my age. She's pretty, blonde, and visibly uncomfortable as she looks down and away. There's something polished about her; she has clean, trimmed nails and a nice haircut. She's beautiful in a timeless way; she could get in a time machine and be the most beautiful woman in the room no matter the style or decade.

"Danielle, you're naked," Darla says. She glares at me, letting the awkward silence hang in the room to let me know how inappropriate she thinks it is. My skin flushes hot and I freeze, unsure of what to do.

"I forgot my clothes," I say, unsure of why I sound so apologetic. I'm not completely naked; I have a towel. Behind the hot wash of shame still crashing over me is a tickle of annoyance that Darla thinks it's an issue being naked in my own room after a shower. Does she live in a world where people bathe fully dressed? I bite back the feeling and swallow it.

"This is your new roommate, Erin."

Erin's eyes brush over me, then flick away, looking at the floor. It is like looking into a mirror. We are both in the limbo of our decisions.

"Hey," Erin says without looking up. She's in hospital clothes and has no belongings with her.

"Hi," I say. What else could I say? *Hey, nice to meet you, I'm crazy too.* "That bed is mine."

"Okay," she says and walks over to the unclaimed bed.

I feel stupid. But I don't have anything to say. I'm out of pleasantries, and thinking of any is more exhausting than I can manage. "Sorry."

"You and me both," she says.

It occurs to me she thinks I'm apologizing for being almost naked and not for being an inarticulate asshole.

"Please put on some clothes." Darla waits, looking at me.

"Okay." I shuffle to the tiny dresser to pull out my hospital-issued attire. This season's crazy-chic is all the rage; everyone's wearing it. I take out a pair of drawstring pants and a cotton t-shirt.

"In the bathroom, please," she says with contempt and disgust as if I was going to drop my towel and give them a show.

47

"Erin, do you need anything?" Darla asks, giving Erin a long look before staring me down.

"No..." Erin says, looking at the window. I question if she what she really meant was that there was nothing that could be brought, nothing that could be asked for that would sate her soul. I know the feeling. Darla leaves the room, closing the door behind her.

The bathroom door clicks closed behind me and I hurriedly get dressed.

"Why are you here?" Erin asks through the door.

The question surprises me, probably because it's the first time someone has asked me that. It seems like it's something that should be asked. "They said I had a psychotic break, that I hallucinated things," I say, opening the door.

"You don't sound convinced."

I shrug.

"I took too many pills. Or maybe not enough," she says.

The matter-of-fact tone sends a chill down my spine. How do I respond to that? I look at my hands and she looks out the window. I want to ask about a thousand questions. Each question sounds so intrusive. I want to know. I have a curiosity about her.

"And now?"

She looks at me. "Now what?"

"Do you still want to die?" I ask.

"Only when I'm awake," she says and turns back to the window. I'm nodding. I can understand not wanting to be awake with the addition of being afraid to sleep.

"Can you do me a favor?" Tears creep up from my chest, threatening to spill down. In a roundabout way, I'm asking for help, something I'm loathe to do. My heart thunders in my chest as if it's trying to free itself to silence my mouth.

"What's that?" she asks.

"Can you stay alive while we're roommates? I just don't know if I can stand losing someone. I mean, I don't want to encroach on your free will or anything. I just... I need people to stay alive."

"How long do you think you'll be here?" Erin looks at me, but now she's seeing me. She weighs something: maybe if she can wait that long, or maybe if she gives enough of a shit to grant my wish.

"Who knows? I think their modus operandi is to drug us to the gills, verify some semblance of sanity, and then shove us out the door with a prescription in hand." Wow, that sounded more jaded than I'd meant it to.

"Probably; they can only keep me for three days. I think we'll be okay for a few days," she says, and I feel relief.

The conversation brings something else to mind; I hadn't thought about how long I'd be here. Nothing waits for me outside these walls. I want out, but to go where? If I haven't been evicted from my apartment yet, I will be within the month. I have no job and no income. My health insurance will lapse soon. And when that happens, what will I do?

There is a knock at the door, then it swings open. "Hi." Ivy looks at us both, smiles, and nods before leaving, shutting the door behind her.

My eyes rest on the closed door but my attention stays with Erin.

"What did you hallucinate?" Erin looks at me, biting her fingernails.

"Bad things..." My voice trails off. I can't really form the words. It seems worse to say it out loud. If it only exists in my mind, I can continue to question whether it's real or not. I'm too unsure of my perception, of what actually happened, to say it out loud.

"Well then, maybe it wasn't a hallucination, because the world is full of bad things." She says it like it's a fact that since it's bad, it must be real.

10

Before

It was payday, a last-minute stay of execution. Or at least paying my rent on time would keep my roommate from murdering me in my sleep.

I burned through the entire amount because of the teetering stack of bills that I'd finally been brave enough to open. Everything was paid and a few days later, my 401(k) cash-out would be deposited, minus fees and penalties, putting put me ahead for the first time. I could save it for an emergency, or I could build a new computer. I was accustomed to my pick of terrible options. Having good options felt indulgent.

Rainy's Burger Joint was an unassuming 24-hour burger place off a main road with no indoor seating and a half a dozen tables outside. Rudder said this was the best burger place that was within driving distance and open in the middle of the night. Which probably meant it was the only place I could drive to, eat, and get back to work within the thirty minutes allotted for my lunch break. With a little money in my pocket, the cool night air smelled like possibilities and French fries. The guy behind the counter mumbled the number on my ticket. I picked up my food, and went to grab a seat and watch the traffic go by—what little traffic there was at 2:30 a.m.

A guy sitting at the far table was hunched over something, a red backpack next to him on the bench. Silkscreened on the back of his black shirt were the words *You are not what you own*. Rudder was so enraptured in what he was doing, he didn't notice my approach.

"Hey," I said.

He startled, closed a book, slid it off the table and into his backpack in one motion.

"Oh hey, Danni Dan."

"You know that's not my name," I said, taking a seat, not waiting to see if he invited me to join him.

"Technically your name isn't Danni either."

"Said the guy whose name is Rudder." I rolled my eyes.

He chuckled. "I legally changed it. So yeah, it's technically my name."

"You changed your name legally, and you picked Rudder?"

"I couldn't say my name as a kid; it came out like rudder. Eventually everyone else called me that too. Just made sense to change it. What about you? I assume Danni is short for Danielle."

"Yeah, but *Danielle* sounds like ruffles and bows. That's not me." I opened my burger and took a big bite as if to punctuate my point.

He raised an eyebrow and waved his hand as if to say *Well, there you have it.*

I nodded in understanding, conceding that he could be called whatever he wanted to be called.

"How's the night shift?"

"The time crawls by."

"There's a DVD drive in the computer in the corner; everyone brings in their own. They usually lock them up when there's a new person."

"Right. I'm untrustworthy." I shoved French fries in my mouth.

"Not you per se, but we've had some really flaky people on third shift. I've been called in to work so many twelve-hour shifts on weekends, I also lost my second job."

"Yeah, but with the overtime, would you need the second job?"

"Ha, that's funny. No. If they call me in to work a long shift, they just give me days off during the week to keep me from going over forty hours."

"That's shitty," I said.

"Hey, take my key. I usually have a movie or two in my drawer so I can at least have some noise on in the background when I'm working alone. It helps pass the time and it makes it less weird to work alone."

I took the key. "Thanks. I appreciate that."

He nodded and shrugged as if it were nothing.

I slurped the last drops of my soda and shook the ice in the cup, scowling at it.

"What are you doing here at this time of night?"

"Lunch break. My second job is just down the street and I told you about this place."

"Why do you have a second job?"

"Do you always ask personal questions of people you barely know?"

"I didn't think it was that personal. You volunteered that you had a second job. It's just weird. You have a girlfriend with expensive tastes? A pack of kids to feed?"

He swallowed.

"I guess that's a yes then."

I locked eyes with him, waiting him out.

He sighed. "I'm saving."

"For?"

"Why do you care?"

"Mostly because you don't want to tell me." I smiled. It usually worked on guys, but he didn't grin, look deeply into my eyes, or inch closer. "Okay, fine. Don't tell me. What's the gig?"

"Passion Palace."

"Is that a porn shop?" I asked.

"Adult bookstore," he corrected.

"You'll tell me you work at a porn shop, but you won't tell me why you're saving?" I narrowed my eyes as if it would help me figure him out.

"You're nosy."

The roar of a sport bike broke the quiet night and came to a stop at the corner, as the rider minded the red light. Rudder and I looked at each other and then at the motorcycle. The light turned green, the rider revved the engine, hit the gas, and popped a wheelie at the light. On the other side of the intersection, the passenger fell off the back of the bike and onto the pavement. He bounced and skidded like a stone skipping across a lake.

We were on our feet, running to the ejected passenger in the middle of the road. The bike kept going, unaware he was light one person.

"Are you okay?" Rudder leaned down and offered his hand to help the guy up.

"Yeah, I'm fine," he said. His words were delayed; he sounded dazed or drunk. He ignored or didn't see Rudder offering to help him up and pushed himself up off the pavement.

"Can I call anyone for you?" I asked.

"He'll come back," he said, looking off into the distance. "This has happened before."

My head jerked in surprise. "And you keep getting back on?"

"That's what you do. You keep getting back on. That's life, man." He started walking in the direction of his friend on the motorcycle.

The roar of the motorcycle grew louder as the rider returned to retrieve his lost passenger. I watched as the dazed man walked to him. The motorcycle pulled up to him and he got back on. I stared as they drove off.

"What the fuck was that?" I asked, not expecting an answer.

"A life lesson," Rudder said, watching the bike ride out of sight.

"What's the lesson?" I motioned with my hands.

"The night shift is weird," Rudder said.

"I guess I can get on board with that," I said, tapping a button on the side of my phone to see the time. "Shit, I gotta get back."

"Later," Rudder said, waving at me.

"Bye." I ran back to the table, grabbed my trash, and threw it in as I ran past the trash can. My soda cup bounced out. "Damnit," I said, going back to pick it up and toss it in and then ran to my pickup, hoping I wouldn't be late getting back.

11

Before

I HIT THE CURB pulling into the parking lot. Then I hopped out of the car, slamming the door, and ran to my desk before I was late. *Don't be a fuckup. Don't be a fuckup.* The words reverberated in my head. The only thing I needed to do was be on time, keep my head down, do my checks every night, and don't fuck up. I'd come dangerously close to violating the first of the very short list of rules given to me. I checked the time again on my phone; I had exactly three minutes to get back to my desk.

Movement caught my attention. A tall man in dark clothing walked along the perimeter of the building. The patch on his short-sleeved button-up shirt was likely the insignia of a security company. What kind of security guard doesn't investigate a person barreling into a parking lot at 2:30 in the morning? I swiped my badge at the reader. The door beeped, clicked, and granted me access into the stairwell. I took the stairs in short, quick steps, spinning at the landings until I reached the third floor, two floors below ground. I ran down the walkway.

I made it back to my desk a minute later than I should have. Mike, the other graveyard tech, didn't look up when I walked in. He didn't speak much, which was fine with me. But it made the nights drag. I opened my mouth, then stopped. I was going to ask about the security guard, but he was watching TV. Anything I asked would be met with monosyllabic responses or grunts.

"Backups done?" I asked.

"Uh-huh." Two syllables. I stand corrected. The clipboard hung next to the monitors; the second walk through of the night hadn't been done yet.

"I'm going to do the checks." I grabbed the clipboard. Mike grunted behind me and I wasn't sure if that was an *okay* or a *thank you*, but I didn't care. I reviewed the clipboard to verify what tasks needed to be completed: Datacenter LED checks, rotate backup tapes. I exited the office into the open-air walkway and the concrete stairwell. My steps echoed, disrupting the silence.

It was the stillness that got to me. No wind, no crickets. If I let myself focus on it, I questioned if this place was a type of purgatory. Rudder said the thing that made it weird was a type of sound. It was the opposite. Noise might be the only thing to keep me sane. Sound was my friend. I hit the push bar on the fire door at the bottom of the stairs. It opened like a jack-in-the-box, and I popped out like Jack, but I was the one in for a shock.

I faceplanted right into the security guard's chest. He was tall and thin. I had to crane my neck to look up at him as I backed away.

"Hi," I said. "I'm so sorry."

He gave me a smile and a nod, then ran a hand through his black hair. Momentarily speechless due to surprise and embarrassment, I stood dumbstruck. Way to make a first impression. His eyes were the color of blue gray storm clouds over an ocean. They seemed to deepen in color the longer I held his gaze.

"Hello. It's fine," he said. A strange smile crossed his face, an amused smirk.

"I'm Danni. I'm new," I said, looking away to avoid those eyes.

"Hi, Danni. I'm Ian. I'm new too." His eyes glinted in the light.

"Oh. How long have you worked here?" I asked.

"I have a few buildings I check on, but I've only been on this one for the last month or so," he said.

"Weird. A little longer than I've been here." I put my hands on my hips as I tried to think of something else to say and not sound like an idiot. "Did they just start to need security or are you just newly assigned?"

"I just go where they tell me to." He shrugged with a *whatcha gonna do?* smile.

"Well, at least I got the chance to introduce myself, so you know I'm not breaking in. I work here."

His brow wrinkled and he gave me a long look, followed by a wink. "I might still think that."

"You're right. I definitely have that air of the criminal element," I said.

He gave me a strange look. I shifted from one foot to the other. He said nothing. If it was a staring contest, I lost. I blinked first. "I should do my checks." I pointed the clipboard at the datacenter door.

"Yeah, of course. I'll see you around, Danni," he said, then turned around and walked away.

"Later," I said and turned to go to the datacenter. He was familiar and unsettling at the same time. I'd never seen someone's eyes change color as I looked at them; they went from blue-gray to dark blue. I wondered if I'd imagined it. Maybe it was the light playing tricks on me. The hair on the back of my neck stood up. My chest tightened and I had the sense I was being watched.

He walked the perimeter, not looking in my direction. Infrasound. It was like Rudder had said. It's just the weird acoustics of the building. I shook it off and badged into the room. I flipped the light switch and squinted in the lights. It was either too dark to read the clipboard or the pure rage of the afternoon sun. No middle ground.

I walked up and down the rows, checking the LED lights on all the servers in their tall black racks. The displays glowed through the metal mesh doors. I scanned up and down the rack: green, green, green. The first two rows of severs were all happy with blinking green lights and steadily humming away. Color affects mood and green lights all the way down were a good sign. It was reassuring.

Beep. I froze. The sound was faint. I silently counted to thirty, waiting for it to beep again. I breathed a sigh of relief; it was a hiccup.

Beep. Shit. The constant rush of air drowned out the sound of the noise, making it difficult to tell where it was coming from. I stood still, like a cat about to pounce.

Beep. I jumped to my right. The sound was coming from the front of the room.

To the right of the door, against the windows was the computer room's air conditioning unit. The massive beige box, at least eight feet wide and about six feet tall, had a small LCD display and a few buttons. I stepped closer to it.

BEEP. I jumped and laughed at myself. I should have expected it to be louder. The LCD wasn't backlit, making it difficult to read.

The letters scrolled across the LCD: POWER LOSS DETECTED. That was odd. It obviously had power. The room shook; the window rattled in its pane and the large air conditioning unit roared and shuddered back into operation. I took a step back and put my unsteady hand over my heart, trying to catch my breath and shake off my fright. The shift in air pressure and the vibration of it roaring into life had caused the window to rattle. More creepy sounds.

Beep.

"Why are you complaining? You have power." I tapped it. I always talk to computers and electronics in general. They tend to work better when you talk to them, or maybe it just made me feel better.

"Ugh, fine."

The phone was on the opposite wall. I stomped over to it, hearing my footsteps clomp loudly on the hollow raised floor. I dialed the help desk extension. "Help Desk," Mike answered.

"Hey, Mike." I had to plug one ear to hear anything on the phone. "The AC unit is beeping, and it has an error. It says, *power loss detected* but it's running, so it has power."

"What?" he asked.

I repeated myself this time, yelling it into the phone receiver.

"Oh yeah, that happens. There was probably a power fluctuation, but not enough for the generator to turn on. Hit the Enter button three times and it'll clear."

"Okay," I said. The line clicked in my ear. "Hello?"

Well, at least I knew he could form full sentences when he wanted to.

I put the phone receiver back, then walked back to the unit and tapped Enter three times. The message cleared. I waited, watching to make sure it behaved. I sighed and resumed the checks. I pulled the backup tapes and loaded the ones for tomorrow night. I walked down the ramp that brought the raised floor down to the same level as the outside walkway. The rush of the 90-degree night air embraced me as I left the 65-degree computer room. The door swung closed behind me and the windows rattled again. I shuddered, relieved to leave that icebox of a room where I couldn't hear myself talk or think. The clock on my phone said it wasn't quite three in the morning. Three hours to go and suddenly I didn't feel so optimistic.

12

After

"IT'S SO HOT IN here. Why do you keep closing the vents?" Erin asks through the darkness. Apparently, she can't sleep either.

"I don't like them open." I'm sitting awake in the dark. I'm waiting and watching. The dreams have returned and I'm sleeping less and less. Every moment, I'm on high alert, waiting for the shit to hit the fan.

"That's a strange answer." She shakes her head and opens the vents. "It's Phoenix. Air conditioning is the miracle that allows us to exist in this inhospitable hellscape."

I cringe and turn back to the wall. There's no telling what I'm waiting for. Maybe it's for ghosts or monsters or for the texture of the wall to become a mouth and talk to me. But I'm waiting, and I'm watching.

"I need to get out of here," I say.

"Why don't you fill out the form to release yourself? It's only a three-day waiting period and then you're out," she says. Erin's evaluation hold had passed but she was still here, despite saying she was going to leave as soon as it was up.

"Why?" Why haven't I? Maybe it was because until the last few days, I'd been sleeping ten to fourteen hours a day. But it must be something more. "Maybe I want to be sure I'm not crazy."

"Whatever. That's weak," she says.

"Why don't you?" I ask. I don't care about the answer. I'm just turning her question around on her.

"I know who I am on that side of the door. And I'm more afraid of that side of the door than what they'll do to me on this side."

"What does that mean?" I ask. She's piqued my interest.

"Death is on the other side of that door for me, at least right now. I want to know it's not breathing down the back of my neck before I step back into the real world."

This was a possibility I hadn't considered. Could it be true for me too? Death might be waiting on the other side of the door for me. What if the mental health ward of this place is just a way station? It's just a place where death can't get to you. How ironic would that be, that I could only be sane in an insane place?

"Do you really believe that?" I ask.

"I tried to kill myself. I couldn't even succeed at that," she says.

"Why did you want to die?" I feel a flush of shame. "You don't have to answer if you don't want to."

"Have you ever woken up every day for months and wanted to cry just because you had to be awake? Just because you had to spend a day in your own skin? Every word of my internal dialogue was how awful, unlovable, and useless I am. At some point, I decided I couldn't keep living like that and it felt like the only way not to live with it was to not live. It's not that I want to die, it's that I can't find the energy to keep living," she says.

"Wow, that's depressing," I say.

"Exactly," she says. "It wears you down, little by little, word by word, till you're so exhausted just being awake that you just don't want to wake up anymore."

I don't know what it is like to stop fighting. My entire life, I've spent fighting and flailing, just trying to survive and make it through another day without losing my mind. For all I know, I'm on the cusp of not being able to fight anymore. Maybe we all get there at one time or another, a place where we can't fight and can't stand to just *be* anymore.

My eyes flick to the vent and back to the wall.

"Where would you go? What would you do?" Erin asks. "If you weren't here?"

"I'd get a tattoo," I say.

She laughs. "Seriously? That's why you're dying to get out of here?"

A hot feeling rushes over me and I regret saying it. The feeling of being laughed at is familiar and awful.

"What are you going to get a tattoo of?"

"I'm still thinking about it."

"But you want to get out so you can get a tattoo you can't decide on?" Erin's blonde hair is fanned out over her pillow. She turns to me.

"No. I want to get out so I can work and not lose my apartment and my entire life." It didn't make sense to me that this was a foreign concept to people.

"I don't think a few days will be the difference between keeping your apartment or not."

"It is. Sometimes the difference is only a few dollars."

"No one is losing an apartment over a few dollars."

Her cavalier tone is annoying. Responses in me bubble up before I can weigh if I have the energy for a fight. "It happens. They don't take partial rent, so if you are ten dollars short and you won't have those ten dollars until after the fourth, they won't take it. Then you get a fifty-dollar late fee and then a daily fee compounded. That ten dollars ends up costing you a hundred dollars."

"Everyone can come up with ten dollars. You're being dramatic."

"Whatever you say, Scottsdale."

"That's unfair," she protests.

"What part of town did you grow up in?" I ask.

"Scottsdale, but we weren't rich or anything."

She'd never understand what it was like. Some things can't be understood unless they're experienced.

"And don't call me that," she says. "You think I think I'm better than everyone."

I shifted in my bed. "I didn't mean anything by it."

"Yes, you did," she says, her words quiet but firm.

"I'm sorry. I just..."

"Think I'm a selfish spoiled brat who has no business being depressed and that I'm doing it for attention?"

I open my mouth to dispute it, but hadn't I thought something similar? Not the brat part, but that she's pretty, with an expensive haircut and manicured nails. She looks successful and together, other than the crippling depression. The minute I saw her, I sized her up.

"I hate those words. *Did it for the attention*. It's what my family said the first time. 'Don't make a big deal. If we give her attention for this, she'll just keep doing it.' As if somehow ignoring someone with depression and treating them like you don't care that they tried to kill themselves is helping."

Her anger makes me uncomfortable and yet it's calming at the same time. I appreciate the honesty of it and the no-bullshit presentation.

"And if it was *just for attention*, isn't that a sign there is something severely wrong if I'd be willing to risk my life to get someone to care about me being alive? Not that the thought ever crossed my mind. That's not why. But if it was, isn't that a reason to fucking help someone? And isn't attention just the expression of human connection? Wanting the attention of the people you love seems like a pretty basic human need, if you ask me." There's no hesitation in her voice. Her eyes flash with intensity and she doesn't look away. Heat rises to my cheeks and I look away. The way she knows her own mind, even if it's dark and unpleasant, endears her to me.

"I'm sorry," I say.

"About what?"

"That they talked about you like that, and that they weren't there for you."

"See, spoiled brats from Scottsdale have feelings too," she shoots back, and I deserve it.

"I didn't think those exact words but something adjacent to them. I don't think you think you're better than anyone. I think that you're better than me. I'm a train wreck and a place like this was probably always on the itinerary for someone like me."

"You think you're the only one destined for a place like this? You don't have a monopoly on being fucked up."

"You're right. Judging other people in a mental hospital is like the pot screaming at the kettle about the government tapping my phone."

Erin smirks. "You're funny."

She's not laughing. I'm not sure if she means I'm funny because I make her laugh, or I'm funny like I'm not right in the head. In all honestly, both are correct. I hope she didn't think the second one.

"What did you do, before this?" I ask.

For a moment, the only sound is her breathing. Maybe she fell asleep. "I worked downtown in an office. I don't think I'm going back though."

"Did you lose your job?" I was sure that I'd lost mine.

"No, I'm on leave. But I don't want to go back. Everyone knows. Tales of my insanity are retold at water coolers throughout the company. I'm a big draw."

That's something I hadn't considered until this moment: People at my work were likely speculating about what happened.

"Who were you before this?" she asks.

"That sounds like an existential question I don't know if I'm prepared to answer."

She sighs.

"I worked the graveyard shift on a help desk. It's not that exciting. I'm a computer geek, and before that, I was a poor kid from a shitty part of town."

"Why are you here?"

"I'm the in-house entertainment," I say, half believing it. I know how to entertain.

"No, seriously. I told you," she says, and she has a point.

"Did you?" I look over, wondering if I missed something or if the drugs caused a memory lapse.

"Too many pills, or not enough." She repeats something she's said before. There's more to the story; she's oversimplifying it to move the conversation along. As outspoken as she is, there's something she's holding back.

How do I explain what happened when I don't understand it? "I did something bad," I say, with both shame and relief in admitting it.

"If that's all it took to end up here, everyone would take a tour of duty in the nuthouse."

My laugh is sharp and abrupt. If only it were that simple; the words don't carry the weight of what I did, the severity of it, and the enormous guilt I feel.

"We've all done bad things," she says.

"Are you always like this?"

"Like what?"

"So certain. Does everything in your head come out your mouth?" I recoil a bit at the sound the words make. I mean them as a compliment.

"What do you mean?" She tilts her head.

"I'm not used to people being this honest." I pause. "It's nice."

"I lied a lot over the past year or so. 'I'm fine. I'm happy. It's just allergies.' It's exhausting pretending to be okay all the time. After this, we'll never see each other again. I don't see how I can still be alive in a year, so here I get to be honest. If for no other reason than to have a break from pretending." She lets out a sigh that sounds like a thousand-pound weight is falling off her shoulders.

"I hope you're wrong, that you make it past a year. We could hang out after we get out of here." The words hang in the silence. I like her, even if her honesty is only out of exhaustion. Maybe it was never knowing where I stood with Steve, always feeling like he was holding back in so many ways. I craved the truth, even if it was awful. Erin is the best part of being here.

"Would you act like you didn't know me?"

"Never."

"If people asked where we met?"

"I'll tell them we did time together."

She laughs and the sound is a gentle melody in my ears.

"And not to ask questions or we'll shiv them like the last person that asked too many questions." Another laugh rewards me for my joke.

The door opens. I feign sleep, letting my body go limp. I'm waiting for the sound of the door closing, but it's not coming.

"It's past lights out, ladies. Stop talking. You better be asleep by the time I come back," Darla says. After a long pause, the door clicks closed.

"I don't know about you, but vague threats always put me right to sleep."

64

"We probably should get some sleep," she says. There's hesitation in her voice, a reluctance I'm intimately familiar with. But like everything else, I don't know what's real and what exists only in the folds of my brain. Now the hesitation is mine, unsure what to say in response.

"Goodnight," she says.

"Night." I say the only thing I'll allow myself to say.

13

Before

THE RINGING PHONE SHATTERED the silence and jerked me out of a light sleep. I picked the handset up, having fallen asleep without my headset on, and hit myself in the head with the receiver.

"Fuck..." I said, close enough to the handset that I'm sure they heard me. My boss would be hearing about it. *Awesome.* "Help Desk; this is Danni. How may I help you?"

Static. The other end popped and buzzed. A faint voice said the words, "We're down."

"What's down?" I adjusted the cord on the phone.

"This is Bravo building. We're down," a man said.

I reached for my headset and hung up the phone, thinking it must be the cord. "What's down?"

"Everything. Nothing works," he said.

None of that was helpful.

"Is your computer down or is the entire Fab down?" *Fab* was lingo for the building where they fabricated semi-conductors. If no semi-conductors were being made, then I was going to have to wake up half the company. If his computer was down, I logged a ticket and told him to move to another one. Big difference.

"I... it looks like things are coming back online. Never mind," he said.

"Can you give me some more information? I need to log it for my shift turnover report," I said.

The line was dead. He hung up and he didn't give me a name or a number. Shit. I was going to have to either not mention it or tell first shift I didn't get any information and look like an idiot. The night was not going well.

Due to my unscheduled nap, I was late for the first round of checks. Still breaking rule number one. Rechargeable flashlights were plugged under the desks, in case of power outages. The generators kept the datacenter humming; there was no emergency lighting near the help desk. So there were flashlights. Since the floors were poorly lit, I took a flashlight on my rounds. The guys didn't. I didn't care if they made fun of me; it just meant I was smarter than they were.

The third floor was quiet. The stillness reminded me of a cave where occasional noises came from deeper in the caverns. I told myself it was the building settling. Like I was settling for this job. Or it was infrasound. I walked the floor, passing empty workstations with cubicles half disassembled. The area was labeled *Sales*. As recently as five years ago, I'm sure this area was bustling with action and even late at night, there would be a sales guy making a deal with an overseas client. All that was before. How many of them are still looking for work? I shuddered. Unemployment was more terrifying than an abandoned building.

I swept the light over the room. The stillness seeped into everything.

The rest of the floor echoed the silence of empty offices and lost jobs. The light from my flashlight caught the dust hanging in the air.

Nearing the main exit, I shut off the flashlight. Light from the walkway lit the rest of the way. The night sky's scattering of stars was a negative image of the dust in the beam of my flashlight. I leaned over the railing and looked up. I felt like I was looking up from the bottom of a well, a feeling I couldn't shake any time I looked up from what had to be over thirty feet below ground. I imagined that if it rained, the courtyard would fill like a bathtub and I would drown. My body shuddered involuntarily. I moved on, taking the stairs down to the fourth floor. My steps reverberated against the cold concrete walls of the stairwell. I swung open the door and stumbled, then caught myself. My jaw hung open as I stammered for words. If any had come to mind, I would have been afraid to utter them.

The wingspan of the moth was easily larger than the width of my hand with fingers spread. I didn't know that they grew to that size. It was black and brown with a line of iridescent purple across it. It perched on the planter just outside the stairwell. An irrational fear gripped me that if it took flight, it would come for me. The body was large and fleshy, as if it had never fully shed its caterpillar form. I was locked in a staring contest with two dots on its wings; they were unblinking eyes. I pulled out my phone to take a picture. I had to know what it was. I snapped the picture and examined the two-and-a-half-inch screen on my flip phone. The photo was grainy at best, and I wondered why cell phones even had cameras if they sucked so much.

I reached out with the clipboard, tapping the planter. It didn't move. I tossed the clipboard, aiming not at the moth but next to it, but it landed on it and clipped one of the wings. The moth took flight and I ducked and screamed. When I peeked from beneath my hands, the moth was gone. I touched the clipboard where it had touched the moth and examined my fingers.

"That was stupid," I siad. My ears popped. A quiet, high-pitched noise sounded as if it was coming from all around me. I put my finger in my ear, rubbing in an attempt to knock the sound out of my head.

I still had a job to do, so I made my way to the datacenter to do the checks. The lights were off, leaving only the emergency lights on. The server farm seemed to glow amber; my stomach sank and my pulse raced. I checked my phone to make sure I hadn't missed any calls. Maybe the guy who called was right; maybe the whole Fab was down. I ran down the aisles. The LED scrolled a random mix of letters, numbers, and symbols. The only characters that were clear were the words *Panic Fault*. I pulled the pen out my back pocket and jotted down all the information from the first server. I compared it to the next and the next. None of it made any sense. Each server had redundancy; multiple hard drives, multiple power supplies, and the individual servers were not teamed or connected. It failed all logic that they would all have the same error at the same time. It was akin to every car on a block not starting at the same time. It just didn't happen.

My phone had zero signal down here. I went to the phone mounted on the far wall, next to a clipboard with every contact in IT, cell and home numbers. I scanned the list, trying to figure out who to call. Do I call my boss or maybe the on-call server person? I didn't know any of the names. The page was dated; it was almost a year old. Many of these people didn't work here anymore and if I called, I'd be waking up someone who wasn't going to be that happy about it. To be fair, even if they're paid by the company to be woken up, they still are never happy about it. I was torn between not wanting to ask for help because I wanted to show I could manage this on my own and knowing that I needed help.

I took a deep breath, hit nine, and then found Rudder's number so at least I wouldn't be waking anyone up. The lights dimmed, the fans inside the servers slowed as they lost power, and I was able to hear myself think. Then everything came back. All the fans kicked on, on high. The noise was deafening. I dropped the receiver on the floor, but the sound was drowned out by the massive air conditioner turning on. The glow emanating off the servers switched from amber to green.

I ran back to the first row of servers in their big black cages. The lights hummed along, happy and green. *How could this be happening? It's not possible.* I ran down the rows, scanning all the racks, looking for anomalies, and found none. Everything was as it should be.

I clanged open the metal door on a server rack and pulled out the keyboard. A small LCD monitor popped up. I punched the keys and logged in to check the uptime. The server reported that it was last rebooted twenty-three days ago. I pulled up the event log and frantically scrolled through. There were no server errors and no warnings in the last hour.

The phone was still on the floor, so I picked it up and put it back on the hook. Air circulated in and out, making the room breathe and sigh. It was in a constant fight over the temperature. Nothing would ever be silent here.

I looked at the servers and then the phone, unsure of what to do. I couldn't wake people up unless something was down. Nothing was down, but I didn't know what it all meant. This was something the server admins would want to know about. It would go on the shift turnover report. I wasn't going to ignore it and pretend like nothing had happened. Everything in me wanted to sweep the whole night under the rug, but my fear of getting fired kept me on the straight and narrow. I made the note on the bottom of the checklist and continued checking the rest of the servers. Everything was green across the board.

It was almost one in the morning; another hour or so and I could take lunch. I walked over a perforated floor tile, shivering in the gust of cold air. The temperature gauge on the wall read sixty degrees. It was eight degrees colder than it had been before. I rubbed my arms and made my way to the door. It was ninety degrees outside, but at least I could defrost on my way back to my desk. The door swung open and on the bench in front of the door was the moth, unmoving. The door slammed behind me. I jumped, and the eight-inch moth took flight. I ducked, screamed, and covered my head with the clipboard.

The moth flew to the other corner and then the far end before disappearing. My heart thumped in my chest like a piston about to be thrown through the block of an engine. I tried to catch my breath. I stopped, tried to shake it off, and even laughed at myself a little. Moth: 2, Danni: 0. My body was still cold from the computer room, but the air was hot. Ian, the security guard, darted around a corner. *Or was it him?* Maybe it was just a shadow. My heart rate began to come back down to a normal pace. I decided to take a walk around the building before heading back to my cave.

14

Before

TWO LAPS AROUND THE building in the night air cleared my head and settled my nerves from a roar to a quiet thrumming. In the parking lot, the world made sense again. I reminded myself that Rudder said the building was creepy. I shook my head to rattle the feelings loose. It should be creepy. It's a job graveyard. How many of the people they laid off were able to get something quickly without a lapse in bills? How many had to live off unemployment and food stamps? How many... No, I can't keep doing this to myself. I have a job. I may be in a job graveyard, but I'm not going to starve.

The parking lot was empty except for my car and one other. Maybe Ian was still here, darting around corners. I glanced at the phone to check the time and make sure I hadn't missed any calls while I was walking around. It was a quiet night. *Knock on wood,* I thought instantly. Nothing will make you superstitious like working IT. Saying "it's quiet" is the kiss of death; at least I didn't say it out loud. A tall figure appeared from around the corner of the building. What was Ian still doing here?

"Hey Ian," I called out to him, taking hurried steps in his direction. Working alone two nights a week without a single person to hear talk or breathe was a type of isolation I wasn't prepared for. Ian waved back at me, put his hands in his pockets, and continued walking toward me.

"Hey, were you here earlier?" I asked.

"Earlier when? I've been here for a bit," he said, looking around.

"Maybe an hour or so ago. I thought I saw you but didn't think you'd still be around if it were you. But you seem like the person I should be telling if there are suspicious characters walking around."

"You think I'm a suspicious character?" His smirk seemed to say to me *if you only knew.*

"Just if it wasn't you, it would be suspicious. Because who else would be wandering around here in the middle of the night? I mean, besides me."

"We've already determined you're suspicious." The way he towered over me made me feel like an ant under a magnifying glass or a bug that he might pull the legs off to see what happened. He smiled and I dismissed the thought. I was tired and it'd been a weird night.

"Usually, I hear bad influence, but I'll take suspicious character."

He seemed loosely put together, like his bones were connected with rubber bands. I wanted to like him, but no part of me trusted him. Caught between my desire for human contact and my impulse to keep him at a safe distance, I just kept talking. "How many buildings do you visit in a night?"

"A few," he said, cocking his head to the side, his hands still in his pockets. So much for small talk.

"Do you come by once per night or a few times? Is it on a schedule?" I asked.

"What's with the twenty questions?"

"I like to know what to expect so that way, I'm not freaked out. So, I can be like, 'Oh, it's about time for Ian to be here. I shouldn't have a heart attack because I see someone walking around.'"

"Sorry; I can't be much help. We'd be a shitty security company if we announced our schedule. People could case the place once and know when we aren't here."

"Do people really case office buildings?" It seemed ridiculous to me. I guess they could steal computers or office furniture. Or they could steal the printer, but I'd help them roll that out of here.

"Enough that companies see a reason to hire security companies." He shrugged.

"Have you noticed anything weird?" I cut to the chase.

"Weird how?" he asked with a raised eyebrow.

"Just weird in general. The second shift guy says it's because the building is underground and it's infrasound. Like sound that's lower than the human ear can hear, and he says that's what makes it creepy." I bit my lip. I was babbling.

"Infrasound. Haven't heard that one before. I'll have to look it up when I get to a computer." He hunched down, squinting at me, studying me. "Have you seen anything weird?"

"I work the graveyard shift in a ghost town. Everything is weird." I wasn't about to tell him I had dreamed or imagined a door and a monster and then woke up on a bench without remembering how I got there. I didn't want him to think I was insane, or maybe I didn't want to confirm to myself that I was going insane.

He exhaled and gave me a slow smile. "I could see how that would do it."

"Do you work for the alarm company or is it a separate company?" I asked.

"Separate."

I nodded. It made sense.

"What's the company name—you know, in case I see something and need to call?"

"SWF," he said, turning his shoulder to me with the patch of the company name. "I should get going to my next site." He gestured toward the other car in the parking lot.

"Right, of course. I should get back." The cell phone rang. "The fun never ends," I said, holding up the phone.

Ian waved.

"Help Desk; this is Danni." I answered the call, waving back.

"Hey, how's it going?" Rudder said.

"Are you checking up on me?" I dropped my keys, gave an exaggerated sigh, then bent down, snatched my keys, and roughly shoved them in my purse.

"You called me," he said.

"What?" I paused, reaching for the stairwell door.

"Well, someone called me from the datacenter."

Right; he wasn't the asshole. I was. "Sorry. I dialed and dropped the phone. There was a—" A what? It wasn't a glitch. It wasn't a hiccup. "There were some issues, but it self-healed." The worst answer in all of IT. I entered the stairwell and let the door slam behind me.

"Did you put it on the turnover report?"

"Not yet," I said.

"Don't. Report the shit that's still broken or the stuff where we know what happened."

"Uh, okay."

"The dayshifters have a negative view of second and third shift. If we tell them stuff like that, it's just fuel."

"How's your night going?"

"Well, it's a Friday night in a porn shop. It's going about how you'd expect."

"That sounds very funny or very gross."

"You've basically described my job," he said flatly. "How's yours?"

"Well, I haven't gone insane and burned the place down yet," I said, laughing.

"If you burn it down, then I find another job or they move us to a different building. If you quit, that's when I have to work twelve-hour shifts."

"Right, sorry. For a second, I thought you might care about my welfare, but now I see the error of my ways."

"Well, as long as we have an understanding."

"Crystal clear. Hey, what's in the drawer tonight? I haven't checked yet. What's the movie recommendation of the night?"

"You're not at the desk?" he asked.

"Just talking a walk outside. It'd be a break if I didn't have to answer the phone."

"*Scarface*, *Terms of Endearment*, and another Godzilla flick."

"You have eclectic taste, my friend."

"I like monster movies."

I took a moment to consider that and decided it could apply to all three movies in different ways. "Anyway, pass. Can you get something a little more current?"

"I see the current stuff when it comes out. I'm trying to fill in the gaps."

"Do you take requests?" I asked, hoping that maybe I could get something in the rotation that would be a good movie to watch in the middle of the night.

Scarface is a classic; *Terms of Endearment* is a good movie for a cry… but good movies to zone out to while you pass the time… nope. I wanted something mindless and familiar.

"You know you can bring your own movies if you don't like my selection."

I frowned.

"Hey, I gotta get back," he said.

"Sure. Those dildos won't restock themselves."

"No, they won't. Talk to you later," Rudder said.

"Later," I said, snapping the flip phone closed as I badged back into the stairwell.

My quick footsteps echoed down three flights of stairs. There was a rhythm to going down the stairs fast. One misstep would mean more than losing the rhythm. It would mean landing at the bottom, black and blue. I tried to push the image out of my mind of my blood running down the steps.

The conversation with Rudder lightened my mood. Maybe we were becoming friends. It was good to have friends at work. So often I'd been the odd man, er, odd woman out. Having friends that were actually friends in the office was good, instead of guys who just wanted to date or sleep with me.

Two flights down, I exited the stairwell on the third floor and hurried along the walkway back to the office, hoping the phone didn't ring before I got back to my desk.

I made it through the main doors and down the hallway, passing the break room. A crash shredded the silence. It sounded like a five-pound bag of rocks being dumped. I jumped and my legs went weak. Disoriented, I searched for the source of the noise and realized it was the ice machine dropping ice. I laughed. The phone call, the strange errors, the moth. I tried unsuccessfully to find something interesting on the Internet that was also work appropriate as the clock slowly ticked away.

15

After

I CAN'T RUN FAST enough because the ground beneath my feet is like wet sand. The thing behind me is getting closer. I look back, but there's no visibility through the haze. My mind races faster than my feet, trying to name the sound, but every search comes up with an error: *Cyclic Redundancy Check*. The words flash across my vision in a dialog box with an OK button. "Seriously," I say, flicking it away with my hand. It disappears as my hand eclipses the button.

My right foot sinks as I put my weight onto it. I trip, falling on all fours. I get back up and start running again. The more I try to run, the more my feet sink into the ground. It could be faster to slow down, but the frenzy in my head doesn't let me consider it.

A wailing that sounds like a dying calf reverberates through my head, joined by a chorus of falling trees. It's getting closer. I trip again. My useless mouth flops open but nothing comes out. I'm incapable of making sound. The word *help* is loud and screeching inside my head, but my tongue is unable to form the word; I emit a strangled, airy whisper.

Behind me, a figure materializes out of the mist. It's inhuman, without a distinct head or neck, and towers over me at least double my height. I run, the silhouette of the thing chasing me through my mind, cross-referencing it against known animals and shapes. *What is it?* The rush of blood bangs on my eardrums, mixed with my raspy breath.

Stabbing pain rings through my head as I'm knocked backward. I look up from the flat of my back at a large blue wall. On the royal blue wall is a block of grey text, most of the words a stock message. My eyes are trained to go straight to the error and find the text: IRQL_NOT_LESS_OR_EQUAL.

"Fuck," I whisper. Everything I try is useless. The things I know I can do, like running and screaming, are impossible. My body betrays me, refusing to respond to my demands. This is more terrifying than whatever is chasing me. If I could only run, if I could only see what's coming, if I could only scream for help...

Through the mist, I hear the creature approaching, feel its eyes on me. Every hair on my body stands on end. I'm frantic, looking for a power button or a keyboard or anything to make the screen go away so I can continue running. Crawling to my feet, I bang on the royal blue wall. I cackle in deranged laughter; my cause of death will be listed as BSOD, a blue screen of death. It's blocked my path and there's nowhere to run. The mist envelops me, hot, humid, and putrid.

A piercing wail cuts through my laughter. Every step it takes sounds like it's chewing on planks of wood. The ground shakes, the vibration travels up my body to my rib cage and I wonder if it will liquify my insides. My mind races, trying to reason out the solution; is it a driver, or a memory issue, or a hardware problem? I could fix it, if only I had a keyboard.

A gust of hot, wet air blows my hair forward; it's behind me. Its sudden grip on my arm is excruciating and I open my mouth to see if my tongue and my lungs remember how to scream. Nothing comes out. I turn to face it; its inhuman fingers look like insect legs. The mist is thick and veils its face as it crouches down while still towering over me.

This time, my scream rings out. Its face, if it has a face, is hidden from me but I can feel that it's pleased with my terror. The insect-like fingers move up my body to my chest, hovering over my sternum. The pain is searing.

"Danni." The sound of my name cuts through the mist as my body is rocked back and forth; I startle and flail as I realize where I am. I'm in a bed in a mental health facility. Erin crawls onto the bed next to me, on top of the covers. "Shhhh." Her voice comforts me. "It's a dream."

Erin's face is inches away from me. I rub my eyes and she rubs my arm.

"You were screaming," she says, drawing her eyebrows together.

"What was I screaming?" She's so close, we're breathing the same air.

"Most of it was nonsense and whimpering. At the end, I think you were yelling 'F8.'"

I laugh and cover my face even though she probably can't see the flush of my embarrassment in the dark.

"What? Is that funny?"

"Yes, it's hysterical. I'm having computer error nightmares. I was trying to reboot my dream into safe mode. Awesome."

"Maybe next time, it'll work. Safe mode sounds like a good thing for dreams," she says. She's still rubbing my arm.

Why is she being so kind to me? I feel a flash of anxiety and discomfort because I realize that I'm a burden. She's trying to calm me so I don't have more nightmares and continue to keep her up all night. A silence settles over us as I admire the curve of her lips, her delicate features, and her beautiful brown eyes. Those eyes are locked on mine and I look away.

"Thanks for waking me. I'll try not to keep you up." I pull away and she gives me a blank stare.

"Um, sure. Yeah, of course. It's fine. I'm a light sleeper." She shakes her head as she gets up and returns to her bed.

The last thing I want to do is step over the line with the only person I feel I can talk to. There's something wonderful about her. I can't do that to her; she has enough to deal with without me pushing her into a situation she doesn't want to be in. But I can't help but feel like I said the wrong thing at the wrong time. I put my hand over my heart; the skin beneath stings. Pulling my shirt down a few inches, I expose the scratches on my chest. Great. I'm hurting myself in my sleep.

16

Before

THE CLOCK HIT 2:30, I forwarded the phone to my cell, and ran out of the building like it was on fire. Rudder was at his other job. I wasn't above stalking some guy I barely knew at a porn shop.

The bell on the door announced my entrance. A guy near the back casually flipped through a bin of VHS tapes. Rudder glanced up from his red notebook, gave me a head nod before closing the book and sliding it off the counter.

"Oh my god. Kill me," I said, flopping my torso on the counter where Rudder was reading a magazine.

"We don't do that here," he said and turned a page.

"I'll pay extra." I pulled myself up and gave him an evil grin.

"Do I know you?" he asked.

"I'm only like your best friend on earth."

"Oh right. What's up?" He set the magazine down on the counter.

"Well, I think the world is falling apart, or maybe it's just work. Reality ceases to make sense when I'm in that building."

"Sounds like a job."

"Basically. But worse," I said. "Have you ever seen one of these?"

I pulled up the picture of the moth on my phone.

"What is that? A butterfly?" he asked.

"I think it's a moth, but it's huge. You can't tell from the picture, but it's bigger than my hand." I held my hand up with fingers spread to demonstrate how big it was.

"That's pretty big. Have you been drinking on the job again?" he asked. I squinted at him and scrunched my nose.

"No. I get high on my coffee breaks." I shrugged.

"And you're not sharing?"

"I'm a selfish bitch."

"True," he agreed. I flipped him off.

"I'm serious; it was huge. You've never seen one there?" I held up the picture again.

"Nope; that's freakish. Maybe it got lost on the way to wherever it was going."

I considered the possibility, then nodded. He was probably right. Just a freak thing.

Rudder loaded a few boxes on a cart and pushed it from behind the counter. I walked with him as he began stocking shelves. "Is this a good place to pick up chicks?"

"I wouldn't know. Also, flirting with the customers is specifically against the rules."

"Yes, it's the one universal truth that a company policy will keep a man from acting inappropriately."

"I'm celibate." He kept moving as I stood there looking slightly confused.

"Like, by choice?"

"I don't know if it's by design or by choice. It's just how I live."

"Huh. I didn't know that's a thing."

"I find the whole thing bizarre."

"Which thing? Dating? Or sex? Because if sex is bizarre, it just means you're doing it right." I grinned at my own joke. He ignored me and continued to stock the shelves.

"Attraction in general. Physical appearance is such an incomplete record of who a person is. I reject the idea that just because a person has a symmetrical face that I have to want to stick my dick in them."

"Incomplete?" I guess we were getting serious.

"Yeah. What can you tell from looking at a person? Most of what you see on the outside is how they want the world to see them based on their haircut and clothes they put on that morning. And often, the person they want you to see isn't the person they are."

I stopped, letting it sink in. There was a story behind that belief. Rudder was a puzzle. It'd be rude to ask what was behind the pieces, but I still wanted to know.

He shrugged. "Besides, bodies are kinda gross. So many fluids: sweat, saliva, and mucus."

I blinked a few times and considered asking how someone with an aversion to bodily fluids ended up working in a porn shop. But like many things with Rudder, I decided to just accept because acceptance doesn't require understanding. It's his business.

I picked up a clear plastic device off the cart, two smooth curved pieces that looked like a duck bill. I squeezed the handle and the duck bill opened. "Quack, quack."

"There's something wrong with you," he said.

"What's this thing?"

"Please put that down, and you know damn well what that is." He took it from me, not giving me a chance to put it down. I chuckled.

"So, you're not interested in sex, but you work in a porn shop?"

"Yes," he said.

"What are you saving for?" I grinned.

"I have work to do. Shouldn't you be getting back?"

"Do you get days off from the stroke hut?"

"We prefer the term *whack shack*," he said. I raised my hands in a dramatic *well, excuse me* gesture.

"I'm off tomorrow. It's my only day off from both jobs."

"So what is there to do in this one-horse town?"

"I was going to go to the Radio Ballroom."

"I love that place and I'm off tomorrow too... Mind if I invite myself along?"

"Sure." He shrugged, and I didn't know if he really meant it or not.

"Can I bring a friend? I might be able to drag my neighbor away from his computer for a few hours and force him to socialize."

"Sure, why not?" Rudder said.

81

"You'll like him. He's cool."

My cell phone rang. It was a work number and I held up a finger to Rudder. "Work. I gotta get this; hold on." I flipped the phone open, "Help Desk; this is Danni."

"Hi, my account is locked. Can you reset my password?" the voice on the other end said.

"I'm offsite at the moment. I'll be back in twenty minutes and can reset it then. What is your name and extension and I'll give you a call back?"

"I'll just call back," the person said and hung up. I closed the phone with one hand and tossed it onto the table. "These people are so fucking rude."

"Don't forget stupid," he said, shaking a finger at me.

"So stupid."

"Don't you love working a shift alone and not getting a break?"

"Right? I wonder how they could get away with it."

"We used to have three per shift so there were always two people working at the same time. It made it easier to take breaks, go to the bathroom in peace."

"What happened?"

"Rightsizing." He put air quotes around the word. "And attrition. As they laid off office workers, they said they didn't need as many of us."

I shook my head. "And we'll let them, because we need the job," It was true. There was so much that we would tolerate because of the job market. They could work us twelve-hour days and make us answer calls on breaks and we'd do it.

"Do you need to go back?" he asked.

"Eh, after I grab lunch. They're the dumbasses that forgot their password," I said.

17

Before

BEFORE I LEFT WORK, I struggled to keep my eyes open. In the lobby before exiting, I had my sunglasses at the ready, putting them on before I got to the door. I would be transformed from barely awake and barely functional into wide awake and barely functional. I drove against morning traffic, allowing me to zone out. I needed to be alert enough to drive, but not so much so that I couldn't fall asleep after I got home.

Sliding the key into the lock, I still didn't know which it would be. Would I be asleep in five minutes, or would I be awake for the next five hours? A small nudge in either direction would determine if I'd be able to sleep. Turning the knob, I hoped that my roommate wasn't home. She hadn't been around much for the last month. Britters was barking on the other side of the door.

"Hold on." I hurried to close the door and stuff the keys back in my pocket before she could make a break for it. I didn't see the inside of the apartment until the door was shut and I turned around. I'd been robbed. The room was empty with the exception of an old thrift store recliner, which was mine. No couch, which was my roommate's. No television, which was hers. All her pictures were missing from the walls. Slowly, the image solidified in my sleepy brain, and I knew before I saw the note on the counter. But wait. Britters was still here.

I snatched the note off the counter and skimmed the contents.

Danni,

I'm moving back in with my mom be-
cause you don't listen to me anymore and
you don't understand me. My mom won't
let me bring Brittney with me. She's yours
now, she likes you better anyhow. And since
you've had use of my dishes, my couch, and
my TV for the last month and you're keep-
ing my dog, I shouldn't have to pay the last
two months left on the lease or the electricity
bills. Don't call me.
-Abby

It was a breakup letter. I laughed. I was furious, but I laughed. For some reason, she thought she had to sneak out in the night like I was some abusive boyfriend.

"Oh my god. This is too much."

I picked up Britters and walked out of the apartment and across the landing to Carlos's apartment. The door was unlocked; I tapped on it as I walked in. Carlos was at his computer and didn't turn around.

"Motherfucking campers. Come back and I'll shove my BFG up your moth-erfucking ass," Carlos yelled.

"Your blood pressure. A man your age should try to stay calm," I said. Carlos wasn't even thirty, but he talked like he was fifty, had seen it all, and had wisdom to spare for us young whippersnappers.

Carlos flipped me off without turning around and then returned his hand to his mouse. "Fuck this," he said and punched some keys on his keyboard. "Bunch of fucking fourteen-year-olds have no fucking morals or respect for the game."

"Did you tell them to get off your lawn?" I joked.

"In fact, I did." He lit up a cigarette.

"Have you moved from that spot since I left for work?" I asked.

"To piss, sure."

"I don't know if that counts," I said.

"So how was having a job?" He put a clove cigarette in his mouth and reached for his lighter.

"Awful. Can I go back to being unemployed?"

"Not funny," he said as he lit the cigarette.

"Sorry," I said. "In other news, I no longer have a roommate." I handed him the note. He took a few seconds to scan it.

"What is she, like twelve? Who does this?" he asked.

"Right?" My muscles tensed and I couldn't keep myself from smiling. I probably looked deranged, but I didn't care. Every judgmental thought I had about her was confirmed by this one childish act. I pushed back the nagging guilt in the back of my head reminding me that I wasn't winning any prizes for world's best roommate. I was messy and sometimes late on bills. "I think this is the first breakup letter I've ever gotten."

"And that's a bitch move, leaving her dog behind," he said.

"Yeah, I'll judge her and talk shit about her. But I'm actually glad," I said.

"You don't say?" He smirked at me and exhaled a puff of smoke.

"But seriously. She doesn't think she has to pay her half of the bills because I used her dishes for a month? I could buy more than ten sets of those dishes for how much her half of the bills is for the rest of the lease." It hit me that what I'd set aside from cashing out my 401(k) was about to disappear, paying her half of the bills. So much for that new computer I was going to build. That KT7ARAID motherboard with onboard RAID controllers was now a pipe dream.

"Don't forget the dog," he said, patting his lap so Britters would jump up. I set her on the floor and she leapt into his lap.

"Okay, six sets of dishes and the dog. But I love how she's decided what her stuff is worth and chooses for me that I'm paying because she can't stick around, be an adult, and own up to her responsibilities."

"Kids these days," he said.

"Hey, you doing anything tonight?" I ask.

"Quake and schooling the kiddies on gaming etiquette," he said.

"Take a night off from mentoring today's youth and come out with me." I motioned toward the door as if I was trying to coax him out. Carlos scowled and recoiled.

"Out? Where?" He eyed me with suspicion.

"The outside world. It'll be fun. You can meet my coworker. You'll like him." I nodded at him, trying to get him on board. "I'll pay your cover."

"Maybe," he said and spun back around in his chair.

"Okay. I'll be back tonight. I need to get some sleep. Come on, Britters. Let's go do your business and then sleep." I patted my leg and she jumped off Carlos's lap. I connected her leash and opened the door.

He waved at me without turning around while logging back into his game. I hummed to myself, happy to have a weekend plan and a little bit of money. I thought to ask Carlos if I was able to get out of my lease, could I move into the second bedroom at his place. But I didn't want to put him on the spot and make him feel like he had to say yes. The chances of the apartment letting me break my lease without a heavy fee were nonexistent. Plus, he hadn't suggested it, so he probably thought it was a bad idea.

***

Waking up was painful and disorienting. I took a minute to figure out what time it was.

The clock wasn't always helpful. When I woke up, it was six and I had to pull the blanket away from the window before I could figure out if it was morning or night. The sun wasn't down yet; it was almost dusk.

Six o'clock at night. Time to make coffee.

I pulled myself out of bed and shuffled to the kitchen. By seven o'clock, I'd had three cups, breakfast, and a shower. My hair and makeup were done. I sat on the edge of my bed, bored and ready to go with nothing to do and no television to distract me. Rudder was coming around 11 p.m.; the plan was for him and Carlos to have a few drinks because somehow, I had ended up as the designated driver.

I had an old boombox, but the antenna didn't extend all the way anymore and it didn't get the best stations. I stared at the white walls. Even Britters was still asleep. There was nothing to do; no new email, no one online to chat with. The emptiness of the apartment echoed inside my chest, making me feel empty there as well. The lack of furniture seemed to accentuate how alone I was. Before, I could turn on a TV for background noise. Now I lived alone in a two-bedroom apartment without enough furniture to fill a studio.

The walls started to close in. I could go next door, but Carlos was probably still asleep. I wanted to crawl into bed, but it was the loneliest spot in the whole place. It was still early in the evening. I picked up my phone.

"Hello," Steve said.

"Hey, what's up?" I asked.

"You called me." I could hear the smile in his voice.

"I was just sitting here thinking..." I trailed off. This was our game.

"Thinking about what?"

"How long it's been since I've seen you. And more specifically what we did the last time I saw you," I said. I used the voice; the tone was a beckoning hand. He was silent for a moment, and this was either when he would have said, "oh really" or "I don't think that's a good idea." I held my breath and closed my eyes.

"I've been thinking about it too," he said.

That was the response I wanted.

"I'm free for a little bit. I have plans later though." I wanted to make it clear I wasn't asking him to spend the night, giving him the easy out. I could picture him looking at the clock and deciding if he had time before whatever plans he had that night. He always had plans, always something to do and somewhere to be.

"Well, I wouldn't want to make you late for your plans."

"My plans aren't for three or four hours; I dare you to make me late." I let my voice drip with playfulness, knowing full well what it did to him. I could spin his brain with just a few words. I abused this talent at every opportunity, something he both appreciated and hated about me.

He laughed. "I have to be somewhere at nine. It's not far from your place; I could swing by."

I clicked my phone closed. I knew exactly what I was doing, but my head spun like I'd just come off a Tilt-A-Whirl. It was an intoxicated type of tunnel vision. As soon as he left, he'd regret coming over. He'd call a few days later, talking about how we have to stop doing this. He'd mean every word in that moment. With the right tone of voice, word choice, subtle glance, some of his defenses would come down. Just the ones that kept me out of his bed. I had no hope of knocking down any other walls. I didn't play this game alone, but usually, it was me doing the reeling and him the resisting.

Punctual Steve knocked at my door thirty minutes after he hung up. I let him in and realized I hadn't said anything about my living situation.

"Were you robbed?" he asked, looking around. I hadn't bothered to clean up.

"My roommate broke up with me." I pointed at the note on the counter. He walked to the counter and read it.

"You're obviously better off. Even if you have to pay a little more, at least you aren't living with a psychopath anymore," he said.

I laughed. "Childish and self-centered. Psychopath might be a tad harsh."

"Absolutely not. She's a train wreck. Did you read this? What kind of adult abandons their commitments and responsibilities because their roommate doesn't listen to their incessant whining?"

"See, now you're just trying to sweet talk me." I smiled and tilted my head. I also realized that I complained a lot. Maybe that was it. Maybe I was too negative.

"And now you have a dog. That's pretty much a win-win." He put the note down.

"True. I'd ask if you wanted to watch something on TV. But I don't have one."

"I see that," he said. "What do you have?"

"I have a chair. It's very comfortable, even if it looks like it's seen better days and several different owners and the inside of at least one thrift store. So, if we sat in here, you could sit and I'd either have to sit on your lap or worship at your feet. I also have a bed, and a radio. I believe you're familiar with my bed."

"It seems that's the only place where two people can sit," he said as if it were a foregone conclusion.

"That would be correct. Would you like to sit on my bed, which now also doubles as a couch? I can make you a drink."

"Sure. What do you have?"

"I have beer, coffee and Baileys... maybe some vodka and soda."

"Vodka and soda please," he said.

"Two drinks coming up." I went to the kitchen, opened a beer for myself, and poured him a vodka and soda. When I returned, he was sitting on the edge of the bed. I sat next to him, handed him his drink, and traced a finger along the top of his thigh. The sound of his breath quickening sent electricity through me.

"We shouldn't do this," he said without looking at me. He took a drink.

"I know," I said.

"I shouldn't be here," he said.

"But you are." I smiled. The word was on the tip of my tongue, to ask him why. Why does he still come if he doesn't want to be with me? But I didn't care as long as he kept coming. There was more to it, something complex and beneath the surface that I hadn't figured out. And maybe that was the reason I kept coming back. I couldn't let it go. One of my many flaws: until I understood something, it became an obsession.

"What are we doing?" he asked.

"Having a drink," I said. No part of me wanted to have that conversation. He sighed, but he was here.

"I've had a shit day. I just need to take my mind off it. I don't want to have a long emotionally draining conversation about what it means or to be told again that we're not getting back together but you still care. I need to not feel the way I feel. That's it. It's simple. I'm not asking for anything else. Just be here. Just take my mind off everything."

"I do know how to take your mind off things." He grinned, and that look alone could make me intoxicated.

"Yes, you do," I said. He brushed my hair back and made me forget the night I'd had. I was euphoric. It felt like a victory and a renewal wrapped into one.

18

Before

"Okay, Britters." She leaned against my leg. "I'm going out for the night. It'll be like I'm gone for work, but I'll be home earlier." She jumped and barked like she understood. I checked my makeup and changed into something more club appropriate: hip-hugger black vinyl pants, matching halter top, and my '90s grunge combat boots, a perfect outfit for going out on a Sunday night. I tossed Britters a treat so she wouldn't run out the door, and I made a break for it.

Carlos was still playing a first-person shooter on his computer.

"Wassup baby?" I said.

"Hey." He didn't look away from the screen.

"Go get changed. Rudder should be here soon," I said.

"What's wrong with what I'm wearing?"

I eyed his worn undershirt and baggy jean shorts. "Everything. Go fucking change," I said.

Carlos went into his bedroom, grumbling something about me being a bitch. Then there was a knock at the door. I opened it.

"Hey, you," I greeted Rudder.

"I'm sorry. I must be in the wrong place. I was here to pick up my mousey computer geek friend." He looked me over.

"No one's ever called me mousey," I laughed. He was dressed in black jeans and a black t-shirt with the name of a German band I'd never heard of.

Carlos walked out of the bedroom wearing a shirt from the same band. "You have to change," I said.

"I just changed. What's wrong with what I'm wearing?" he asked. I stepped aside and pointed at Rudder's shirt.

"Brother," Rudder said. Carlos smiled, walked over, and they slapped hands.

"Rudder, this is Carlos." I did introductions even though they seemed to already be hitting it off. "You're really going to go as twinsies?"

"Tequila or beer?" Carlos asked Rudder, completely ignoring me.

"Both," Rudder said.

"Good man." Carlos went to the kitchen, poured shots, and pulled out a few beers.

"None for me. I'm driving." I held up my hands, refusing drinks I wasn't offered. "Although I don't know how I pulled the short straw."

The guys had a good buzz on when we showed up at the club. The bar lost all its magic when the lights came up. But with the house lights off and strobe lights going, it transformed into one of my favorite places, where rational thought was replaced by the beat of the music. We danced until it was questionable whether it was god awful late or god awful early. An hour before close, the guys were still dancing off the booze out on the dance floor and I needed a little break. I hit the bar; it wasn't staffed but had a large orange water cooler like the ones used at construction sites. The Sunday night crowd, while it had started as a crowd, had slowly thinned to a few dozen hard-core night people.

I drained the cup of water, trying to cool myself down, feeling the sheen of sweat evaporate, leaving my skin cooler but clammy. A tall man with a large bull ring piercing though his nose walked up to the bar. His long black hair was slick against his head, the sides shaved and tattooed. I respected the dedication; in my mind, there was not much worse than a fauxhawk. Commit or don't.

"Hey," he said.

I nodded in time to the music. "Hey."

"How are you tonight?" he asked.

"Pretty good," I was able to say honestly. "Although tonight is almost over."

"The night only ends when we want it to." He smiled and motioned to clink plastic water cups with me. I returned the gesture. We chatted for a few minutes about music. He didn't ask me the boring questions, *Where are you from* or

What do you do? His eyes locked on mine. I looked away to avoid the awkwardness of sustained eye contact, but when I looked back, he was still boring into my eyes with his. His intensity was captivating and intoxicating. The club fell away and we existed in a bubble.

"You here with friends?" he asked.

"Yeah, those idiots on the dance floor." I motioned to Rudder and Carlos.

"Boyfriend?" he asked.

"No."

"Do you have a boyfriend?" he asked.

"No," I said, not thinking he was the type to apply for the position. Also, I wasn't taking applications.

"What are you doing after this?" His eyes traced me up and down.

"Sleep," I said.

"Sleep is for the weak. We're not weak," he said.

"Sleep is for the daylight hours," I corrected.

"Come over to my place; I have beer. We could hang out for a while," he suggested, somehow sounding both casual and carnal at the same time.

"Oh, I'm driving. I'm the designated," I said, hoping that would close the conversation.

"Did you drive your car?" he asked.

"No, it's my friend's." We'd taken Rudder's van.

"Give them the keys. I can take you home later." He smiled and the light hit a fleck of gold in his hazel eyes.

His smile was a mystery that I wanted to unpack but I leaned away involuntarily.

"No; they've had a lot to drink. They probably haven't danced it all off yet. And I can't bail on my friends. That would be uncool," I said.

"They'll be fine. Come hang out with me," he said.

My mouth hung open, not finding any words. The pace and volume of the music slowed and lights started coming up. Carlos and Rudder were by my side before I could make sense of anything.

"Hey," Carlos said. He gave a head nod to the other guy, and I realized I never got his name. He didn't look at Carlos or Rudder, but extended a hand in greeting without taking his eyes off me. The interaction had gone from intriguing to mysterious to downright creepy.

"Closing time." Rudder pointed up at the lights that drained the magic from the club, turning it into just another room with a shitty linoleum floor.

"Right. We should go," I said, standing up. Bull Ring Guy stuck to my side as we walked out. In the parking lot, the guys were getting antsy, wanting to leave. The guy was really starting to weird me out, but there was a secret in his eyes I was trying to figure out. What was he really after? We stepped outside and I did a double take: his eyes were hazel a moment ago, but now they were blue. Not just blue, a specific shade of blue; they reminded me of storm clouds. He was another riddle I didn't know how to walk away from.

"We'll be in the car," Carlos said. He took the keys and walked away.

"They're fine," Bull Ring Guy said. "Come over and hang out. Just a few beers."

"I have to go," I said, but my feet would not move.

"What should I call you?" he asked. "Give yourself a name that only I'll know."

Alarm bells went off in my head. But I didn't move. It felt like he recognized something inside of me, something that I was unable to name. In a very short period, I felt connected to him, but wary at the same time. Following him down this path would be life altering, and I wasn't sure if that was good or bad. Would Alice have been better off not falling down the rabbit hole? This rabbit hole could be a snake pit.

"You're like a battery of energy. I can feel it," he said. Red flags and alarm bells became a blaring siren.

"I should go."

A noise drew his attention away from me and to the other side of the parking lot. Rudder's beat-up minivan squealed in complaint as Carlos tested its turn radius doing donuts in the nearly empty parking lot. Then I noticed a private security guard walking through the parking lot.

"Shit. Later." I called out the hasty goodbye and ran across the parking lot to the van. It came to an abrupt stop; the window rolled down. Rudder leaned out.

"I saved you from the creepy dude," he said.

"Jesus. Get out," I commanded. I opened the driver's door. "Move over."

Rudder moved to the passenger seat; Carlos was in the back, laughing. "Let's get out of here," he said.

I put the shifter into drive and pulled out of the parking lot, smiling and waving at the security guard. "I can't believe you guys. I was having a conversation. I can't trust you with car keys for two minutes."

"We were helping," Rudder said from the back.

"That guy would devour you," Carlos said.

"You're drunk," I said.

"He looked like he was into some freaky stuff. Believe me, we saved you," he said.

"I'm capable of saving myself," I said. It rang hollow in my ears.

We didn't hit any red lights on the way back to the apartment; the lights seemed to be timed to the fifty-five miles an hour I was driving, until we stopped for a left turn. I'd shaken off the strange interaction with the guy at the bar. I tapped the wheel in time with the blinker and the music. The street was empty, no cars in either direction, except the headlights coming up behind us. I tensed, worried that the security guard had called the police because of Rudder's parking lot antics. My eyes were glued to the rearview mirror.

19

Before

"Is THAT HIM?" I asked. Carlos and Rudder both turned to look. "Shit. I think that's the guy from the bar."

I was trying to remember; we'd talked for almost thirty minutes. Did he say he lived on this side of town? I couldn't remember.

"Is he following us?" Carlos asked.

"Fuck," I said.

"I can drive," Rudder said.

"Too late." The light turned green and I slammed the gas pedal to the floor. The minivan strained as it leaned into the turn. We were a mile from the apartment. My mind raced. I couldn't lead him directly to where I lived. But I also wasn't going to let him chase me around the streets at four in the morning.

"Hold on," I said, and I turned left from the left lane instead of from the suicide lane. I turned onto a neighborhood street, taking the first right as headlights appeared behind me. "Fuck. He's following us."

I took another quick left, speeding through the sleepy neighborhood, convinced he hadn't seen the last two turns and I'd lost him. When we got back out to the main street, I darted across the road into the apartment complex parking lot and parked in the first spot I found.

"This isn't near the apartment," Carlos said.

"I don't want to park near the apartment in case he saw us turn in."

We all piled out of the van.

"I think we lost him," Rudder said.

"Move," I yelled as headlights turned into the parking lot. We ran in between the apartment buildings and around the corner, all three of us with our backs to the wall. My breath quickened, my heart pounding like the beat of a train barreling down the tracks. The sound of an engine revving echoed around the buildings and ripped apart the silence of tranquility of the early morning hours.

"We should run," Carlos said. "Don't stay in place for too long. Follow me."

Rudder and I exchanged glances, but we followed. Carlos led and Rudder brought up the rear. I glanced back; he scanned the surroundings. They flanked me, protecting me, and I was too terrified to spout my mantra that I could take care of myself. I was grateful they were there. I felt so ridiculous, like we were overreacting, and also like the threat was completely real.

We darted behind a cluster of bushes near the pool and listened. The engine revved, but farther away this time. Carlos motioned forward; he ran to the next building and we ran behind him.

The vehicle was getting closer again. I pictured him in his car, circling the parking lot over and over, looking for me. He was going to drag me back to his place to do God knew what, or this was what he did for fun. Either way, I wasn't willing to engage in conversation over it.

We darted between buildings, hiding in dark stairwells and behind bushes. We finally reached my apartment building. The air was quiet again, with a faint sound of traffic. Maybe he was gone? Or maybe he'd stopped near my apartment and was lying in wait.

Carlos held up a finger, telling us to wait. Rudder and I crouched behind bushes. I felt ridiculous hiding, but I was still hiding.

"You okay?" Rudder asked.

"In light of the last twenty-four hours, yeah, I'm still upright. So that's something," I said.

A whistle cut through the air. "Is that Carlos?" I asked.

Rudder shrugged. "Probably."

"Does that mean it's safe? Or stay where you are?" I asked.

"I think it means it's clear," Rudder said.

Carlos poked his head around the corner. "Come on." We walked into the open space between buildings. The glow of red taillights reflected off another car in the parking lot.

"Run," I said, trying not to yell and not to whisper. Not waiting for anyone else, I broke out into a run. Bull Ring Guy could be watching us, laughing, waiting to murder me, or he could have already left. Rudder and Carlos started running beside me. We got to the stairs; Carlos took them two at a time and Rudder brought up the rear.

Carlos got to the door first, dug into his pocket, and promptly dropped his keys. He picked them up and unlocked the door and pushed it open in the same movement. We poured into the apartment, slammed and locked the door behind us. Rudder and I had our backs against the door. Carlos paced and ran his hand through his hair.

"I think we're okay," I said. With the door shut, the sound of his engine revving seemed amplified.

Carlos said, "Turn off the lights." We flipped the light switch off and then sat in the glow of his computer monitor.

"I mean, you looked okay, but not like *try to possess your soul and stalk you home* kinda hot," Carlos said. I halfheartedly punched him in the shoulder.

"Could this week get any weirder?" I asked. "Giant moths, crazy roommates, weird security guard at work, and then psycho stalker."

"What did you say?" Carlos said.

"Which part?" I asked.

"Giant moth?" he said.

"Yeah, at work there was this enormous moth. So weird," I said. "It was as big as my hand," I said.

"You still have the picture?" Rudder asked.

"Yeah. I took a picture. I totally forgot." I flipped open my phone and tapped at the buttons until the grainy image was on the screen. I held the phone out to Carlos.

"Mariposa de la Muerte," he said in a reverent voice.

"What? Wait, I know that word. *Muerte* means death," I said.

97

"It's the butterfly of death, or the Black Witch Moth. My abuela told me about it. I've only seen one once. It flew into her house and my uncle died." He crossed himself. "A month later, but she never forgot that."

"Carlos, you're an atheist." I looked at the picture on my phone.

"Yes, but I also knock on wood when someone says it's been a long time since the mail server went down. You don't leave that stuff to chance. It's a harbinger of death. Did it fly to all four corners?"

"I don't know," I said. "Maybe."

"You should have told us before we left."

"How was I supposed to know the death butterfly was a dark omen?" I asked. He gave me look.

"No one is going to die." In truth, I was on the cusp of something, something I couldn't describe or define, and I couldn't say what would and wouldn't happen.

We sat in the dark, waiting and listening for any sound that he was still outside waiting for us. In the dark and silence, the feeling that we were overreacting grew. I fell asleep on the couch listening to Carlos and Rudder playing video games.

20

After

"WHAT WAS THAT ABOUT?" I follow Erin down the hallway back to our room. She's been acting strange all morning and then left the group therapy session abruptly. "Slow down."

She reaches the door to our room and swings it closed in my face just as I reach it. Frustrated, I open the door and enter the room as she is closing the bathroom door behind her. "Will you just talk to me?"

"What's the point?" she yells from behind the closed door.

"What's wrong? I'm exhausted. Please just talk to me." The anxiety that normally feels like a gnawing at the back of my brain is blaring in my ears like a siren. Every moment since I got here has been disjointed and painful, except for the moments with Erin. I can't lose her. They check on us every twenty minutes, feeding us pills and examining us to make sure our thought patterns aren't too aberrant but not so normal that we shouldn't be here. It's like being watched from behind glass as people walk by as if we're in a zoo. Every moment I'm here is a moment where I'm being watched and measured. It's exhausting and would be unbearable if it weren't for her.

Was it something I said? I replay the morning in my head. My mind is mush and I can't figure out the order of events. Retracing the morning takes effort. What happened? I woke up. Erin was already up and had left the room. Ivy convinced me to shower, I missed breakfast, and didn't see Erin until the morning's group therapy session. Begging and cajoling wouldn't do any good, but I don't want to leave her alone. But that's so me, isn't it? I can't leave anything alone.

"It's like grade school," I say, unsure where I'm going with this. "Sitting in a circle, forced to talk about our feelings. I've never been good at that." I pause for a few beats to see if she responds. I'm met with silence. "I was in the fifth grade, in the music room. We were sitting in a circle on the floor, waiting for the teacher, and the most popular boy in class spoke to me. He never spoke to me; most kids didn't. Kids are mean; if you didn't have a triangle logo on your butt, you were no one. I didn't have brand-name clothes. All my clothes were hand-me-downs or from thrift stores."

I trace my hand over the door. "He asks me, 'Why do you wear the same shoes every day? Don't you have any other shoes?' They were old ratty sneakers, probably as old as I was. Maybe he didn't understand that some people only have one pair of shoes. But that's what it makes me think of, sitting in a circle, waiting to see if someone points out my obvious shame in front of everyone. I close ranks and shut down."

There's an apology in my voice even if it's lacking from my words. I don't know what I'm apologizing for, but I feel the same as I did in that circle on the music room floor, that there's something wrong with me and I need to make it better. What I want more than anything is to help her; the responsibility of it hangs heavy on my shoulders even though that's not where it belongs. I take it on because I don't know how not to.

"Joke was on him though. Those weren't even my shoes." I laugh. It sounds forced and hollow in my ears. I slide to the floor, waiting to see if Erin comes out or says anything as I play back the entire thing in my head, looking for the thing that I said wrong. Maybe she didn't like how I talked to the counselor leading the group. Before she'd opened her mouth, I'd made up my mind about her: Something about her irritated me and made me angry. Maybe it was her designer shoes or her glowing smile. She had real shoes, she could leave anytime she wanted, and I bet she had a nice car too. In a few minutes, I'd imagined a whole life of privilege and plenty. It brings out a side of me I don't like. The claws come out, hackles go up, and I feel the urge to tear her down to the ground. It thought I'd kept it check, but if Erin is this upset, maybe I wasn't as successful as I thought.

"Whose shoes were they?" Erin says through the door.

The door opens and swings out a few inches.

"My mother's. I grew out of all my shoes. She didn't have money for new ones, so she gave me a pair she didn't wear anymore."

She's unnaturally still. Her eyes find me and then look away.

"Why are you sad? I mean, I know you said you were depressed. Are you sad because you're depressed or are you sad about something else?"

"I didn't think you were listening." She hugs her knees to her chest.

"I listened to everyone," I say, remembering the woman whose husband was killed in a tragic accident, another who had her child taken from her during a schizophrenic episode. Each one a knife in my chest, knowing that I lost my shit because I was afraid of losing my job and my inability to walk away. "I don't see how it's supposed to help us get better, listening to everyone talk about their shit. Does it make you less sad? Because it just makes me feel guilty." I grimace and bite my lip because the words out loud sound awful.

"Why would you feel guilty?"

"Why are you sad?" I ask.

Erin rolls her eyes, then looks at me.

"I'm afraid of not being able to pay my bills. Every day I'm here, I think how I'm not going to be able to pay rent. I don't even know how much this is going to cost. How can I afford this? My insurance will cover some, but if I'm not out of here before my insurance gets cut off, what then? Do they kick me out because I can't pay, or do they keep me here and let me get into more debt?"

Erin squints at me. "Really?"

"I'm saying, this is what I'm worried about. Everyone's stories are just so gut-wrenchingly painful and here I am saying I'm worried about my job and paying my bills. I'm insufferable."

"It's more than that. You're minimizing because you don't want to talk about it."

A hot flush washes over me. We're talking about me. We always seem to talk about me.

"Why are you sad?" I ask again, hoping she won't ignore me.

"I don't know. I wake up sad, I fall asleep sad. It's all I am at this point."

"I don't believe that."

She frowns. "My head doesn't care what you believe."

"I just mean that you're more than sadness or depression or whatever you want to call it. You're also kind. You comforted me last night. You're pretty and funny." I want to keep going, but her eyes are turning glassy. Compliments aren't helping anything.

"I just don't see the point."

"In what?" I'm not expecting her to answer, but I still ask.

"Do you really think it's healthy to use people diagnosed with severe mental illness as a measuring stick for how fucked up or not fucked up you are?"

I consider it.

"Would you feel better if I assured you that you're sufficiently mentally ill to be here?"

I cringe; terror grips my chest at the idea of her knowing how truly screwed up I really am. "I know I am," I whisper.

Erin won't let me redirect the conversation to her or deflect from the things I don't want to talk about. What did she say at group therapy? *Everyone lies.* That's what she said. Does she think I lied to her? I want to ask her again why she's sad. She'll give me a non-answer or change the subject again.

"Do you think I lied?"

"I..." she looks at the wall. "Not in so many words."

"Please just tell me."

"I thought you liked me, and I felt stupid. Because you don't."

"But I do like you. Why would you think I don't?"

She sighs. "You were gone when I came back this morning. Then at group this morning you didn't even look at me and sat on the other side."

"Oh, I just plopped down in the closest chair. Then I felt committed because I didn't want people to think I was switching chairs to get away from them. And you already have to be around me 24/7. I thought maybe you could use a break from me." I shrugged.

"That's it?"

"Yes."

Erin studies my face. I exhale and the air feels lighter again.

"I trusted the wrong person," she begins.

I hold my breath, afraid to move, worrying I'll break the fragile trust I am trying to build.

"Someone I trusted. Someone I thought I could love betrayed me. I was in college, put on academic probation and nearly kicked out because it upended my life. My family's patience for my depression had been wearing thin already." She pauses to take a breath. "There was a Christmas party. This last try, wasn't my first try." She glances at me and then looks down.

I shift on the bed, not wanting to seem too interested and not disinterested either.

"I was supposed to show up, be the perfect daughter, going to the perfect school, so they could look good in front of their friends, coworkers, and an assortment of neighbors they hate. Anyhow, I wasn't well because of the mix of pills and alcohol. They dumped me in the furthest room of the house and told me to sleep it off. I called a friend, they called an ambulance and the perfect party wasn't so perfect."

"That's fucked up."

"They told people I had to go to bed early because I was leaving for Durango the next morning. They left me there, on the floor. Because of it, I don't talk to them anymore, or they don't talk to me. It's been years. I've been on my own. I know: I should be over it. It's been years. I'm afraid people will leave and if they don't leave, I'm afraid they'll hurt me."

I feel bad for making fun of her before.

"It's not why I'm depressed. I was depressed before that ever happened. But it made it worse, a thousand times worse. They cared more about appearances than my life. It reinforced my worst fears, and I spiraled."

"I'm sorry they did that to you. You didn't deserve that."

"I mean, I did challenge our 60-year-old neighbor to a drinking contest and then picked a fight with him when he declined."

I grin. "You know, I like you more and more every time you tell me something about yourself."

She laughs, and it's the first laugh since I met her that isn't self-conscious or restrained.

"You're so strange. You like me more because my parents disowned me, or because I was drunk and stupid?"

"Did you pick an argument, or did you throw a punch?"

Her face turns a deep shade of pink. "I missed entirely and knocked over an end table."

"That's awesome, I mean it's an awful story, but I bet he had it coming."

"He did." Erin half smiles, and then looks at the door. "I don't trust easily."

"Neither do I." Despite this fact, I trust Erin. Her honesty about everything—good, bad, and ugly—makes me like her. "I'm sorry someone did that to you. It's really fucked up."

"Thanks." She shrugs.

I have to remind myself to keep it in check. My track record with roommates isn't great, and I'm not far separated from my last awkward living situation that went downhill fast because she was a neurotic head case and I lack the ability to keep my mouth shut. Don't get too attached, because these four walls are temporary, and after this, Erin is going to go back to her life and never look back. I should do the same.

21

Before

BEFORE I LEFT MY apartment, I cranked down the air conditioner as low as it would go and cracked a window. The electricity bill was in my roommate's name. A three-hundred-dollar electricity bill would be a fun surprise for her. I layered on socks and sweaters when I was home and slept with two blankets during the day. She probably wouldn't pay the bill and they'd disconnect the electricity, but it wasn't in my name. Why should I care? I'd just reconnect it in my name.

As I locked the door, I felt a spark of joy in sticking it to her. Outside my door, an extension cord hung from the light between Carlos's door and mine. There was a light switch adapter in the socket. Carlos's door was cracked open, the cord disappearing into his apartment.

"I said moo, bitch!" Carlos yelled from inside his apartment.

I nudged the door open to find Carlos at his desk and Rudder with his computer at the normally vacant spare desk. All the lights were off and the only thing that had power in the apartment was their computers.

"What's this?" I motioned to the cord.

"We got to the cow level." Rudder smiled at me, pointing at the screen.

"Shit. Run," Carlos called out. Rudder returned focus to the screen as both of their characters on screen ran in the other direction from bipedal cows wielding halberds into another horde of bipedal cows. "Damnit, not that way. Back, back."

The cows walked around saying *moo* very matter-of-factly and swinging their weapons.

"That hurt," Rudder said. "Running."

"Don't run," Carlos said. "Too late, and we're dead."

"What's with the cord?"

Carlos and Rudder spun in their chairs. Carlos lit up a smoke. "Fucking electric company. The unemployment check didn't come till yesterday; I deposited it, but I have to wait for it to clear before I can pay the electric. I told them I'd pay them today, but they wouldn't give me a day. Probably so they can also charge me the reconnect fee. So I had a few bucks and bought the light socket adapter. With that, an extension cord, and a few power strips, we're back in business. The power should be back on as soon as they send someone out, which they take their sweet time doing."

"You know it's over ninety degrees out, you don't have AC, and you decide to run two computers in the dark with the door cracked open?"

"Yeah, and? It's a dry heat."

I rolled my eyes.

"You know I have AC and it's like sixty degrees in my apartment. Just relocate."

"No way; it'll be back up any minute now and it took us two hours to set up the network," Carlos protested.

"It only takes two hours to set up the network because you spend half that time making everyone share out their drives so you can pilfer their porn."

"That's half the point."

"I think it took three hours; too many IP conflicts." Rudder shook his head.

"There are two of you; how many conflicts could you have?"

"Before the power went out, we had more people."

"Where?"

"Two on the coffee table and a few on the floor." Carlos pointed at a few spots.

"You didn't invite me," I said.

"You were at work." Carlos looked at me, confused.

"How long have you been in here? I've been back and slept since."

"Oh wow," Rudder said. "The time just disappeared. I have to be at work in four hours. I need to get some sleep."

"You wanna crash on the couch?" Carlos asked.

"No, I need to get home. Cool if I leave my computer here?"

"Yeah. Come back and play more when you get off. I'll even have electricity."

"Great. Talk to you later." Rudder grabbed his backpack and headed out the door. "See you later." He waved to me and walked out the door.

"You had two dollars and you spent it on a light socket adapter instead of just coming over?"

"You've been avoiding me since the other night." He pointed at me with two fingers with his clove cigarette wedged in between.

"Are you guys like best friends now or something?" I asked, not wanting to discuss how I had been avoiding talking about being followed home from the bar.

"He's cool. I was thinking about seeing if his lease was up soon. I could use some help with the rent. I'm running out of things to sell."

"You barely know him," I countered, unsure of why I'd care if Carlos and Rudder were friends since I was friends with both of them.

"He's a good guy and I need a roommate if I have any chance of keeping my apartment."

"He's kinda weird," I said.

"My evil little sister, we're all pretty weird. What's your deal?"

What *was* my deal? "I suppose if I wanted to keep my work and personal lives separate, I shouldn't have introduced you two."

"Exactly." Carlos nodded and turned back to his computer. "We've all got our own shit. Rudder's just been through different shit than you."

"I think the night shift is getting to me. I barely see anyone besides you and people I work with. Wait, what did he tell you?"

"About what?"

"You said he's been through different shit. What shit?" I asked, suddenly far more interested in this conversation than I had been a minute ago. Carlos knew things I didn't. The part of me that loved figuring things out perked up. Another piece of the puzzle that was Rudder was about to be revealed.

"If you want to know, why don't you just ask him?" Carlos said, spinning back in his chair and knocking the ash off his smoke.

"In the thirty minutes our shifts at work overlap? It's a little difficult to transition from shift turnover to deep childhood trauma." I took the seat at the computer Rudder had abandoned.

"We didn't delve deep into childhood trauma. We talked about video games. You know he'd never heard of Asteroids? He just said that he had a super religious upbringing, and he didn't play video games or watch movies. So, he's catching up."

"That sucks," I said. A wave of guilt hit me for being excited over the potential for juicy gossip when the truth was kind of sad.

The room lit up and the air conditioner kicked back on.

"Now if you'll excuse me, I have to retrieve my corpse from the cow level."

"I was going to go grocery shopping and run errands, but I can do that later. Want some help?" I grinned.

"Sure. I'll wait in town for you."

22

Before

TUESDAY, I RETURNED TO work expecting nasty emails about everything that went down Friday night, but there was nothing. By the end of the week, I questioned if it had happened how I remembered it. It was a hiccup. Technology sometimes doesn't make sense and does weird things. When that happens, just reboot and move on. So that's what I tried to do. Reset and move on.

I hadn't seen Ian, the night security guard, all week. Like he said, they randomize the schedule to be unpredictable. He probably came by when I was inside working. I had a nagging thought in the back of my brain that I had seen him, or rather, he'd seen me, through the eyes of the creepy stalker at the bar. Even though it didn't make any sense, it was something my mind entertained.

The phone had rung three times in the last four hours, busy for a Friday night. I spent the time between calls checking the cord on my headset, setting it on the other side of the phone farther away from my computer with no improvement. The static on the line doubled my call time because I had to ask everyone to repeat themselves. The last call was especially painful. A woman called saying the Internet was down because when she clicked on the blue *E* on her desktop, nothing happened. Yes, the entire Internet is down because your browser won't work. They think a reboot is magic, and I'm a genius for fixing the issue in a five-minute call.

"Shit, where is the stupid fucking clipboard?" I stood up and looked around, checking all the desks and around the room. Giving up, I forwarded the phone to my cell phone, grabbed the flashlight, and headed back out to find the clipboard.

I could print a new sheet, but it had the checks from first shift and second shift on it. It should have been filled out to turn over to the next shift in the morning. I traced my steps on the third floor. I walked down the dark hallway, the one I had first walked down for my interview for this job. I swung the light around on any surface where I might have set it down.

The air shifted, dropping in temperature by at least ten degrees. The unused sections of the office were usually warmer because they didn't want to spend the money to cool the whole floor. Even though three of the four floors were underground, it would get warm. At night the temperature dipped into the 90s, and the courtyard at the bottom was open to the elements. The Phoenix sun was brutal and unforgiving for six months out of the year that it would left the scorched earth of the desert sizzling well into the night.

A faint rustling noise came from behind me at the back of the room. My feet cemented to the floor; I held my breath, afraid to make any noise. The rustling sound came from all the corners like there was something all around me, closing in. The hair on my arms stood on end. I was covered in gooseflesh from neck to ankles. My back became warm. I stood in at least a ten-degree temperature differential. Sweat beaded on my forehead even though it was on the cooler side. I squeezed my eyes closed and stood as still as I could.

I strained, listening for any hint of what was making the sound, but it was silent. The room was still except for my ragged breath. My body refused to move. What would be behind me if I turned around? My back was to the exit. My only options were to go forward or back the way I came. Neither sounded safe. But safe from what? My breath quickened and I forced myself to open my eyes. On my left, a shadow crossed in front of the blinds. It had to be Ian.

I spun on my heel to head to the exit. The flashlight's beam didn't penetrate the darkness. I tilted the flashlight toward me to check and looked down, blinding myself. *Wow, that was smart, Danni.* I blinked and shook my head. The screen burn on my eyes from the flashlight lingered, dominating my field of vision as I struggled to readjust to the darkness.

I stepped forward into the hallway and the temperature normalized, and my quick steps became a hurried trot. I got to the empty reception desk, turned right, and burst out the door so quickly, I couldn't stop myself from bashing my knee on the railing.

"Motherfucker," I yelped. The open-air courtyard absorbed the sound like I was in a room coated with acoustic foam and not an open building with hundreds of square feet of exposed concrete.

With fresh air in my lungs, I dismissed my fears and laughed at myself. It was just my overactive imagination and sound vibrations; infrasound, like Rudder had said. *Remember, Danni, your job is to do the checks on time and not fuck up.* Find the clipboard, get back to the desk, and hunker down till the next round of checks, then again till the sun comes up. Simple.

I took a slow breath in and out, holding the railing to steady myself. The courtyard was dark; the grass looked black. My footsteps echoed as I took the stairs, and I was grateful that something sounded and felt like it should. I opened the door into the courtyard, took two steps out, tripped forward, and caught myself. My mouth gaped open; my jaw shook as I scanned the courtyard and the walkway. It was impossible.

What I'd thought was faulty lighting was a blanket of moths ranging in size from an inch to almost a foot-long wingspan. The ground was so thick with them that they climbed over each other, some taking flight and then landing on another. I screamed and slapped my arm as something crawled up it. A moth flew at me and then toward the courtyard. I ducked and covered my hair. My eyes went wide; I didn't know if they would ever close again. I spun to get back to the stairwell; a caterpillar inched along the handle. The walkway was littered with caterpillars and moths. Even in my shock, I wondered how both could be here; they should all change around the same time, with the weather. It wasn't spring. It was late fall.

I covered my hand with my shirt and pushed the caterpillar off the handle, swiping my badge to get back into the stairwell. It beeped but did not open.

"Fuck," I said. I put my back to the wall. My eyes were locked, riveted on the sea of insects covering the ground. It moved and flowed like a river of wings and insect legs.

I couldn't run. I could barely walk without stepping on something. I inched along against the wall, shifting my eyes back and forth to avoid touching anything but unable to look away from what had to be tens of thousands of insects writhing like a pile of mating snakes, every moment petrified that if I disturbed one, they would all react.

I took a hair tie off my wrist and gathered my hair in a low ponytail, tucking it into the back of my shirt. My eyes darted spastically, drawn to everything that moved.

I couldn't get into the stairwell. If I could get to the other stairwell, I could wait it out.

I inched closer and closer to the door to the datacenter. If I couldn't get into one, I would get into the other. I decided it as if it were a fact. The door to the stairs was twenty feet away and the datacenter was thirty, not a straight shot but by the walkway. Moths landed on my jeans and I brushed them off.

The air conditioning unit in the datacenter kicked on. The glass shuddered in the windowpane. I screamed and clapped my hand to my mouth to muffle the noise, but it was too late. Tens of thousands of moths took flight. I couldn't hear my screams as their hideous wings brushed my hands, arms, and face.

Tears streamed down my face and I fell to my knees, still holding my hands over my mouth. My eyes were clenched closed like a fist. The world seemed to be made of flapping insect wings. Something crawled across my head, and I slapped it off. My breath was jagged and I couldn't get enough air.

All I needed to do was stand. *Come on, Danni. Get the fuck up.* Pushing against the ground, I forced myself upright and my eyes open. Everything looked like a scrambled cable channel with only flashes of an image through the wall of static. Eighty percent of the image was flapping wings and the other twenty percent was the building and the door I was desperately trying to find.

There! The door!

I ran for it, mouth closed, eyes open. My foot landed in front of the door and in the same motion, I swiped my badge in front of the badge reader, it beeped, the light turned green, I turned the handle.

The door opened; I went into the stairwell and slammed the door behind me, brushing my arms and running my hands through my hair to be sure I didn't have any of them on me.

A few had followed me into the stairway. They flapped in confusion, flocking to the light and away from me.

I ran up the steps. My heart pounded in my chest and I gasped for air. I took the three flights of stairs so fast that I was light-headed by the time I reached the first floor—the ground level.

At first, the door stuck. I put my weight into the metal pressure bar and the door gave all at once. I tumbled out onto the sidewalk next to the parking lot. The door clanged shut and rang into the night air. I was hyperventilating.

In my rush to get out, I hadn't formed a plan. My purse and keys were at my desk. All I had was my badge to get back into the building or my feet to just walk away. I could go to Rudder's other job, but if they carded me at the door, I didn't have my driver's license.

The next five minutes seemed the most pressing; if I could figure out what to do in the next five minutes, that would take care of things. I was stagnant and undecided, two seconds from calling my boss in the middle of the night and quitting. I'd take the verbal abuse that I'm sure would follow. It might even be a relief.

I crumbled to the ground, running my fingers through my hair, brushing it in a self-soothing manner. My eyes wouldn't focus on anything. I smoothed my hair over and over. Time passed, and I was unaware of how long I'd been outside.

"Danni?" a voice said. I turned toward the sound. It was Ian.

"Hi," I said. The ground was hard, my legs were falling asleep, and everything was stiff. I pushed myself up and stood.

"Are you okay?"

"No."

"Did something happen? I just got here and saw you sitting there," he said, looking around, perhaps for a perpetrator or something else that would explain my state.

"I..." Words failed me. What could I say? There were bugs and I freaked out. Wow, I could hear how it sounded and still I said, "There were moths. So many."

His eyes widened and mouth opened and then the expression washed off his face, replaced by a smile and those storm blue eyes, clear and calm. What wasn't he telling me?

"I've seen a few, just you know, around the lights, drawn to the lights like a moth to the flame," he chuckled. "You have a phobia or something?"

I wrinkled my brow. The look I gave him wiped the smile from his face. He looked around and then back at me. Heat rose up into my chest and threatened to come out my mouth in the form of words. His words were so dismissive and reductive of what I'd experienced. I didn't have a phobia of insects, but I might after that. "It's not like that," I said.

"You want me to check it out?" he asked, swiping his badge at the door and holding it open. He didn't ask me where it had happened; he knew it was inside. Although, if they'd been out here, it's likely that I would have gone inside to avoid them. Part of me wanted him to witness it too and see him try to wrap his mind around it. The other part of me wanted it not to be real. But I also didn't want to look like a girl whose whole world was shattered by a few bugs.

"Well, you have to do your rounds anyhow. And I need to get back to my desk." I looked at my phone to check the time. I'd been outside longer than I thought, and I still didn't know where the clipboard was. It was almost time to check on the backups.

"If you're too scared, I can go and come back and let you know," he smirked. I have an older brother; I know when I'm being laughed at. I gritted my teeth and crossed my arms over my chest.

"I'm fine. It's fine," I said. It was just some bugs, no big deal. I mean, it was a lot of fucking bugs.

He held the door and motioned with his hands in an *after you* motion. I exhaled loudly and reentered the stairwell. My stomach churned and everything in the core of my being was screaming that I shouldn't go back in. I took every step slowly and deliberately, taking deep breaths as I went, steeling myself for what was in the building. At least this time, someone else would see it.

Ian opened the door on the fourth floor. A single dead moth laid on the ground. The courtyard remained unchanged, nothing but the green of the fake grass and the planters. The only moth was the one dead one on the ground that I must have stepped on when I ran for the exit.

"Was that the moth?" He smiled at me, his lip curled, and I sensed a laugh on its way.

"It had friends," I said.

"Is that your clipboard?" Ian asked, pointing to the bench outside the computer room.

"Yeah," I said. Walking over to it, I snatched it up and walked away, feeling his eyes on my back and not caring. "I have work to do," I said without turning around.

I tried to push it all away. Had I imagined it? It all seemed so real, so visceral. Had my brain taken one moth and repeated it thousands upon thousands of times? Was it exhaustion? Paranoia? I had a job to do, a paycheck to earn, and now a dog counting on me. I sucked it up and got back to work.

23

Before

TRAFFIC LURCHED FORWARD, THEN became a wall of brake lights.

I slammed on the brakes to avoid smashing into the idiot in front of me. Traffic slowed, likely due to an accident or people trying to catch a glimpse of an accident on the opposite side of the freeway. No one is happy on the I-10 at 7 a.m. It's purgatory on wheels. No matter how much people yelled at the other drivers, we sat stuck, waiting, hoping it would end soon.

The only thing waiting for me was a mostly empty apartment, a dog, and a bed. I followed a white box truck and fought to stay awake since I had nowhere pressing to be. The sun glared down. Even with tinted windows and sunglasses, it was still an assault on my eyes.

I was two days away from the weekend—the two days I worked alone. I dreaded those two days of the week. The days that I worked with Mike were boring to the point it was practically torture. Even though he barely talked, it was still a comfort having someone there. Everything went wrong on the days I worked alone. Was it the weird sound vibrations? But when strange things happened, Ian, the security guard, always seemed to be nearby. I was missing something, a part of the equation that would make everything fall into place.

Traffic stopped again. I slowed, still behind the box truck. There was something strange about Ian. I couldn't quite figure it out. His words and mannerisms twisted around in my mind, looking for something that filled in the blanks.

Traffic moved forward and I mindlessly accelerated. I stared at the back of the box truck till my eyes went out of focus. My little pickup felt so small next to it.

Its metal bar was at the level of a car bumper. I zoned out, mesmerized by the mundane delivery truck.

Everything snapped back into focus as I watched my vehicle slide toward the truck. The bar underneath gave with no resistance as I slid under it, heading for it like an embrace. Outside my body, I watched myself opening my arms to greet it, as if I was meeting my destiny.

The top of my truck sheared off. The bed of the truck struck my neck. The force sheared my head from my body; it flew through the back window, where it came to rest in the bed of my truck. It rolled as everything came to a stop. My eyes turned storm blue, then closed.

I blinked. The truck was at a full stop. I threw my weight into the brake with full force. A puff of grey smoke emanated from my tires. My heart thundered in my rib cage, feeling like it might explode. A hot rush of adrenaline and panic rose from my chest; it was hard to know if it was the near miss or if it was the image of my own head flying from my body. The thought of my impending demise felt like an embrace. But wouldn't it be a relief? If my head wasn't attached to my body, I wouldn't have to go to work.

I tried to shake the feeling off. It was a dream, right?

That was the most terrifying part of all, that death seemed like a better possibility than spending another night at that job. Both felt like death. Going to work felt like insanity, but not going meant losing everything I'd worked for. When all options feel like death, what choice do I choose?

I checked my right rearview mirror, jerked the wheel, and entered the right lane to exit the freeway. The car behind me honked the horn and the driver flipped me off. I waved.

At the exit ramp, I turned left and reentered the freeway going the other direction. With any luck, Rudder should just be getting off from his other job. I didn't know what help he could provide, but I didn't want to be alone. I needed adult supervision, but I couldn't articulate why.

24

Before

RUDDER WAS WALKING OUT of work when I called him to see if he'd meet me for coffee. Walking into the diner was like walking into the 1970s. Rudder waved me over to his table. I slid into the booth covered in worn burnt orange vinyl, flipped over a coffee mug, and poured a cup before saying anything. The first sip was bliss because it was diner coffee. The free work coffee tasted like it'd been burned into existence by sheer hate. In comparison, this was bliss.

"What's new with you?" I asked.

He wrinkled his brow. "Nothing. You didn't sound good on the phone."

I sighed and relaxed my shoulders. "I'm not okay."

"You look like a cat that went through the spin cycle."

"I look like a wet cat?" I said, pouring another packet of sugar into my coffee.

"It's a metaphor," he said.

"It's a shitty thing to say."

He tilted his head down and gave me a long look.

"Fine, it's true. I'm a fucking mess," I said. "Yes, it's work. It's a nightmare and I don't know what to do."

"Quit," he said. The word came out like it was the most simple, easy thing to do. Like it wouldn't upend my entire life and I wouldn't lose everything.

"It's not that simple. I'll lose my apartment."

"Get a different one," he said.

"Moving is expensive," I said. "I don't see how that's a solution. Also, I have to get a job to have an apartment."

"You can't get another job?" he asked.

"The one great truth of job hunting: It's easier to get a job when you have a job."

"You can work with me at the porn shop. Same hours, different problems." He shrugged.

"I can't pay my rent with that." I flipped through the menu.

"This is very circular," he said.

"Because it is. It's dominos. My life is teetering on the brink. It's almost comical how little it will take to tip me from semi-functional pseudo adult into unemployed and homeless," I said.

"Don't you have family here? You have a place to go then, right?"

"You have no idea what I'd do before that became an option. I'd find a nice cardboard box and take my chances on the street. It's almost winter; Phoenix is lovely in December. It could be good—you know, until April when I die of heat exhaustion."

"Ha, ha," he said. "Okay, so you can't quit, you can't move, and you can't keep working there why?"

I set the menu down pausing to come up with the right answer. *Friday and Saturday shifts are cursed? The building is only haunted on the nights I work alone?*

"You remember the other night, when we were followed back to my place by that weird guy?" I ask.

"Yes, I remember creepy dude," he said.

"Something strange happened while he was talking to me," I said.

"All of it was strange."

"I'm serious. Weird things have been happening around me, especially at work."

"Like what?"

"Like the power fluctuations and then this one time, all the servers went nuts all at the same time, which is statistically impossible. Then there are these giant months. Carlos called them... what did he call them? Something Death. Black Witch Moth thing."

119

"You're still upset about that moth?" He asked it slowly, as if to point out the insanity behind what I was saying.

"No, not *a* moth. I saw tens of thousands of them. A moth that yeah, might venture this far north but generally doesn't. And then there were enough of them to blanket the courtyard."

"Blanket?" He squinted at me.

"Tens of thousands of them," I repeated. "They were everywhere. You've never seen one there?"

"Nope." He took a sip of coffee and then looked at the waitress walking up to us.

"It freaks me out just thinking what happens if the power goes out and the badge readers stop working. I have nightmares that it rains and fills with water, like a giant bathtub, and I drown there."

The waitress stood at the end of the table. My words hung in the air; I smiled at her, trying to move past talking about my demise.

"Ready to order?" she looked at Rudder, her eyes darting to me and then back to him.

"French toast, no meat," he said.

She turned to me but pulled her arms in closer to her body.

"Special, over medium with bacon. Actually, can I have the bacon that comes with his French toast?"

"Sure." She repeated our order and left with the menus.

"Tens of thousands?" He raised his eyebrows.

"I'm not exaggerating," I said. "It was horrific. My skin is still crawling."

"What did you do?"

"I ran to the stairs and got out of there. But then Ian showed up. He's always there when these weird, creepy things happen. And we went back into the building and they were all gone."

"Ian?" he asked.

"Yeah, Ian. The graveyard security guy."

"Do you think it's possible you imagined it? Maybe you fell asleep and had a nightmare or something?"

"No, it happened. There was one of them dead near the door to the stairs."

"Just one?" he asked.

"Look, I'm not crazy. Then we got followed home by the weird guy at the bar. But as he was talking to me, his eyes changed. The turned blue, just like the security guard's eyes. Then they changed back. I didn't imagine it. I saw it."

"I'm not sure what to say. That sounds impossible. It sounds like you're under a lot of stress."

"Don't do that thing," I said.

"What thing?"

"The thing where you're saying nice things and empathizing but what you're really doing is thinking that I'm losing my shit and I just need some sleep and a juice box, like a crazy kindergartner. I'm not losing my mind. I might feel like it. But these things are real. I saw them. I felt them." I was starting to become angry, and I realized I was raising my voice. I focused on my coffee and said quietly, "It's real. What do I do?"

"Let's operate under the assumption that everything is real, and that work has a power issue, a moth infestation, and a weird security guard that I've never seen. What does it all add up to?" he asked.

"I— I don't know," I said. That question hadn't occurred to me. Something was going on and it meant something. I just didn't know what. "You've never seen him?"

"No. I don't think there is a security company. Or if there is, I've never seen them. We have an alarm system and if there's one thing I know about work, it's that if they can get by without paying a warm body to do something, they will." He poured another cup.

I soaked in this new bit of information. What if there wasn't a security company monitoring the building?

"You don't know what you're dealing with or what it means. It could be good. Maybe they are moth fairies and they grant wishes or some shit," he suggested.

"It feels like something is happening. Help me figure it out. Carlos said the moth is a harbinger of death. So that means someone might die. What if that someone is me?" I placed my hand over my heart.

"You're not dying," he said.

I pushed my hair back. "You don't know that."

"So how do we figure it out?" he asked.

"Well, we're geeks. Figuring shit out is what we do."

"Okay, Troubleshooting 101. When did the problem start?" He looked at me over his coffee cup.

"Soon after I began working in that weird building."

"Second question: Can you reproduce the problem?"

"Unknown."

"You think it's the security guard? But he wasn't at the club that night," Rudder pointed out.

"Yeah, but the weird guy's eyes changed color to the same as Ian's. It was like Ian was looking at me through that guy's eyes. Or rather, Ian's eyes in that guy's head."

"That's weird," he said.

"I agree," I said. "There was a security guard at the bar."

"But a different guy?"

"Yeah. Uniform could have been the same." I brought the coffee up to my lips, taking in the smell.

"Was it distinctive?"

"No." I sat back and looked out the window, hoping to find answers there.

"We have two bits of information. It's somehow related to work and possibly this guy Ian. We think he is... what? Evil? A demon? A wizard?"

If I didn't know him, I would have thought Rudder was making fun of me. "I think he's a person. But there is something off about him. Like when I told him about the moths, he gave me this odd look like he was shocked and then he played it off. Like the time my older brother told me that spiders fall from the ceiling and then laughed at me for looking up before I entered rooms for the next month."

"Like he's tormenting you?" he asks.

"Yeah," I said.

"Maybe you should ask him," Rudder said and took a sip of his coffee, looking at me over the top of the cup.

"Just ask him. And believe what he tells me? Why would he tell me the truth?" I asked.

"Well, you can at least see his reaction. Hey, what company does he work for?"

I blinked, "Some acronym... what was it?"

"You could do a search for the company. It's a little strange that they'd only send one guy every time and that you're the only one that sees him. I can't work seven days a week for the same company. So why haven't you seen anyone else?"

"This is also a valid question. We have more questions than answers."

"What now?" he asked.

"We isolate the variables until we have a theory that seems workable." I nodded, agreeing with myself. I was going to get to the bottom of this.

"You can still quit," he said. "But please don't."

I shook my head. It was too late for that now. I was committed, not just to figuring out the mystery but also committed to getting a regular paycheck. I had a plan: figure out what was going on, make it stop, keep working, keep making a paycheck. Simple.

"We need to see if his presence increases the weirdness and then we can say that he's causing it," I said.

"Correlation is not causation," he said as our food was delivered to the table.

"Well, correlation is all I have to go on."

25

After

SINCE MY WORLD WENT shitshow-sideways, time has had no meaning. It drains and drips through the day with no regard for the speed at which the Earth rotates around the sun. Of course, that's probably the disassociation talking. I'm alternating between fighting unconsciousness and begging for sleep. I take the pills they give me because the worst thing that could happen to me has already happened. In group, they would say that's a positive thing: Nowhere to go but up. As if people don't die on mountaintops. I'm out of my mind. Even if I'm not crazy, I'm still nuts. Was it even real? The question haunts me as much as the memories.

"Are you awake?" Erin asks.

"Yes. You too?"

"No. I'm deep in REM sleep dreaming about unicorns and popsicles."

"Do you ever wonder if you're just crazy?" I ask.

"You mean while I'm lying awake in a mental health ward?"

"Well, when you put it that way..." I roll over onto my side and prop my head up with my arm.

"Did you have an official diagnosis in mind for me?" Erin asks, not looking in my direction.

"I don't mean you per se. I'm not in a position to diagnose anyone."

"So, you mean just run of the mill crazy, in a general sense?"

"Not really. I meant more that I've been trying to figure it out. Ask myself where I went wrong and ended up here..."

Erin laughs a laugh like sandpaper. "Baby girl, you can do everything right and end up here. If you did everything wrong, you end up dead."

"I thought I was going to but now I don't know if it was real or not."

"Does it matter?"

Erin's question sits heavy with me.

"Shouldn't it matter what's real?" I've clung to the idea for so long that only real and authentic things matter.

"Was how you felt real?" she asks.

"Yeah, but that doesn't make it any more real, does it? How I feel isn't important if it's not real."

"How you feel put you in a hospital. I suggest you start caring more about how you feel. Maybe that's what led you here."

"Why are you here?"

She sighs and the air is still and quiet. Maybe it was inappropriate to ask. I open my mouth to apologize and say that she doesn't have to tell me when she speaks.

"Have you ever woken up and started crying? The thought of being awake and having to live and breathe in your own skin all day is so exhausting and awful that all you want to do was sleep?"

I tried to imagine it and couldn't. Things were bad but never that bad, or maybe just not yet.

"I'm sorry."

"Don't."

"Do you feel like that now?" The stillness of the room sucks all the air out. I'm afraid of her answers but can't stop myself.

"It's blunted." Erin turns on her side, facing me.

"And after you leave here?"

"I can't think about that now. How did you get here?" she asks me. "Are you one of the lucky ones that knows enough to check themselves in?"

"Lucky?"

"Yeah. One of the ones that comes in on their own two feet, knowing that they need help."

"I don't know how I got here."

"You don't remember?"

The question bothers me. I don't have the luxury of forgetting, yet there's something inaccessible. So many things from the last month are burned into my memory that eclipses everything. As if it's taking over my life, my identity, and everything I've ever known.

"What about you?"

"I was unconscious." Each word is a soft piano key, the sound of which reverberates out, carrying meaning not in the combination or words and letters. Do I ask the next question? Do I let her volunteer it?

"Everyone is so keen on keeping me from trying again but once I get out the door, no one will give me a second thought."

"I'm sorry," I say, because I can't think of anything else to say.

"Me too. Sorry about everything. Sorry I didn't do it right the first or second time."

"Why are you telling me this?"

"Because it doesn't matter. Because no one cares and the truth isn't going to change that."

"Why did you do it?"

"It made sense at the time."

"You said that before. I think you just don't want to answer."

A thousand questions rush through my head, all of them more intrusive than the last. My curiosity about her is growing. I want to know about the darkness inside of her and hold it up to my own, or maybe I just want tips in case I end up where she is.

"There was a moment, after I took the pills, that I was relieved. I don't know if it was because I expected to die, or if it was my mind and body slowing. If I could feel like that all the time, maybe I wouldn't think about dying all day every day."

The weight of it hung in the darkness. "Why do you want to die?"

"You misunderstand. I don't want to die. I want to stop being in pain. It feels like the only way is to stop existing. So don't make that mistake. I don't want to kill myself. I'm exhausted and carrying a two-thousand-pound weight with me every day. I wake up knowing that I'm going to have to carry it through the day.

People will compliment me, but really, they're just saying that I should be happy about carrying this every day. They see that I'm fortunate and I should be happy because I have so much of what they think they need to make them happy."

It's like she's reading my mind. She is beautiful, she has an education and a good job, but here she is, and I don't understand it. But thinking about it, I don't understand why I am here either. I don't know why I'm seeing these things.

"I have to believe it isn't a constant state of being. That someday I'll be better. But if I didn't think that was possible, what then? What do I say?"

"There's nothing to say." She pauses long enough that I notice the crickets chirping outside our window. "Well, there is. It's just that most of the things people say are more isolating than helpful. I don't need to be cheered up. It's reductive. A cheery platitude isn't enough to fix this, and people act like it should be."

"What should people say?"

The room is silent except for the sound of her breathing.

"Something that is honest, but kind. I almost died. What do you say to people who almost died?"

"I'm glad you're still here."

"Do you mean it?"

"Yes. You said honest."

"If you knew me, you wouldn't say that." The bedsprings complain as she rolls over on her side, away from me.

"So it doesn't matter what people say then because you'll invalidate it."

I sit up in bed. Erin's back is to me. Movement in the light coming in through the window draws my eye. A moth circles frantically because it's trapped inside. My mouth gapes open. My body won't move.

"It doesn't matter because everyone lies." Erin's words are far away. "Danni?" She's less than four feet way but her voice is floating down to me at the bottom of a dry well.

She touches my arm. I jolt backward, jerking away so fast that I fall to the floor. I push myself backward with my feet; my mouth is open, and unintelligible sounds come out. I'm without language. Words run through my mind but none of them gel into sentences.

"What's wrong?" Erin approaches, her hands out at her sides.

Words are failing me. The world is failing me. The lights are too bright, and every noise is like a drum inside my head. The walls are moving in. "Out. I need out." The sound of words coming out of my mouth is shocking. I reach for my head, unsure if I should cover my mouth, my ears, or my eyes. My face is wet with tears. I'm sobbing tears of devastation and confusion.

"Shh. It's going to be okay. I need you to take a breath. We can't go outside; we need to breathe. With me... In"—she breathes in—"and out..."

The air comes in in jagged, stuttering breaths.

"Just focus on me. Just breathe. In... Out..." She's the softness they were trying to achieve with the beige walls, but I am incapable of calm and a rush of anger joins my confusion.

I suck in a breath. There's a moth flittering at the light. It's an itch I can't scratch. I focus on Erin's face and wipe my tears. I'm panicking. The details of every object appear in high contrast; it's like trying to listen to five songs at top volume. Every sound replays in my mind like an echo and as a result, I can't hear anything. Erin's words are drowning in a sea of everything. Focusing on her voice and connecting her words to meaning takes every ounce of my concentration.

"That's good. In... out..." She looks at the door and then back at me. "Can I help you?"

I don't know the answer to this simple question.

I nod. I can barely speak. Breathing is a challenge. I watch the floor because the floor is quiet. Erin pulls me up; I don't offer help or resistance, but I allow her to bring me to a standing position. The door is so close and the other side promises safety if I can just get through the door. I grab the knob, expecting it to be locked, but it turns and the door opens.

I rush out the door.

"Where are you going?" Erin hisses after me.

Footsteps thud behind me and I break into a run down the hallway in the opposite direction of the nurse's station, not wanting to be seen. The wide hallways close in.

Stumbling, I catch myself and barely stay on my feet. I pause, unable to process directions. I don't want to look back; something could be chasing me. The TV room is empty and I turn, my back to the wall, waiting for what's coming. The lights are flickering—no, not flickering. They're strobing and drawing shadows on the floor. I look up, expecting to see a thousand little insects fluttering around the lights. There are none.

Erin stops next to me. She's looking out the windows at the night sky. It's everything I'm not; clear and calm. It feels like a lie. My skin is crawling. My breath is ragged.

"We need to go back. We shouldn't be out here. It's a panic attack." There's tension in her voice and I think she's trying to convince herself it's nothing.

The room is spinning, like a carnival ride that's pinned me to the wall with centrifugal force. My stomach drops as I'm hit with waves of nausea. "No, no, no, no, no." The sensation makes it hard to stand. My knees buckle and hit the floor. Glass rains down from the windows. I cover my head and scream.

Erin crouches on the floor next to me and clasps my hand. I pull her to me, trying to shield her from the glass. I push shards away, so she doesn't hurt herself. Blood smears on the linoleum. The hand I injured in the datacenter is bleeding. The wound isn't reopened, but blood is still flowing from the not yet healed flesh. My eyes can't be trusted. Blinking, I try to reorient myself in the spinning room.

Erin holds my head in her hands. Her eyes are wide and fixed on mine. I don't have answers to provide her; I don't know what's happening to me. The glass is gone. There's no blood. The footsteps of the staff approaching us slow as they get closer. They're either trying to figure out what's going on, or if I'm dangerous, like a wild animal. I feel wild.

"It's going to be okay," Erin lies.

"Everyone lies," she had said to me earlier, and I know from the look in her eyes she doesn't believe it, but she has no other words to offer me. I want to believe.

Darla and an orderly watch and we disentwine from one another. Erin helps me to my feet. The room is dark and quiet other than the sounds of my breathing. Darla's eyes blaze. I don't want her to see me cry, but it's too late. Tears are steaming down my face, and I bring my hands up to cover myself. They help me back to bed and give me more medication, either to calm me or to make me sleep. I'm not sure which, nor do I care as I wait to slide into unknowing unconsciousness.

26

Before

Mariposa De La Muerte. Harbinger of death.

Carlos's words echoed in my mind. I avoided the stairs, not admitting to myself it was because I was afraid.

Last week, I'd been hit with a wave of vertigo. The entire stairwell swung and shifted around me. My stomach dropped out, as if the floor had also dropped and I was falling. When my vision steadied, the lights dimmed and a shadowy lump lay on the landing below. It looked like me: bloodied and broken. I blinked and the landing was empty.

I wrote it down in the notebook, dated with a note: *disoriented, imagined or hallucinated falling down stairs, No Ian.* Then I rated every entry on severity, a scale of one to ten. Last week had a 6 next to it.

Things had been quiet since my talk with Rudder, as if it had a calming effect on the building, or on me.

I reached the courtyard.

"Ian?" I said, looking around the empty courtyard. I was trying to call his name and see if it would summon him. No answer came back, no movement. The courtyard was devoid of life; even the grass was fake. Minutes ticked by while I waited. The only sound was the hum of the fluorescent lights. I tapped the clipboard against the bench next to me. Looking around one more time, I gave up and walked to the computer room to do my walk-through.

I worked by the dull glow of the emergency lights because it was better than being blinded by the fluorescent shock of the datacenter fully lit. It also made the lights on the servers more visible. A server in the first row blinked amber, indicating a failed hard drive. The LED display read: *Drive 3 failed*.

I made a note on the walk-through report. First shift would call support to open a case and the replacement drive would be delivered within four hours. I collected the information they needed to open the ticket: the server name, the row the server was in, and the serial number of the server.

A droplet of sweat dripped down my back. The cheap outdoor thermometer with a cheerful rainbow read eighty degrees. Not hot by Phoenix standards, but by datacenter standards, it was sweltering. The air conditioning unit display didn't have an error on it. I propped open the door to the outside. I dragged a floor fan from the back of the room to the door and pointed it inside the room to get some of the cooler air circulating.

I scanned the checklist. There was a check for the temperature on the list, but no information on the expended range or threshold. I tapped the enter button on the air conditioning unit a few times. Then I kicked it with my foot, not hard, just enough to feel like it would do something. I had to decide—call someone and maybe wake them up or wait and check again later and then definitely wake someone up. Who the hell do I wake up for a cooling issue? That's not a server thing. There wasn't a facilities contact on my list.

I couldn't leave the door open to cool the room from the outside. I also couldn't stay in the datacenter all night while the room cooled. The unit was running; the air coming out was cold. I walked the remaining rows of servers and found a space heater. Worse than that it being in a cool row, the aisle where two rows of server racks faced each other and were supposed to be pulling in cooled air and blowing hot air out the back. The hotter the air it pulled in, the hotter it was when it came out the other side. Overheating could cause performance issues or even spontaneous reboots.

"Assholes." I pulled the plug and rolled it off to the side. The cool row was supposed to have perforated floor tiles so airflow could circulate through the raised floor and pull hot air out, but someone had swapped all the vented tiles with solid floor tiles. I shook my head at the floor and then went looking for the tile puller.

It was on the other side of the room.

I grasped the large handle and planted the two large suction cups on the tile. The two-foot-by-two-foot tile felt like it weighed thirty pounds. I pulled hard and stumbled backward, not expecting it to be as heavy as it was. I regained my balance and nearly dropped it on my foot. I lugged it with me as I searched for the misplaced vented floor tiles. I pulled the handle on the tile puller to release the suction and it thumped onto the floor, then used it to remove the vented tile and replace it with the solid one. I carried the tile back and stopped for a moment to catch my breath. One down and four more to go. It took me about ten minutes to swap the five solid tiles with five tiles intended for airflow. Sweat dripped down my forehead as the temperature in the room dropped steadily. A chill shook my body as the cold, dry air brushed my skin.

The thermometer had been near the space heater, so it had registered a higher temperature than the room had been overall. With the temperature dropping and the floor tiles back where they should have been, I took a deep breath.

"Unbelievable," I said under my breath. Someone didn't care about proper cooling principles because they were cold while working on the servers and then just left it for someone else to deal with. I wondered if second shift skipped the checks or just ignored it. I went to put the tile puller back where it belonged because someone had to be the responsible one.

Footsteps approached from the back of the room. They weren't quite footsteps, unless what was ambling toward me was a bear.

"Shit," I said. My stomach dropped as I remembered propping the door open to get cool air circulating. The fan had moved, pushed out of the way. Or had I placed it a little off center? The exit was farther away than whatever was at the back of the room. The tiles creaked under a massive weight.

I looked to the back of the room and back at the door. Run or investigate? *It's nothing*, I told myself. *It's not a person; it's just the building shifting.*

I picked up the flashlight and walked toward the sound. I couldn't leave an unauthorized person in the datacenter. I could get fired. I shined the flashlight down each row as I walked down the aisles, holding my breath between steps.

I caught movement out of the corner of my eye and shined the flashlight toward it. My breath quickened. There was nothing there.

I sighed in relief and shined the flashlight down the next aisle. Despite the temperature steadily dropping back down to where it should be, perspiration beaded on my forehead. A rush of cold air hit me; my muscles tightened and twitched.

The thing moved in the distance, no more than twenty feet away.

I froze, afraid to breathe. My thumb found the power switch on the flashlight, and I slid it into the off position while cringing at the soft click it made.

I wanted to shine the light on whoever or whatever was in the room. My survival instincts screamed at me to run for the door. Instead, I ducked behind a row of servers, hoping that whoever it was would find their way out, like a fly in the car when I open a window to let it out.

A shadow moved across the back wall. It faded away like a passing dust storm, just to reappear on the other side of the room in my peripheral vision. The thermometer's needle dipped to sixty-three degrees. I turned the flashlight on and pointed it in the direction of the shadow and it disappeared again. The light from the flashlight diffused and faded out about five feet from me. I hit the flashlight against the palm of my other hand.

I took a step toward the shadow, letting the flashlight point down. It made some sound between a hum and a buzz. I was transfixed.

It drew closer. It wasn't a shadow. It had a form and it moved, but it appeared to be made of the absence of light, or it absorbed light like a black hole.

I stumbled backward and dropped the flashlight. It came closer. It was inhuman in its form and movements; the arms were long and the shoulders too high. It had no neck. The figure was so unnatural in its proportions that it sickened my stomach, but it was incorporeal at the same time, like a swarm of insects. It was getting closer, and I didn't know if I should run or wait. A strange part of me wanted to walk into it and let it consume me.

"Danni?" Ian called to me from the open door.

I screamed and pivoted, and I was enveloped by the shadow. My skin erupted in gooseflesh, and I shivered in a way that was more like a convulsion. Shock rippled through me. I shook as if dunked in ice water, but the air was hot and humid to the point that it was swampy. It lingered on me.

"Ian," I called to him. He was standing outside the door. Pressure surrounded me and something was pushing in on me. I clenched my fists, held my arms out. My screams sounded far away, my ears felt full and wet, like having swimmers' ear. The sensation was hideous. The shadowy form squeezed me. I was enveloped by it like a translucent cocoon that muffled my screams.

Ian grabbed my arm. The shadow faded and evaporated. I shook and hugged myself before crumbling to the floor.

"Are you okay?" he asked.

I shook my head, unable to find the words.

"What happened?" I looked up at him from the floor. I didn't believe his feigned confusion. He rubbed his brow and flashed a strained smile that didn't touch his eyes.

"Did you see it?" I asked.

"See what?" he said, blinking at me.

"That thing." I held out my hand, requesting help getting up. He took it and pulled me into an upright position.

"What did you see?" He watched, measuring me. I didn't trust my eyes enough for the thoughts to form or for words to come out of my mouth. I'd sound like a crazy person, and maybe I was.

He avoided eye contact, but nothing in his demeanor said he was surprised to find me screaming and freaking out. Maybe he thought it was a matter of time till I lost my shit. Screaming my head off in the middle of an empty room sounded like the behavior of a crazy person, unless he had seen it too. If he wasn't surprised, and didn't think I was crazy, that left one explanation: He knew. Or maybe he was involved. He'd showed up again exactly when things were getting weird. I suspected he was evaluating my response to it. Maybe I was a lab rat. Ian asked, "What did you see?" not "What was it?" They're the same question, but they aren't.

"I'm fine," I said, even though he hadn't asked.

He shrugged and walked out of the computer room. I walked to the door, turned on the light, and shut the door behind him, then went back to my checks. These were only the first round of checks for the night. The thought sent a shiver down my spine.

It was only Friday night; I still had to do this twice the next day. Not to mention twice a day five days a week until I got another job. I squeezed my eyes and mouth closed, then opened them, trying to push out the thoughts. I wrote in the small notepad, *Friday, shadow thing(?) in computer room. Ian is complicit or actively causing*.

I flipped the notepad closed and it was decided. I needed to do something about Ian to make him stop whatever it was he was doing. Seeing him saunter out of the computer room without a care, completely unaffected, was what I needed to convince me. And now that I was sure, it was time to do something about it. It was time to formulate a plan. I dialed the phone.

27

After

"WHAT HAPPENED LAST NIGHT?" Erin looks ten years older when her brow furrows like that.

I pull my knees to my chest on my bed and sit with my back to the wall. It's lights out and we should be asleep. The floor is quiet except for the occasional footsteps, doors opening and closing. It runs like clockwork. Depending on my frame of mind, it either helps keep track of the time or makes me lose my mind.

"I don't know." I say it because it's true. I have no idea what happened. The days are scrambled and I'm not sure which yesterday she means. "What happened?"

"You lost your shit." She watches me, measuring my reactions.

"That doesn't really narrow it down."

"That's funny," she says, a faint smile teasing her lips. But I didn't say it to be funny.

"I don't remember which night was last night."

"Oh, sorry. I thought you were kidding." She looks away, "You ran out; you seemed really freaked."

How am I supposed to explain what I can't understand?

"I thought I had the market cornered on fucked up and neurotic." She pauses so long that I look over to see if she's asleep.

"Are they helping you?" The question comes out of my mouth from nowhere. Maybe because it's a question I ask myself: Is it helping?

"It's hard to say. I still feel useless, it still hurts to be awake. But before, I felt like I was teetering over the edge and now I feel like I'm an inch from it," she says.

"If we measure progress in inches, then that's a yes?"

"I'm so used to one step forward and two steps back that inches feel like nanometers."

"Movement is good, though. It's the stagnation that gets me. The thought that this is just my life now. That every day is going to be a repeat of the worst day."

She nods. "Movement feels like stagnation. It's just part of the roller coaster."

I sit with her words, rolling them over in my mind. What if the roller coaster wasn't just the ups and downs of life, but the distraction keeping us from realizing we always just end up in the same place at the end? "It's like we're trying to describe the same thing but with different words because nothing feels quite right."

"Maybe. Makes sense; we're uncomfortable in everything, even in our own words." She rolls over in bed, turning toward me.

"I'm worried you're going to get better and leave."

"Why?" She props herself up on her elbow.

"I like being around you." The words come out at just above a whisper.

"Really? You act like you don't care."

"It's not you." Every word that comes to mind to try and explain myself just sounds insane. Instead, I'm keeping it to myself, worried that my words will only make things worse.

"It feels like it's me." Erin roughly fluffs her pillow and plops her head back down, looking up at the ceiling.

"No, it's me. I'm not a fully functional human and that's got nothing to do with you. I don't feel like I belong anywhere." I let the words hang in the room like curtains I might take back.

"You mean you don't think you belong here with the crazy people... like me," Erin says, not looking at me.

"No, I spend time questioning not who I am or where I belong but rather asking myself *what* I am. It makes sense that I'm here. I've spent a life disconnected in some way, checked out and disengaged. Doesn't that make me crazy too? And

I don't want you to leave because you're the only person that could understand that."

"Is that it? You want someone to understand you?"

"Doesn't everyone?" I ask.

"It's a selfish reason."

"Maybe I'm a selfish person." The words were meant to just be contrary to what she said, but as I say them, they feel truer than I'm comfortable with. I exhale an exhausted sigh, a sign of surrender. I don't want to argue. I push and she pulls. I pull and she pushes.

The door opens; Ivy pokes her head in and scans the room. She nods at me, notes something on the clipboard, and shuts the door behind her. In my mind, a twenty-minute clock starts, because that's how long it'll be until she's back.

"It's funny how much a mental health hospital is like my last job."

Erin turns her head toward me and shoots me an annoyed look.

"Except I'm the one that used to carry a clipboard and do the checks, but on servers instead of on people. Everything is acronyms and codes that only mean something to the people doing the diagnosing. It can go from peace to panic in minutes."

"Yes, exactly the same," Erin said. "I'm sure IT is exactly like a nuthouse."

I shrugged; it lined up to me. The main difference, aside from the obvious, is that I am surrounded by women instead of men. The more I think about it, the more it tracks. I don't get paid for this, but taking care of my mental health is a type of work.

"Erin." My voice is soft and almost apologetic.

"What?"

"I don't know what's real anymore." Every word out of my mouth feels like admitting failure. I feel a tear on my cheek and realize that I'm crying. Not a downpour, just a drizzle.

"Yeah, you said that you hallucinate. That's part of it, hon." She no longer sounds annoyed with me for keeping her awake.

"I know, but I don't know if I believe they aren't real."

"Well, that's why you're here."

I nod, sniffle, and wipe the tears away. "But if it's real, then the meds won't work and I'll never leave here. But you'll leave. Everyone else will leave."

Erin inhales deeply and sighs out the air. "Well, I guess if that's the case, you should just focus on how it affects you."

"What do you mean?"

"Well, whether or not it's real, you still experienced it, right?" Erin sits up in bed.

"Yes—" The word comes out as a question.

"And it was traumatic, right?"

"Yes." This time, I say it with absolute conviction.

"So, deal with the trauma."

"While I'm still being traumatized?"

"Are you being traumatized because it's happening or because you don't know if it's real?"

"I..." I tilt my head and weigh the question. "How do I separate that out?"

She shrugs.

"Why are you sad?" I ask.

"That's reductive. I'm not sad; I'm hollowed out. I'm morose."

"Why?" I press.

"Why is the sky blue?"

"There's a scientific reason for that. I don't remember exactly what it is."

"Exactly," she said as if it explained everything.

"You're morose because of science?"

"Not what I was trying to say. I'm sad because the chemicals in my brain are trying to murder me. I have a parasite inside of me. It's coded into my DNA and no matter how much I know that, I still feel like a worthless piece of shit that doesn't deserve to live."

"I'm sorry you're in pain." I push myself off the bed and stand beside her. Reaching out to touch her shoulder, I hesitate and pull back. Instead, I sit next to her on the bed.

"You can touch me. I'm not diseased." Her shoulders curl forward, her head hangs. She looks like she's trying to curl up into the fetal position while sitting.

"I didn't know if you wanted me to." I still don't know what to do to provide comfort. It's a fight between what I think is the right thing to do, what will make her uncomfortable, and trying to not make things worse. Sometimes, as I'm actively trying not to make things worse, that seems to be the outcome anyway.

She leans toward me and I reach out my arm and receive her in a half hug, my arm around her shoulders and her head on my shoulder. I smell her shampoo; it's the same one we all use here, but somehow it smells sweeter.

"You're just using me," she says.

The words paralyze me and I struggle with how to respond. "How am I using you?"

"It's easier to try to fix the depressed girl than it is to deal with your own shit. Once you figure out you can't fix me, you'll move on like everyone else does."

The words are a sharp knife that cuts so deep and fast that for a moment, I don't feel the depth of the wound. "Can I care about you, be fucked up, and be running from my own shit at the same time? Maybe all those things can be true simultaneously."

"You care about me?" She lifts her head and furrows her brows.

"Yes."

"Why?"

"I'd love to answer that question, but I have a feeling I'm talking to the chemicals in your brain that are trying to kill you. No offense to you, but I'm not their biggest fan."

She scrunches her eyebrows together. "I guess that makes two of us," she says in an uncertain tone. "I'm exhausted."

"I should let you sleep," I say and withdraw my arm from her shoulders and rest my hand in my lap.

"Stay." Her hand overlays mine as she looks into my eyes. "It'll help me fall asleep. Please."

I nod. "Of course."

Erin is snoring softly and I'm close to drifting off when I hear the door open and Ivy pokes her head in for her nightly check.

28

Before

"Double bacon burger and fries. Veggie and fries. Double-double and fries," the guy behind the counter window called out. The sun was still finding its way over the horizon. The morning sun was tempered by the overcast sky, but I still wore my sunglasses like a vampire.

"Why don't they have numbers?" Carlos asked me. Rudder was already up and retrieving the food. I shrugged.

"They serve great burgers twenty-four/seven. I don't ask questions." I smiled. Who cared about inefficiencies at the burger joint down the street from work? I was starting my weekend. My whole body was lighter as if I'd shrugged the world off my back, if only for two days. But also because I had a plan.

Rudder set the trays on the table and I stuffed fries into my mouth, savoring the hot salty fried goodness and chasing it with a soda. "I asked you guys to meet me here because I either need you to tell me I'm insane or for you to give me ideas to help me."

"Is this the whole *work is haunted* thing?" Rudder asked.

"It's not haunted, per se."

"Then what are we dealing with?" Rudder asked.

"I don't know. Weird shit," I said.

"I'm going to need more than that," Carlos said.

"Fine, so you guys were there when the creepy guy followed us from the bar. I don't remember if I told Carlos this, but his eyes changed," I said.

"Like changed color?"

"Yes," I said. "Exactly. But more specifically, they looked like the security guard's eyes."

Carlos raised an eyebrow.

"I'm serious. He has very specifically colored eyes. They are striking."

"Assuming that's what happened, what does it mean?" Carlos asked.

"He's watching me. I think he is messing with me. It's all connected back to him. I told you about the moths..."

"He's watching you through someone else's eyes?" Carlos said slowly.

They both nodded. I continued, cringing as I said it, bracing for Carlos's response.

"...and the flock of tens of thousands of them."

"Excuse me? What?" Carlos said, blinking at me.

"So yes, that's a thing that happened. Ian was there that night. He was there the first time I saw the moths and tonight, he was there when this shadow thing accosted me in the datacenter."

"Shadow thing? You're losing me," Rudder said.

"The short version: It was a shadow, but it kinda swallowed me and squeezed." I knew how it all sounded. If it hadn't happened to me, I'd say it sounded like a fun B horror flick. "Ian was there, right as it was happening. He looked worried. If I was crazy and it was a figment of my imagination, he would have looked at me like I was insane. But there wasn't a trace of surprise on his face."

It all made sense in my head; making sense out loud was another thing entirely.

"What do you want us to do?" Carlos asked.

"Come to my work next weekend, around the time I do rounds. Hide or something. I need someone else to see it. Usually, things only happen when I'm working alone. Maybe nothing will happen. But it might help. And if you do see something, then at least I know I'm not insane and help me figure out what to do about it."

"This sounds insane." He gave me a long, hard look.

"I know." I bit my lip and looked down. I hated asking for help more than anything. It didn't make it any easier knowing he thought I was nuts.

I made eye contact with Carlos, trying to convince him of my sincerity. "Look, I know how this sounds. But you know me. When things have been nuts in my life, it's usually about some ill-advised hookup or money. And you know how I am about this."

"You don't care who hears you complain about your messy life, but you'll be damned if you ask for help," Carlos recited like a reluctant schoolboy.

"I'm asking for help." A tear welled in my eye. I blinked and inhaled deeply, pulling it back. Saying everything out loud, and seeing the way Carlos shifted in his seat and how neither of them wanted to look me in the eyes, solidified how insane I felt. It only sharpened my resolve. If nothing happened, if I was imagining everything, then it was an answer. Which would be better, being right or being insane? Being mentally ill could be a better possibility.

Carlos stared off into the distance.

I didn't know what to think about everything that I was going through. It seemed Carlos didn't know what to think either. Rudder's phone rang, saving us from the awkward silence. I paused letting Carlos digest what I said while Rudder finished his short phone call.

"I have to cover half of third shift tomorrow," he said, retuning his attention to his food.

"That sucks," Carlos said, his shoulders dropping. "So much for game night."

"What happened? If it's third shift, why didn't they ask me to cover?" Even though I felt a wave of relief that I didn't have to go into work tomorrow.

"You'll get a call later; they'll probably ask you to cover the other day he works alone. The boss didn't tell me why, just that he needed me to. I'm texting Jason; he always knows what's going on. It's a little early though; he's probably still asleep."

The guys returned to eating in silence. I pushed my fries around, then took another bite of my burger, watching them as I chewed slowly.

"We can still game before work on Wednesday," Rudder offered.

"As long as it's not before noon." Carlos took another drink. I wanted to scream. My life, or at least my sanity, was hanging in the balance and they were scheduling their next playdate.

A short, electronic ringtone cut the conversation short. Rudder flipped open his phone.

"I guess Jason is up. Wow, he says the Mike, the other third shift guy, fell down the stairs, broke his leg, and hit his head."

My chest tightened and my breath quickened. I dug into my purse next to me. "At work?" I asked.

"Yeah." Rudder zoned out, staring at his phone. I removed my wallet, phone, and keys from my purse as I searched frantically. Grabbing the notebook from the bottom, I flipped it open, riffling through the pages. When was it, a week ago? Two weeks? I found the page, threw it on the table and pointed at the entry. I didn't need to read it; I had lived it. It was the entry about getting vertigo and feeling like I was going to fall down the stairs. I thought I saw a body, my body, at the bottom of the landing.

The guys turned to each other and communicated without speaking. Carlos jerked back. Rudder covered his mouth with the palm of his hand. A jittery, excited feeling expanded in my chest along with a rush of relief. This was the first validation I'd gotten, that it wasn't something that existed only in my mind. Maybe I wasn't losing my mind after all.

Rudder shrugged; Carlos nodded. "What time should I be there?"

"I'm thinking around midnight, maybe one. Things seem to happen after my first round of checks," I said.

"It's one of the few nights off I get. It's the start of my weekend." Rudder looked down the street.

"Please. You won't be working, just hanging out with us." I smiled, trying to convince him it would be fun.

"Anything I should bring? Snacks?" Carlos asked.

"LAN party at work?" Rudder said.

I rolled my eyes. "Keep it off the corporate network please?"

"Deal. I'll bring a hub and we'll set up a local network."

"Quake or Diablo?" Carlos asked Rudder.

"You need more than two for a good game of Quake."

"Good point," Carlos said.

"Three. There are three of us," I said, not that three was enough.

"Right, of course," Carlos said. I rolled my eyes at him.

"And maybe a few movies in case we need to pass the time," I said, hoping I wasn't going to spend the entire time listening to them yell at each other while gaming. I was sure that nothing would happen with him there. I wasn't asking for witnesses; what I wanted was a security blanket so I could have a night off. A night where I wasn't worried about what might be around every corner. Just Carlos's presence would ward off anything strange. I was sure.

29

After

I WALK OUT OF the doctor's office feeling more confused than when I went in. I follow the hallway around, passing the nurses' station. The phone rings as I walk past, sending a shiver down my spine. I switch directions, walking over to the desk so I can see the phones. Ivy is here with the receiver to her head; she's nodding and writing something. Getting off the phone, she looks up at me.

"Hi," she says.

"That's not the same phone," I say, feeling the blood run out of my face.

"No, we got new ones. They're pretty fancy; they say they plug into the computer port so they're better. I don't know how it makes them better." She looks down at her paper and finishes what she was writing.

"VOIP," I say.

"I'm sorry," she says with a head tilt. "You okay?"

"VOIP. It means Voice Over IP. It's the type of phones they are. They work through the network instead of a PBX phone system so they're easier to manage." I acronym vomit on her unnecessarily.

"Oh, good. For a second, I thought you were having some type of medical emergency I'm not qualified to diagnose." Ivy smiles.

The phone rings again. I realize what it is, the thing that's making my skin crawl. They are the same phones as the one at the help desk; the ring is the same. The sound permeates the air; it's so loud, I can feeling my inner ear rattle. I cross my arms over my chest, rubbing them as if I'm cold. I reach for my cell phone to check if I've missed any calls forwarded from the help desk phone. I don't have a phone anymore, which is good because if I did, I would have thrown it against the wall and earned myself another round of sedation.

I dig my fingertips into the flesh of my arms as Ivy hangs up the phone.

"Can you make it stop?" I ask.

"Make what stop?"

"That stupid, insipid, phone." The words come out chopped and tense.

"God, I wish." Ivy shakes her head, not looking at me.

The lights flicker and I'm digging my fingertips into my arms so hard, I can no longer feel my fingertips. The electricity goes out. The daylight coming in through the windows supplies the only light. The floor of the hospital ward settles into an uneasy quiet.

Ivy looks at a blank computer screen as if it's still displaying an image. A nurse at the desk stands over a printer, now nothing more than a paperweight without electricity. She picks up her print job and reviews the page before stuffing it into a folder. There's a glow down the hall from the only room that has any lights. A faint beeping noise reverberates through the floor. It's quiet, but there... beep, beep, beep. The room down the hall must have a battery backup or generator because nothing else has power.

The phone rings again, and I startle. The phones are POE, they get power over the ethernet connection. If they are still ringing, they still have power. Which should make sense; the switches in the network closet should be on battery backup or a generator. Every muscle in my body involuntarily shivers.

I blink and everything is as it was a moment before: no power outage. All the lights are on. Ivy is on the phone; the nurses and staff are milling about like nothing happened. Even the faint beeping has stopped.

I want to scream at them. How could they not see or react to what I was seeing? It isn't just about having someone validate my reality. It is as if I keep stepping outside reality and bringing everyone with me, but they don't know. They can't see.

I had planned on returning to the day room to watch TV and pass the time. Scanning the room, I decide it's too much. I'd rather be alone in my room.

I change course and head that way; Erin turns and sees me. We lock eyes and I turn toward the sanctuary of our room. The door clicks closed behind me and I exhale, glad to be away from the others. Maybe I'll have a few minutes of solitude before they come in to check on me.

The door opens and closes softly behind Erin. "How was your appointment?"

The hallucination of the power outage, if it was a hallucination, eclipsed the mix of feelings about my appointment. I wanted a moment to myself and some space to sit with only my thoughts. But looking at her face, painted with concern, washes away my irritation. I exhale and shrug, looking for the words.

"I told him I was on the wrong meds," I say. "But I don't know if it was the right thing. Do you get the sense all they do is nod and not actually listen to anything you say?"

Erin nods, taking a seat on her bed opposite mine.

"Why do you think it's wrong? The meds you are on aren't doing much besides turning you into a zombie. Don't get me wrong: You're cute when you drool, but you're not the most scintillating conversationalist."

All the words she's said are lost on me except for one. Cute. She said I was cute. But she said it in the context of me being a drooling, gonked-out zombie. Does she mean cute like a drooling, dozing toddler? Or something else?

"Danni?"

"Sorry. I thought the hallucinations weren't the problem. But now I'm not so sure."

"Yeah, not likely that the docs would agree with that. I'm sure they are of the opinion that all hallucinating is bad."

"The meds make my brain feel soupy. Not chicken noodle, like broccoli cheese," I say, twirling my hand in the air.

"Broccoli cheese brain?" She links and unlinks her fingers as she fidgets.

"It's thick, hard to stir, and tastes delicious in a sourdough bread bowl," I say.

"You're funny. Is chicken noodle brain still bad or is it the ideal?"

"Maybe it is the ideal. Chicken noodle soup is comforting, and it has noodles. Maybe that's where the phrase *use your noodle* comes from. Normal, rational people have chicken noodle brain and I have broccoli cheese, which has zero noodles, leaving me unable to use my nonexistent noodle." My reasoning is sound.

"Did he change your meds?"

"Yes. I'm switching to an antianxiety instead of antipsychotics. Not just a new drug but an entire new class of drug. Yay me."

"Maybe it'll keep you from yelling in your sleep and waking me up at night."

"Sorry." I shrink into myself. "I didn't know that was still happening. I'm sorry I woke you up."

"It's fine. Stop apologizing. You don't need to apologize once, let alone twice."

I look down as I wring my hands.

"Something really bad happened to you, didn't it?"

I look away, turning my attention to the door. It's going to open any minute now. My body and mind run on the clock in this place. One revolution around the sun here is only twenty minutes, but it can feel like hours when I'm waiting for it. The floodgates close and I watch the door. I'm never freer than in the first fifteen minutes between checks.

"Danni." Her voice is music calling me back.

"I don't talk about it." I look away, using the palm of my hand on my chin, cranking my neck to the left and the right, listening to my neck crack and release a fraction of the tension I'm carrying.

"Do you want to?"

It was the question the doctors had asked, trying to draw me out, but when she asks, I consider it.

"I feel like I do all the talking." It's not a no, but it's not a yes.

"I don't like talking about myself."

"Tell me something and I'll tell you something."

"I'm not that interesting." Her demurring would be endearing if it wasn't a sign of her illness. I hate that she talks about herself this way. But my anger isn't at her, it's at a world that doesn't understand or care for us til we end up someplace like here.

The door opens. Darla looks at us. "Checks," she says before giving us a once-over and leaving without closing the door completely. I hop off my bed and gently nudge the door, which then swings closed with a soft click.

"Okay, tell me something uninteresting about yourself and I'll tell you something scandalous." I flash an evil grin.

"Scandalous? Seriously?" Erin raises her eyebrows and eyes me with distrust. "What do you want to know?"

"Whatever. Your most boring factoid? Try me." I return to the spot on my bed and stuff my pillow behind my back, trying to make it more comfortable.

She exhales and rolls her eyes. "I had my heart broken."

"You think that's uninteresting? There's always a story with heartbreak."

"Everyone gets their heart broken at some point. It's the most pedestrian of human experiences. It's like stubbing your toe or tripping over your own feet."

I shrug. She has a point. "Tell me anyhow."

"I fell in love with the wrong person. It ended badly."

"How long ago?"

"You don't get follow-up questions."

I meet her eyes and wait.

"Junior year of college. It's your turn."

"Before I worked in IT, I was a dancer."

She looks unimpressed. "Like a stripper?" she asks.

"Yes, like a stripper. But I prefer *dancer*."

"How does one go from dancing to IT?" She leans toward me.

"Carlos and the guys at the computer club from high school. I didn't know much about computers at the time."

"You were in the computer club? Were you a nerd?" She giggles and gives me a look of mock surprise.

"I wasn't *in* the club. I was nerd adjacent."

"Hanging out with the nerds makes you a nerd," she says, squinting at me.

"They were my friends. I was a poor kid going to an upper-middle-class school. I was so poor, I thought that everyone there was rich. I was a different kind of outcast, but they didn't care. I hung around with them. Carlos is like a brother to me. When I moved out into a place of my own, I got an apartment next to his. Then when dancing began wearing me down and I wasn't enjoying it anymore, he told me I should get a job where he worked. He said I was smart enough. He taught me enough to get through the interview."

"You skipped a part."

"What?"

"You went from high school to taking your clothes off."

"I fell in love with the wrong person. It ended badly," I say with a sly grin. It was true. I'd left a few bad relationships in my wake. I knew enough to walk away from them, eventually.

She rolls her eyes.

"Okay, it was more than an awful boyfriend," I say. "It was fun at first. It was more than fun; it was a rush, holding the attention of an entire room. I reveled in it, until I didn't."

"When did it stop being fun?"

"I've let you get too many follow-up questions. It's your turn."

"What do you want to know?" The slight smile and the gleam she had in her eyes fades. She doesn't want to talk about herself. I consider the options, going for a softball question or something deeper. I want to ask something that will get her talking.

"How did it end?"

Yep, that's me, straight for the jugular. What is it that makes me want to watch someone tear out their guts for me? Like when I was a kid and I wanted to understand how something worked, I'd take it apart. Apparently, I haven't been cured of that habit.

"Love just leads to heartbreak," she says, looking away.

"Please." I give her a smile. "And then you can ask me anything. Nothing is off limits."

The room is quiet and for the first time since I came in, I notice the noise on the rest of the floor. Just when I think she isn't going to answer, her voice pulls me back.

"I fell in love." Her eyes shift from the floor to the door. "But she wasn't. I didn't know she had a boyfriend. When I found out, I tried to save her from him. He thought his girlfriend screwing another girl was hot, thinking it would lead to the inevitable ménage à trois. Then the chick that didn't want to fuck him was trying to steal his girl. He wasn't very forgiving." The punctuation in her sentences is a mix of venom and laughter with pain dripping from every syllable.

"What happened to the girlfriend?" I ask, knowing the answer.

"She stayed with him." Her words hang in the air and I can't find any words. My chest feels tight and I wish that I could help her put it all back inside. I hate that I made her tell me that, but I hate even more that someone did that to her. "I trusted her, and I thought she liked me. But she was doing it for him."

"I'm sorry. That's really shitty."

"I wasn't always like this," she says. I move to sit next to her on her bed. "Not that it's the reason I'm depressed. It's always been a struggle."

"I know," I say as a reflex.

"You don't know. But I'm telling you, so you do. I wasn't always like this."

"Do you want to ask me something?" I say, hoping she'll ask a specific question.

"I don't want to play anymore." She begins to turn away.

I put my hand on top of hers. Our fingers interlace and she looks at me, her eyes still swimming in the pain of her story. I know the story she told is just scratching the surface. The things that she didn't say were where most of the pain is.

"I don't want to play," I say, not meaning the game of trading questions. "I thought I was imagining things. I've been known to hallucinate, you know."

She leans toward me, biting her lip in the most adorable way. I want to be cute, say something smooth, and still give myself an out. Just because she's dated women doesn't mean she likes me. And she's my roommate. Hitting on her could make my living situation awkward. She's the one friend that I have here, and I could risk that friendship. I throw it all out the window.

"I like you and I think you're beautiful. And I don't have a boyfriend or a girlfriend."

I am considering qualifying it, telling her it's fine if she's not interested or if she wants to request another roommate, when she leans in. When I close my eyes, I expect to see moths, but instead I feel butterflies and the softness of her lips on mine. My head feels like it's filled with helium, and heat sweeps through my body. Emotion overwhelms me as tears spill down my face.

"Oh my God, I'm sorry. I thought you—" She shakes her head as she pulls away.

"I do. I am." I ignore the tears on my flushed cheeks and reach for her. "It's just been so long since something good has happened to me."

"I'm something good?" She dips her head, and she leans in.

"Yes. You're amazing. I never thought a girl like you would look twice at me. You just knocked the wind out of me."

She caresses my cheek, wiping away tears. Our second kiss is sweet and uninterrupted by misunderstanding. Her touch sends shivers through my body and I'm weak. She could demolish my heart and my whole world and I'd let her, just to have this moment.

30

Before

"Where's Rudder?" Carlos asked, putting his cigarette out in the dirt. I held the door for him as he walked past me and into the building.

"He's probably at the help desk, wrapping up his shift report. I haven't been down yet." We exited the stairwell onto the walkway. He looked down into the courtyard.

"You weren't kidding; this is creepy. To come in on the first floor and you're on the top floor of a four-story building. It messes with your perception." He shuddered.

"Yeah, and it's only eleven. Just wait till two or three a.m."

"Can I see the datacenter?" He grinned.

"I thought you hated this shit and wanted out of IT?"

"I am out of IT. I haven't had a job in three months."

I paused and played with my badge, concerned that if I was caught bringing someone unauthorized into the datacenter, it could get me fired. But I'd crossed that line just by letting him in.

"Yeah, sure. We have a few minutes." I swiped my badge to the stairwell door and we went down to the fourth floor.

I shielded my eyes from the lights and reached my other hand to turn them off. At the click of the switch, I dropped my hand. "The brilliance of a thousand suns all in one room."

"Damn, that's bright. I can see why you prefer to use the emergency lights." Carlos looked around, stepping into the room. The door slammed shut behind him.

"Here's the giant AC unit, which is fun if you're standing outside and it kicks on." I went into tour guide mode. "And over here are the racks."

"Nice." Carlos yelled to be heard over the AC. "Wow, it's a good-sized computer room."

"These are all the Windows boxes, a few Unix boxes, state-of-the-art tape backup system..." I trailed off.

Carlos walked ahead of me and scanned the aisles. "Is that what I think it is?" he asked as he walked to the back of the room to the giant red tanks that fed the fire suppression system.

"Yeah, it's a Halon system." Not much else to see. I motioned around the room. "So, this is it. Now you've seen it."

Carlos paused.

"We should get back." I raised my voice over the hum of the servers and the air conditioner.

Carlos nodded and we left the room.

"You miss it," I said, still half yelling.

"What?"

"You miss it." I gestured back to the door as we walked to the elevator.

"No." He shook his head. I smiled.

"Don't lie to me. You miss it."

He sighed. "There are parts I miss."

"Like?" I prodded.

"The paycheck," he shot back and hit the up arrow on the elevator.

"Besides that."

"Roasting marshmallows." A half smile appeared on his face and then disappeared.

"Huh?"

"It's a thing we used to say at my last job. Half of the job was putting out fires. System outages, where the company would lose a hundred thousand dollars an hour if it was down. So every outage was measured in minutes and seconds."

The elevator door opened. I pressed the glowing 3 while Carlos kept talking more to himself than to me.

"You'd get the call, and there was nothing I could do because it wasn't my area, so I'd pass the baton to another team. Usually the network team; it's always the fucking network. By the way, they really hate it when you say that. Anyhow, your adrenaline is pumping and there's nothing to do. And that's when you know how awesome your coworkers are when the only thing you can do in the fire is to roast marshmallows over the flames and wait for the fix before you can clean up the ashes. If you have someone you can roast marshmallows with, then you're working with good people."

"So roasting marshmallows means waiting?"

"Not exactly. It's the moments where people get stressed and bitchy or laugh about it. If you can't fight the fire, enjoy it, roast marshmallows over the flames, and crack a joke with a friend."

The elevator doors opened. "Always with the life lessons," I said. "Maybe you should write horoscopes or fortune cookies, old man."

"But yeah, I miss being around my people. That's what I miss about the job."

"You sure you want out?" We reached the outer door of the office.

"Yes, I'm sure. But what I also want to know where next month's rent is coming from."

"We call that living the dream," I joked. "Maybe you can work with Rudder?"

"Do they have a retirement plan?"

"I don't know. Let's ask," I said as we walked up to the opening in the wall where the help desk was located. "Hey Rudder, does the adult bookstore have a retirement plan?"

We reached the walkway and turned at the counter. The desk was empty. All the computers were powered on. Rudder's computer screen was locked but not logged out.

"Did he leave already?" Carlos grabbed a chair and sat down.

"I'm not late; I have a few minutes. He didn't log out. That's weird. Maybe he just ran down to change tapes and save me a trip. Sometimes he does it on his way out. But usually, I'm earlier so I see him before he leaves."

"I'll call him. Nine to get a line out?" Carlos picked up one of the phones.

"Yeah. I have to log in." I went to my computer and entered my username and password.

"No answer." Carlos hung up the phone. I picked up my cell and dialed the help desk number. It rang to all the phones at the same time.

"He didn't forward the phones," I said.

"He was probably in a hurry."

"Probably," I agreed. "Okay, so I've logged in and we have some time to kill before rounds."

"What computer can I use?"

"Come on; let's watch a movie." I opened the bottom file cabinet drawer at my desk and produced three DVDs. "I have *Army of Darkness*, *From Dusk to Dawn*, and *Lost Boys*."

"I'm beginning to see why you think your work is haunted." He spun in his chair.

"These aren't scary at all. Come on. Movie?" I shook the *Army of Darkness* DVD case at him.

"You dragged me here," Carlos said.

"Yes, to keep me company. I'll let you pick the movie."

"I can do both," he said.

"I'm not giving you my password."

"No need. I brought my handy-dandy password cracker." Carlos pulled a CD out of his backpack and grinned. "Sixty seconds and I'll have wiped the local admin password."

"Of course you did. Just keep the computers off the network and uninstall the games before you leave. I'm not getting in trouble if they're monitoring the network traffic."

"Yes, Mom." Carlos rolled his eyes, pulling a hub and bundle of network cables out of his backpack.

"Use that one so you can still see the TV." I pointed to the computer across from mine.

"Got any popcorn?" Carlos asked.

"Check the vending machine. I need to catch up on email before I do anything else. Won't take long. The break room is to the right, and then your first left." Carlos nodded and walked out. I opened my email to read the shift turnover which Rudder sends at the end of his shift. My eyes kept returning to his computer. His chair wasn't pushed in. It was bothering me; it looked like he was coming back. The clipboard wasn't hanging from its hook next to the console computer.

"Carlos," I called as I walked into the dark break room. The stillness of the room made me question if Carlos had been there at all. The air seemed undisturbed. The quiet saturated my consciousness, boring into my brain.

Returning to the hallway, I looked both ways, unsure of what I was looking for. The building was still and silent, like it was abandoned, and also like it had eyes.

"Carlos. Carlos!" It was pointless, but I did it to break up the silence. I paced, calling out to him. The offices were dark; I kept to the dimly lit hallway, cursing that I hadn't grabbed a flashlight. Every step forward was cautious and deliberate; I was both afraid to break the silence and dying to shatter it into oblivion.

The main entrance was illuminated from the outside, light casting shadows on the reception desk that no longer received anyone. I pressed my hands against the glass door, looking outside to check for signs of life. The walkway was deserted. I stepped backward and cacophony erupted in my mind, my inner voice telling me how stupid and ridiculous this was. I was a grown woman in search of a security blanket for something that was all in my mind. I walked briskly back to the help desk to call Rudder and wait for Carlos to come back.

My new resolve seemed to shatter the stillness as I picked up the pace, walking back twice as fast as I had walked away. The smell of popcorn filled the hallway and this time, light shone from the break room into the hall. I turned the corner to the help desk.

"Hey, look who I found." He pointed to where Rudder was sitting at his computer and ate a few kernels of popcorn.

"Where've you been?" I smiled.

"Trying to find the clipboard. You know the good movies are in the drawer next to the TV. What even is this?"

Carlos finished chewing, swallowed, and said, "Don't start. She'll throw you out."

"Damn right I will," I said, knowing no one believed it for a second. But I could talk tough.

"And watch horror movies alone in the dark?" Carlos tilted the popcorn toward Rudder, who took some.

"Is there any other way?" I forgot about the feeling I had looking out into the courtyard, content in being right, that having Carlos and Rudder at work would chase away the dark clouds hovering over me at work.

Carlos threw a piece of popcorn at me. I tried to catch it in my mouth but instead, it hit me in the forehead. Carlos and Rudder laughed, and I'd never been happier to feel foolish.

31

After

It's TIME FOR NIGHT meds. Darla hands me the small paper cup. In it is one and a half of the old drug and half of a new one.

"Are you going to look at them or take them?" Darla asks.

I tilt the small paper cup into my mouth, follow it with water, and then open my mouth, exaggerating, so I can stick my tongue out at her.

She walks away without taking my trash. I shrug. I look at the clock and know that I have about thirty minutes before I'm so zoned out that I fall asleep. But I had three-quarters of the dose, so maybe it will buy me forty-five minutes. It feels like a luxury, like staying up late when you're eight years old.

My mouth is dry even though I just washed down the pills. I can't ignore the nagging feeling in the back of my head. What if I'm wrong? What if these meds are the one that push me over the edge instead of bringing me back from it?

A new terror grips me: the possibility that I'm wrong and the insanity that overtook me at my work is not isolated to that place, but rather exists inside me and always will. The little bit of progress the doctor pointed out to me feels like the little bit of purchase my fingers get digging into the dirt while my body is hanging off a cliff. How do I spend my life running from something that exists in my head, or in my soul? It's something I'm going to have to figure out.

There are some places in life you don't know about until you get there; I suppose mental illness is one of those places. Although I believe that everything I went through was real, I won't deny that there is something wrong with me. I don't have words for what that thing is, just that it is a swelling of discomfort.

It starts as a small itch that blooms into a burning that consumes my thoughts and attention. It takes me out of myself, and I feel like my soul has been knocked out of my body and I'm left watching the carnage. They have a fancy word for it: dissociation. It's a severance of a different sort, not from one's job but from oneself.

I wander over to the TV room. I'm trying to figure out what day it is. Is it a weekday or a weekend? I don't know. If it's Thursday night, Erin will be coming to watch sitcoms. It feels like it could be a Thursday. I let myself entertain the idea of having a future, to a time when I have my own apartment again, with a new job and a dog. It hits me all at once, how much I miss Britters and how much I love that stupid scruffy furball and that I'll never see her again. It didn't occur to me to ask Erin if she likes dogs.

I curl up on the couch in the common room and wait. The TV is on, but I'm barely paying attention to it. The clock is the only interesting thing. Maybe I can figure out how much time that half pill represents. Will it take longer to fall asleep, or will I just sleep less? This is the highlight of my day. I watch the clock until...

"Danni," Erin says softly.

I startle awake and try to wrap my arms around myself. I'm freezing.

"You fell asleep. I thought you weren't coming back."

"I'm right here; I'm fine. New meds. I just fell asleep."

"Come home. I need you." She pulls me and I'm struck by how both sweet and dysfunctional it is. All at once, the future I imagine is me, her, and Britters. Living in my shitty apartment, arguing about whose turn it is to do the dishes. At the same time, I know the room we share in the mental health ward isn't a home. We're barely roommates, there's no rent, we don't take out the trash. We barely know each other.

I reach for her hand.

"I'm coming. I just fell asleep."

"You said that." She looks away and pulls her hand away from me.

"Come on; let's get some sleep." I stand and take a step toward our room, then stop dead in my tracks.

"You left me." Tears are streaming down her cheeks. She's angry and desperate and convinced that I've abandoned her.

"I'm right here. I'm here." I brush my thumb across her cheek to wipe away a tear.

32

Before

THE MOVIE CREDITS ROLLED; Rudder's feet were up on the desk. Carlos stretched and yawned. "Past your bedtime, old man?" I teased.

Carlos flipped me off without looking at me.

"I need to pee. Too much coffee," I said, standing up and stretching.

"No such thing," Carlos scoffed.

"Do you need someone to go with you?" Rudder shifted as if he was about to stand up.

"Ew, no. I think I can make it to the bathroom and back," I said.

"Forward the phone," Rudder said.

I squinted at him. "But you're here."

"I am not here, at least not in a work capacity. If the phone rings, you're answering it," he said.

"Fine." I punched the numbers on the phone and returned the receiver back to the cradle. "I'll be back in a couple minutes." I waved.

Something was off. I stood looking over the railing, trying to pinpoint what had changed.

Quiet had settled in and the usual noises in the city were absent. The warm night air was stagnant. I took the stairs down, moving on autopilot, mesmerized by something invisible. The air was thick and heavy, and the lights were dimmed. The stairwell door slammed behind me, but even the sound of that was muffled. Standing in the center of the fake grass, I could smell the faint aroma of freshly cut grass and a sweet, flowery scent.

It was a dream, wasn't it? I walked to the middle of the courtyard, the place where I'd seen the door. That was when it began—after that dream where I saw the door, if it was a dream. It was after that that the first moth appeared and strange things began happening.

Squeezing my eyes shut, I tried to picture it and remember, was it open or did I close it? Maybe I let something out. And maybe, if I can reopen the door, it can go back to where it came from. It seemed ridiculous that I could have caused this. How could I test it? I reasoned that if I could find the door again, I could open it if it was closed, or close it if it was open. And if things improved or got worse, then I could figure out the cause.

Sometimes you must be destructive to fix the issue, like blowing away a user's profile on a computer and creating a new one. Often, that fixed everything. My logic was flawed; I could always back up a profile and restore it if it didn't work. I couldn't back up reality. But it was an idea, another troubleshooting step, and something that I could test. The answer seemed so close; I could feel it. The pieces were falling into place and I was on the cusp of figuring it out. Even if I couldn't figure anything else out in my life, this I could know.

I closed my eyes and mentally walked through the space, like I'd done before. My breathing slowed and I focused my thoughts and energy toward finding out if this was a thing I could see and touch, or something that I had dreamt while dozing off at my desk. It smelled like freshly cut grass. With every step, fresh dew drops on real grass burst beneath my feet even though I was wearing shoes.

I pushed away the knowledge that it wasn't real, there was nothing but artificial turf below my feet. A song danced on a soft breeze that brushed my face and hair. The usually harsh light softened to a warm glow, and it was like a warm embrace or a homecoming. It should have been a dream, but I couldn't deny my senses. It was something between a dream and reality, something *other*. The door I was looking for was *other*, but so was I. Maybe I was called to the door or had called it to me because we were the same.

I turned and it was there, not in the place it had been, but across the courtyard. Willing my body forward, I navigated not by eyesight but by instinct and feeling. The door was surrounded by a sliver of light between it and the frame that stood attached to nothing. I raised my hands, grazed the door with my fingertips, and felt the texture of the wood grain. It hummed at my touch, a sound I felt in my bones. Every inch of my body vibrated. It rattled my sternum. All the answers were on the other side of this door, and a desire to open it thrummed inside of me. The light surrounding the door intensified as the door began opening so slowly, it was almost imperceptible. Without thinking, I took a step back to give the door room to open. As I brought my hand up to brush hair behind my ear, a moth with a ten-inch wingspan landed on my hand. I froze, transfixed but no longer afraid.

"Mariposa de la Muerte," I whispered, a hint of a smile on my lips.

Three more moths landed nearby as if they had materialized from nothing. My eyes widened at the realization that I had summoned them. It was the first bit of control I had over what had been happening. On my hand, the moth's wings gingerly flapped up... and then down... I watched it, my eyes tracing the thin, iridescent purple line across its wings. I brought the moth up to eye level; my breath hitched and caught going into my lungs. I exhaled as slowly as possible. The insect locked eyes with me and the world fell away and we were surrounded by darkness. Light streamed in through the sliver of a crack in the open door.

"Danni." A voice called me from the distance. I paid no attention to it.

"Danni." The voice was louder and demanding, and I turned to look.

Carlos and Rudder were in the courtyard with me; they approached me as if I might explode. Carlos inched forward, his eyes fixed on the ground and the moths around us. It felt like I'd only been here a minute, but also a lifetime. How long had I been down here?

"Danni," Rudder said. "Can you hear me?"

I nodded, not wanting to speak, not wanting to chase off the moth perched on my hand.

"Hey, you can't be here," Ian yelled from the second-floor railing.

"Huh," Rudder said. "He does exist."

"Danni." Carlos tapped my arm.

"I'm coming down," Ian yelled, his voice uneven as he ran to the steps. He was shaken. We were doing something right. I spun around, taking in the whole of the courtyard. The door or the words, which was it? The analytical part of me wanted to test it: throw open the door and see, then use the words and invite in whatever was there. To know the cause and isolate the variables, I should only change one thing at a time. But I didn't have time for that, and I wasn't about to let Ian stop me. He was keeping something from me, and I was going to find out what it was. I took in a deep breath and yanked the door open. It disappeared. Did something change or did the door never exist in the first place?

"MARIPOSA DE LA MEURTE!" I yelled as loud as I could. The door to the stairs burst open and Ian fell out, stumbling and then breaking into a full run.

"What? How?" He swallowed a laugh as his eyes focused on where the door had been, unable to pull himself away. I couldn't tell if he was horrified or elated.

A hot flush spread throughout my chest and I questioned my course of action. Ian's eyes went to the door and then skyward. *He could see it too.* I looked up; the sky was dotted with stars. Black dots like tiny birds flocked in from all directions; there were thousands, maybe tens of thousands of them. They all converged over the courtyard and blacked out the sky, forming a ceiling over the open courtyard.

The ceiling descended on us. The sky wasn't falling, it was flapping its wings and coming down to us.

"Inside. Now!" Ian shouted at us, pointing to the building. He grabbed my arm and pulled me from the door. I thought for a moment that he would slam it closed; instead, he gave it a look and then pulled me away. It was jarring and I began to come back to my senses, taking a moment to assess the situation.

"Third floor," I yelled.

"What?" Ian said, but I was already running for the stairs.

I swiped my badge and held the door open. "Come on," I said. Rudder and Carlos were only a few steps behind me. Ian jogged over. We took the steps two at a time.

"We're going to be trapped in the stairwell," he yelled up at me.

"Then run faster," I said.

We came out of the stairwell. The open space that was the courtyard was a black cloud of wings and insects. It swirled and pulsed, moving in concert like a flock of birds. It moved like a singular creature of one mind. My mouth fell open. Ian grabbed my arm and pulled me toward the door. He took my badge off my jeans and swiped it in front of the badge reader. The door beeped, the lock disengaged, Ian yanked it open, and we ran in.

The door closed behind all four of us. Rudder was doubled over, trying to catch his breath. Ian spread the blinds wide, careless of whether he damaged them in the process, and shook his head at the swarm outside. Carlos, wide-eyed, ran his hands through his hair. "This is bad," he said.

"Why are you doing this?" I asked Ian.

"Me?" he said. "I just got here."

"Well, enlighten me then; why are you always around when weird shit happens?" I said, walking over to him and getting in his face. He glanced at me and I looked outside through the parted blinds.

"Oh my god," I choked, almost unable to get the words out. The pulsing swarm glowed green.

"No time now." Ian released the blinds, which snapped back into place.

"We're inside; we can wait it out. They're nocturnal, right? They should be gone before sunrise. When is that? Six?"

"We can hunker down and play some games," Carlos said. "You like Quake, Ian?"

I smiled and looked back at Ian. He frowned. "How did you do it?"

"Do what?"

His head flinches back slightly.

"I think I need to update my resume," I said. "Even if this weird shit stops, I don't know that I can keep doing this graveyard thing. It's too weird."

"Do we have any food?" Rudder asked.

"Just the vending machine in the break room," I said.

"This isn't a little inconvenience," Ian said.

"Something similar happened the other night; there was a shit ton of moths and then they were gone," I said. The sinking feeling in the pit of my stomach told me I was wrong, that this was different. I so badly needed to believe that it was just another weird thing that would pass, but it was different than it had been the other night. For one, this time I wasn't alone. Other people saw it too.

"This is different. You know it's different."

168

"Tell me what's happening. What did I do?" I asked, getting into his face.

Thwap. Something hit the window like a small pebble or the sound of a bug hitting the windshield at full speed. I couldn't see what it was with the blinds closed.

"What was—" I said.

Thwap, thwap, thwap. The window was pelted in quick succession.

"We need to relocate," Ian said. He raised his arm to usher us out of the room. "Now."

Thunk, thunk, thunk thunk crash. The window broke inward. I ducked and put my hand over my head to shield myself from the glass. Sheets of glass cut through the cheap blinds and landed inches from me. I was knocked to the ground. Pain exploded in my hand as it came down on a shard of glass.

"Mother fu—" I cried out. Carlos was already on his feet. I scrambled up.

"Run faster," Ian said in a mocking tone. We ran down the hallway.

"This way," I said, taking the lead. A noise filled the hallway behind us. It was a living, breathing noise, like a flock of birds taking flight all at once. A sound I couldn't name pulsed like a heartbeat or the bass line of a song. It was like standing next to the speakers at a nightclub wearing earplugs. I ran as fast as I could. The desire to look behind me was like an itch and I was fighting not to scratch.

"Where are we going?" Rudder asked.

"Help desk," I said. My hand was slick and wet. Blood dripped from it; the pain pulsed in time with the building. We reached the help desk.

"In," I commanded.

No one listened to me. I started pushing the sliding wall closed. The guys, realizing what I was doing, came around to help me push, closing off the help desk from the hallway. One by one, we slid in through the shrinking opening until all of us were inside and we were pulling it closed from inside the room. Ian and Carlos were swatting and stomping on the few moths that had made it inside. A few trampled moths with torn wings lay dead on the floor.

"Well, they die. That's good news."

Ian closed his eyes and took a deep breath.

33

Before

"WE CAN JUST STAY in here for a while," I said. The sliding wall closed off the help desk, dampening sounds from the hall. I exhaled and all the tension left my body. I thought I was going to crumple to the floor.

"Your hand," Carlos said. I tried to clean the blood on my hand by wiping it on my jeans. When that didn't work, I snatched a hoodie off the chair at my desk and wrapped my hand with it.

"Ugh, that hurts," I said, gasping in pain.

"You'll need stitches," Rudder said hoarsely.

"Maybe, but for now, no one should go out there," I said.

"We can't stay in here," Ian interjected.

"All in favor of staying," I asked, raising the hand that wasn't bleeding. Carlos and Rudder raised their hands too. "Then it's decided."

Ian threw his hands up and turned away. He rubbed his forehead. The radio on his belt squelched. He pulled in a quick breath and exhaled hard. "I have to radio in," he said.

"And tell them what? There's an insect infestation?" Carlos asked.

Ian sighed.

"What?"

"Can I use that office? I need to check in with my work," he asked, pointing to one of the doors off the room.

"You can't do that out here?" I asked.

"I'm going to use bad words and at least some of them will be about you. So no, I would prefer to do that privately."

"I'm sure I've been called worse," I said. He ignored me and walked into the office, closing the door behind him.

"Why do you think he said we can't stay in here?" Rudder asked.

Carlos shrugged. "Because he's an asshole?"

"Probably," I said. The low rhythmic pulsing reverberated in the room. I couldn't tell if I was hearing it or feeling it; like wearing earplugs, all I heard was breathing and my heartbeat. Or was the heartbeat mine? It was vibrating through my body; it felt like my heartbeat. I put two fingers to my wrist. The pulse in my veins raced, but not in time to the vibration. A horror crept over me, that the heartbeat was of a giant animal that had swallowed us.

"I don't think we should stay in here," Rudder said. He looked unsettled; he shifted his feet and rubbed his arm.

"You good?" I asked.

"No. Something is wrong." Carlos scanned all four walls.

"You're telling me," I replied.

He clenched his fists. "That's what I'm trying to tell you." His sudden intensity caught me off guard. "Can you hear it?" He looked up, down, and all around.

"What is that?"

"The drums of war," he said.

"Oh my god, you're right. It's the drums," Rudder said.

"There are no drums," I said. "It's the building. It has a heart and we're in its veins."

"It's drums," Carlos insisted.

"That doesn't even make sense." I was getting agitated. How could they be so blind? It was obviously blood moving through a body. And we were inside the building. It was alive. I could feel it all around me. My insides twittered and lurched.

"Do you hear that?" I asked. "The walls are whispering. They're telling them where we are. Ian is right. We can't stay here."

"Ian?" Rudder looked down at the floor.

171

"What happened to him?" I asked. I went to the office door that he'd gone through. I placed my palms on the wall. I could feel it; it was almost talking to me. I put my ear against the wall so I could hear the message it had for me. It had to be important; the walls had never talked to me before. The guys talked behind me, but their words didn't matter. Only the building's words mattered now.

"The answer is on the other side of this door," I said, tracing my fingers over the wood pattern. The door opened.

"What are you doing?" Ian asked.

"Looking for answers," I said.

"Shit," Ian said, opening the office door and taking one look at us. "Everyone over here."

I lowered my hands to my sides.

"Okay, so here's the deal. We have something nasty surrounding us from all sides, thanks to numbnuts over here." He gestured toward me. "We can't stay in here. The sound will drive us insane."

"Too late," I said. "Tell us what is going on."

"The less you know, the happier you'll be. I'll tell you what you need to know to survive. Keep moving. Don't stay in one place for long; it's like soaking in it. Don't fall asleep and don't fight with each other," Ian said. He turned toward the walls and began looking at the ceiling.

"I don't understand," I said, walking up behind him.

"You don't need to understand. Not knowing is better for you in the long run. Trust me." A weariness crept into his voice.

"I don't believe that." It was antithetical to everything I believed in. Knowing was half the battle. G.I Joe cartoons wouldn't lie to me. How could he say that not knowing was better? Knowing my shit was a way of life for me. I ate because I knew things, because I could figure things out.

"I don't care what you believe. Belief is irrelevant. Survival is all you should care about," he said. "Guys, find us stuff. Chairs, rope, flashlights, whatever."

Carlos and Rudder set upon the room, sifting through the drawers looking for the items Ian suggested, as he turned to me and continued, "You called it here.

172

And more important than not staying in one place and not arguing with each other is this... You can't leave."

"What?" I asked as he cut me off.

"Listen now, questions later. You called it here; it's tied to you and it's not going to leave you alone. If you leave, it leaves, and then it's out there in the world. Keep it here, in one place. I've called it in to my work, and they'll send people."

"They'll send security guards?" I still wasn't processing what he was saying.

"It's not that kind of security company," he said.

My jaw dropped. "What other kind of security companies are there?"

"Let's just say it's a company that specializes in something more *arcane*." He gave me a knowing look.

"None of that is helpful. What are we dealing with?"

"I called in the cavalry. Just hold down the fort and keep it from leaving the building."

"What if it flies out of the courtyard? I can't stop that."

"As long as you don't fly out of the courtyard, it won't." Ian gave me a reassuring look. "You're going up," he said to the guys, pointing to the ceiling tiles above us.

"Are you sure that's a good idea?" I asked.

"It's not, but there's only one way out of this room, and that's up," he said.

"It's quiet on the other side of the door."

"Quiet and safe are different things," Ian said.

Rudder came back, holding orange extension cords. "We can braid them like rope," he said.

"Great idea. It'll be easier to grasp," Ian agreed. Rudder set to braiding the extension cords together.

"What's the plan?" I asked. "We leave the room, and then?"

"There isn't a plan. Unless surviving is a plan. Don't die and don't go insane. More importantly, don't die because you went insane. That's probably the hardest one," Ian said.

"I'm not comfortable with this plan," I said.

"I don't suppose you have any weapons?" Ian asked.

"This is an office," I said. "No weapons allowed."

"Come on; what else do you have?" Ian asked.

"There's a paper cutter. It has a big blade on it," I said. "It's in the copy room."

"Where's that?" Carlos asked.

"On the other side of this wall," Rudder said.

Carlos pulled out the desk chair and held it steady.

"We'll improvise as we go. Everyone into the ceiling," Ian said, getting up on the chair, then onto the desk and pushing a ceiling tile up and to the side. "Who's first? Danni is the shortest, so she'll probably need the most help getting up."

I flipped him off.

"No fighting," he said.

I grumbled under my breath.

"Up you go."

The guys held the swivel seat steady while I climbed up the wall into the space above the ceiling.

"Lift the tile in front of you," Rudder called up to me.

I reached over the top of the wall, inside the ceiling, and lifted out the ceiling tile next to where I was.

"What do you see?"

"It's the copy room," I called down.

"The joists won't hold you." Carlos said.

"Are you able to lower yourself down?" Ian asked.

"Hey, use this," Carlos said and tossed one end of the braided electric cord up to me. I caught it.

"Cool," I said. They high-fived each other, congratulating themselves on their cleverness.

"I think the counter is close enough." I pushed against the top of the wall. It shifted, revealing that it wasn't as sturdy as it looked. I swung one leg over and straddled it, carefully reaching out with my toes for the counter below, then lowered myself down, hanging on to the braided electric cord. The wound on my hand reopened, smearing blood down the cord. My foot found the counter and I eased myself down and released my death grip. I hopped down from the counter.

"I'm good," I called up.

"Next," Ian said.

Rudder and Ian held the braided cord for Carlos as he came down. I pulled the printer over to the side to make more room on the counter for him. Rudder came over next and while Carlos was helping him, I redirected my attention to my weapon-making project.

I lifted the arm of the paper cutter. "I think I need a screwdriver," I said. Maybe dropping it on the floor would work; it didn't have to be pretty. I put the paper cutter on the floor on its edge and I had one foot on the cutting arm, trying to wrench it away from the flat platform of the rest of it.

"Aren't you bleeding enough?" Rudder blinked.

"What?" I asked. "I'm fine."

"Not for long," Carlos said. He called to Ian over the wall. "Grab the cord. I'll help you over."

"Want some help?" Rudder asked.

"Sure," I said.

I stood on the platform; Rudder wrapped the blade in paper to protect his hands.

"Is it ironic that it's a paper cutter and you're using paper to make sure you don't cut your hands?" I asked.

"I'm not sure ironic is the right word. I'd say reckless," Carlos said.

"It's enough paper; it'll be fine," Rudder said. "Now hold it."

"Famous last words." Carlos stood over us, shaking his head.

I held the main body of it down with my foot and Rudder pushed. It bent, it complained, and then gave all at once. Rudder tumbled to the floor.

"Careful," I said.

Carlos picked up the blade by the handle and grinned like a madman. "I have a machete," he said.

"Why do you get the machete?" I asked.

"Because it's awesome," he said. Then, "Where's Ian?"

"Ian, I'll hold it and you can climb up, or I can pull you up?" Carlos continued, and then said to us, "Can you guys stop fucking around and help?"

175

Carlos set the machete against the cabinets and we stood next to Rudder.

"Ian?" Rudder called out. "We should go back and see if he's okay."

The orange cord tumbled down from the ceiling, I stood frozen in place, dumbfounded, unable to process it.

"You okay? I'll toss it back over," Carlos offered.

"I'm heading outside to brief the team when they get here. You're going to be okay." Ian's hands appeared, holding the ceiling tile as he put it back into place above us.

I pounded on the wall. "We're not leaving anyone behind," I yelled. My ears popped as if there'd been a change in air pressure. "Ian!"

Rudder pulled himself up onto the counter, pushed the tile back up, and looked over the wall. He ducked, letting the tile fall back into place, and hopped down from the counter. "We should gather what we can and move."

"What? No, we stick together," I insisted.

A muffled gurgling noise interrupted me. It was something between choking and gargling, a wet sound that lasted only a few seconds. I managed to resist the sudden nausea I was hit with, keeping down the mix of coffee, popcorn, and junk food from earlier, but it was a close call.

"What was that?" Carlos asked.

"I don't think Ian is going to be joining us. We need more supplies." I opened drawers and cupboards, not sure of what I was looking for but knowing that I didn't have enough of whatever it was I needed.

"We should go back for him," Carlos said.

"No," I said.

"Why the fuck not? I'd do the same for you."

"If you heard me make that sound, please don't. I'd want you to save yourself," I said.

"What do you think happened?" Rudder asked.

"I don't know. But I imagine that's what it sounds like when you choke on your own blood," I said.

"Gross," Rudder said.

"You can't know that." Carlos turned to Rudder. "What did you see?"

All the color drained from Rudder's face. He shook his head at Carlos.

"No, I can't. But you heard it too. Look at me and tell me you think he's okay," I said.

He averted his eyes.

"He decided to go back out there. He made his choice."

"That's cold," Carlos said.

"It's survival. Let's gather what we can and get out of here." I opened the lower cabinets, looked around, and then went to the next one. I couldn't process what was happening, only able to face what was in front of me in the moment. This was survival mode, a feeling I was familiar with.

"I thought you wanted to hunker down?" Rudder questioned.

"That was before. Ian was right: We're in danger, obviously. The only thing we have to go on is what he said—don't stay in one spot for too long," I said.

"He said some other shit too," Carlos said. "What was it?"

"We can't leave. Let's see what we can make out of these supplies. Then we'll find a way to wait this out until backup arrives."

"Okay," Rudder said.

"Guys, he said that it was connected to me, that it would follow me. He didn't say anything about you guys. I can lead it away and you guys can get out. I don't want to take you down with me."

"No." Rudder shook his head.

"We aren't abandoning you." Carlos gave me a stern look.

"Are you sure?" I asked.

"Yeah," Rudder said. "We're sure."

34

After

"I CALLED MY EX this morning." I say and watch her face in the dark, looking for any reaction. Her affect is flat still, so I don't know what I expect to see.

It's lights out when Erin and I talk the most. Or it's when we can be the most honest, in the dark with no one else around. I don't mention the ten minutes I stared at the phone, wishing I could call Carlos. No sense in trying to call Rudder.

"Are you jealous?" Her body tenses and she pulls away from me in bed.

"No, it's not that," she says.

"It's complicated. He wants to know what happened at the job, but I don't know what to tell him. I owe him and I feel ridiculous."

"Did he leave you or did you leave him?" She brings her hand to her lips.

"He left me," I confess, sensing that she would rather that I had rejected him, but I make a point of telling her the truth.

"Did you love him?" Her eyes search mine.

"I thought I did. I used to say he broke my heart, but it's more like he broke my self-worth."

She looks off into the distance, her eyes not focusing on anything.

"What's the murder brain scale today?"

"Hmmm." She looks up, thinking. "Seven-point-three."

I grin so wide that I feel the limits of my face. Every ounce of relief she can get is huge. While she's still very depressed, it's not a ten. I give her a firm, dry kiss on the lips.

"That's awesome. Sounds like the meds are helping."

"Maybe," she says, looking into my eyes. I shake my head, still smiling. "Yours?"

"Four. A solid four."

"Hallucinations?"

"None recently."

"You're still having nightmares." She scans my face intently, watching my response.

I'm feeling hopeful in this moment. That maybe there's a light at the end of the tunnel not just for me, but for Erin as well. Better living through chemistry. The transition from antipsychotics to antianxiety medication seems to be helping. It's this combination of hopefulness and, dare I say, a moment of happiness, which makes me forget where I am.

When the door opens, I'm not thinking anything of it. I'm so used to it by now that every fifteen to twenty minutes someone, usually Ivy, checks the rooms, I barely register it. The door clicks closed and I make a mental note to myself that I need to move back to my bed before I fall asleep and before the next round of checks.

"At least I'm sleeping...when you let me." I smile, pulling her closer to me. Her hair falls into her face and I brush it back behind her ear. The future I'd thought was a silly fantasy is forming into a plan. I toy with the idea of suggesting that after we get out of here, we should move in together and help each other get back on our feet. It's fast. I know it's too soon, so I bite back the idea and just enjoy the moment.

"I think we're going to be okay. Don't you feel that? That things are turning around?" I ask. Maybe it's the medication, or maybe it's Erin. More than likely, it's both.

Erin pauses, giving me a long look.

The door opens and I bolt upright in bed, startled by it because it's different than the normal rhythm of the hospital. The light turns on and I cover my eyes, momentarily blinded. Darla is standing in the doorway, her top lip curled in disgust, shaking her head at us. Coming in through the doorway are two of the orderlies.

"Rise and shine, girls," Darla calls out to us. "It's moving day."

I fall out of bed onto my side, yelping in pain and surprise. Darla smiles. The relief that washes over me that at least I'm dressed and we were only talking, shatters as I process what Darla said. The two orderlies come to either side of the bed. The bigger guy reaches down and grabs my arm, lifting me up off the floor, not waiting for my cooperation.

"We were just talking," Erin protests to the orderly who looks like he's still in high school and extremely disappointed that we weren't caught in a more compromising position.

"No exceptions. We have to separate you." Darla's eyes are devoid of compassion, but a ghost of a smile teases at the corner of her mouth.

"No, please," I beg. My knees threaten to give and the man holds tight to my arm, his fingertips digging into my flesh. I plant my feet, bend my knees and push off the floor as hard as I can, launching myself shoulder first into the orderly. He loses his balance and hits the ground, releasing my arm. His nostrils flare as he pushes himself up off the floor, squaring up his shoulders. He gives me a faint smile and a nod, daring me to try it again. "It's fine. I'm going back to my own bed. We were just talking."

"It's the rules," Darla says. "Erin, come with us."

Tears well up in Erin's eyes. "Please, it's late. We were just talking. Can I just talk to my doctor in the morning? We can figure it out. We don't have to do this."

"Okay. Chuck, can you get Danni? We'll take her to the other ward," Darla says to the orderly closest to me.

My heart races, my fists clench, and every muscle in my body tenses. I feel like I'm not getting enough air and I become lightheaded. My knees threaten to buckle again.

The room fills with smoke. I can't find the source and it happens so fast that it feels like being crushed by a wave in the ocean. The orderly has no issues finding me, as I feel his hands around my arm again. Another set of hands grabs my other arm. I rock back and forth, fighting to loosen their grip or headbutt one of them, not caring anymore if I hurt myself in the process.

"Danni, don't fight." Erin raises her voice.

I inhale the thick grey cloud surrounding me. I can barely see. I cough. I'm bucking and pulling and pushing, grasping for anything I can get purchase on, intent on taking down one of them with me.

"You're hurting her," Erin yells.

They slam me to the ground and then everything is quiet.

35

Before

RUDDER KEPT WATCH AT the doorway to the copier room while Carlos and I went through the drawers and cabinets, looking for anything that could be fashioned into a weapon. A feeling of doom set in as I pulled out pens, pencils, and binders. It was a wealth of office supplies; weapons, not so much. I stared at my haul, dumping it onto the counter.

"Duct tape. Oh, thank god," Carlos said, pulling a roll out from the back corner of a cabinet. He added clipboards, a keyboard, a padlock, and a power cord to my pile on the counter. I picked up the padlock, bounced it in my hand to feel the weight of it. I hummed as I took one of the power cords and secured it around the metal loop. Distancing myself from the guys, I swung it. That would do nicely.

"Yeah, a pile of junk and a roll of duct tape and zero fly swatters." My voice betrayed my lack of enthusiasm for our chance of survival.

"It's good. We've got some good stuff." He looked at me, not breaking eye contact until I smiled and nodded.

I opened the upper cabinets, scanned the reams of paper, and pulled out two canisters of compressed air. "Hey, Carlos? You have your lighter?"

"Yeah, why?"

I held the cans out to him.

"Compressed air? You want to dust the moths?" His eyebrows scrunched together.

"It has a flammable warning on it." I grinned.

"Mine." Rudder took one from me and scanned the tiny print on the back.

"Rudder, backpack." He held it open, and I tossed in the other compressed air can.

"I think we should keep moving," Rudder said, looking both ways down the hallway and then holding the paper cutter blade out to me. "Time to switch."

I took it by the handle and reached for the backpack.

"I got it. Just keep an eye out." Rudder surveyed the pile of stuff on the counter.

"I think with the duct tape and binders, we can make something," Carlos said.

"Maybe there are some printer parts that we can use as projectiles or shields," Rudder suggested.

"No. I just got it working," I shot back without looking.

"That printer is beyond end of life," Rudder said.

"You touch that printer, I end your life."

Rudder mumbled something under his breath.

"I'm like John McClain," Carlos said, cutting the covers off an old 3-ring binder.

"Who?" Rudder asked.

Carlos stopped and shook his head. "After this, we're spending a week at my place watching movies. We need to work on your pop culture knowledge."

"How do you figure?" I asked, trying to refocus him.

"I mean it's no Nakatomi Plaza, but we're in a building with a something evil-ish, forced to survive with limited resources and our wits," Carlos said.

"That's a stretch," I said. "For one, there are no terrorists. There is terror, sure. Our adversary is less Alan Rickman and more *Arachnophobia*."

"Has anyone told you that you suck the fun out of everything?" He gave me a dirty look.

"Yes." I shrugged. "Ian said we have to keep moving."

The pulsing sound returned as if I'd summoned it. A shiver of revulsion rippled through my body and I shuddered involuntarily.

Carlos held up what he'd been working on. The covers of the 3-ring binders were covered in duct tape, with a matching loop on the back. He slid his forearm through the loop. "Bracers. I call them God and Zilla."

"Why?" Rudder asked.

"Because I'm about to beat the shit out of Mothra." Carlos grinned.

"You know Mothra was protector, right?" Rudder asked.

"That you know, but you don't know John McClain?" Carlos shook his head.

"Do you hear that?" Rudder asked. "I think it was the sound. I think we should stay away from whatever is making that noise. It got inside of me and I couldn't stop it."

Carlos was looking off into the distance as he watched.

"Carlos, you good?" I asked.

"Huh? Yeah, sure," he said.

"We need to get moving." I handed supplies off to Rudder, who stowed them in his backpack.

"Yeah," Carlos said in a dreamy tone. "I'm going to check if the coast is clear."

"No one goes alone," I said.

Carlos walked away.

"Damnit," I said, zipping up the backpack. "Rudder."

"On it," Rudder said, darting out of the room to stop Carlos.

My insides vibrated in time with thunderous footsteps. Not human footsteps. These steps shook the floor. It was a slow metronome, but instead of a soft click, it was a heavy clump. An icy breeze brushed my exposed skin, raising goose bumps all over my body. The fine hairs on my arms stood on end.

"Danni," Rudder said.

His voice was distant and the sound of my name had no meaning, as if it were unintelligible babble. I ran my hand along my arm in awe and fascination. The goose bumps and freckles on my arm, and the underlying structure of muscle and bone, fascinated me. I had a sudden desire to see the muscles that move everything and the tendons and bones that hold and move and support everything. The desire to delve into that unknown universe became irresistible, an urge too strong

184

to ignore. Reaching for the box cutter in my backpack, a strange calm washed over me; I was ready to explore the wonders of my own body.

"Danni, we have to move." Rudder grabbed me and shook me.

"Huh," I said, jostled but not entirely dislodged from my daze.

"What were you doing?" he asked.

"Nothing. Where's Carlos?" I asked. I rubbed my arm. Twice I'd dipped my toe into a terrifying and alien mental state. I'd snapped out of it twice. But how many times could I go to that place and come back unscathed? How many trips down the rabbit hole before I became a rabbit or the mad queen of hearts herself? Off with my own head! My pulse throbbed in my ears; in the noise, I heard my name. "Dan-ni, Dan-ni," it whooshed.

"He's around the corner," Rudder said. "He's getting away from the sounds."

"There are earplugs in the datacenter." I grabbed his arm. "Earplugs, because it's the sound."

"I think it's the vibration," Rudder said.

"Um, yeah. That's what sound is," I said.

"I'm hearing and feeling it in every cell my body. Don't you feel it?"

I squinted at him. "One thing at a time. We do what we can deal with and what we know." I had a direction, and we were going to go in that direction. I turned the corner and headed toward Carlos.

"If we can get to the datacenter, why don't we just head up the stairs instead and leave?" Rudder asked.

"He's right," Carlos said, coming from around a corner. "If you have a chance to get out, take it."

"Ian said that wasn't an option. That if we left here, it would follow us. We couldn't walk away from this if we wanted to. It knows us now. I think there's only one way out. Ian called for help before; he was going outside to meet them. We need to stay here and stay alive until they get here."

"That's madness. How can you possibly say that?" Rudder asked.

"Two to one. You're outvoted," Carlos said. "Why do you want to stay? You can't possibly think you're still going to have a job after this?"

"I heard it calling my name," I said. "But from inside me, like it was the sound of my pulse."

"We need to leave," Rudder said, turning and walking toward the exit. Carlos and I followed.

"Rudder, listen to reason," I pleaded.

"That's it; you've lost all reason. This is insanity." He kept walking, gesturing with his arms to punctuate his sentence.

"Ian's probably dead. He's not meeting anyone. Has he done or said a single thing that gives us a reason to trust him? Yet suddenly he's the person you're listening to?" Carlos said.

"We're never getting out of here," I said. Even if we got out, this wasn't going to be over. "Ian said he called in the cavalry, and we just had to survive. He didn't say that we all had to stay. He said I have to stay."

"Stop," Rudder said. "We're in this together. We're getting out, all of us. That's what we're doing now. Because whatever it is, it's over there and we're going this way, and this way is out."

"We all go, or we all stay," Carlos said as he walked off to follow Rudder.

A whisper in my ear said that this was home now. Just like where I'm from, this is a place I'll carry with me everywhere. Like I carry the memory of not having enough food or wearing the same pair of worn-out shoes every day when I was ten. Those things are part of me, and now whether I liked it or not, this was part of me too. You can take the girl out of the datacenter, but you can't take the datacenter out of the girl.

The footsteps were so loud, it sounded like it had tree trunks for legs. Rudder stopped and turned back to me. His face elongated, mouth opened, and eyebrows went up. All the color drained from his face. He took two steps backward and crumpled to the ground.

Don't look. Don't look. Don't look. I repeated it to myself. I walked forward. Carlos grabbed Rudder's arm and pulled him. Rudder didn't respond, then he got up ran. We sprinted toward the door.

It sounded like ketchup packets hitting the ground. Small dark things, less than three inches in length, and they were moving. My eyes and my brain struggled to register what they were. The floor crawled with grasshoppers. Two dozen flew up at me. I yelped.

"Left," Rudder called out. We ran. My foot came down on a grasshopper that didn't move fast enough, and it slid out from under me. I got my left foot down before I had a face full of carpet and insects. Rudder looked back.

"Keep going," I yelled. I didn't want anyone slowing down for anything. I meant when I'd said I wanted them to save themselves. Sometimes saving yourself is all you can do, and I wouldn't begrudge anyone for saving themselves. How many times had I wished I'd been able to save myself?

Glass crunched under my feet. We were close to the door to the outside, the insides of the building. Its empty soul.

Rudder and Carlos barreled through the door and held it for me. "Stairs," Carlos yelled. The door was at least fifty feet away.

"Shit. Hurry." Carlos' voice was hoarse.

They reached the door to the stairwell before I did and had to stand still for a second while I caught up and swiped my badge. Carlos pulled the door open. The three of us ran through and it slammed shut behind us. Rudder ran up instead of down; Carlos and I watched as he did.

"Rudder!" I called out. "Fuck."

"We should go after him," Carlos said, not waiting for a response before he ran up the stairs.

I told myself it was different. We weren't going back for Rudder; we were going toward him. We were moving away from the datacenter where the earplugs were, where our salvation was. I followed Carlos up the stairs.

36

Before

RUDDER WENT UP THE stairs at full speed. Carlos followed close. I trailed behind, going as fast as I could, hoping we could get to him before he ran outside. I stopped short on the second to last step; Carlos and Rudder stood in front of the door. My lungs burned as I gasped for air.

"This stairwell is fire rated. We can stay here," Rudder said, looking at the door as he took a step back. "They can't get in."

"How can you be sure?" I asked.

"It's made of concrete. Those are fire doors, meaning if the building were on fire, we'd be able to stay in here for a few hours and be okay."

"That's not a fire," Carlos said.

The concrete walls seemed to grow and expand with the pulsing as it got louder and louder.

"We can't stay here," I said.

"We're on the ground floor. We can get out," Rudder said.

We went quiet and looked around. A pulsating whooshing sound enveloped us as if we were in the veins of the building trying to pull us back into its heart.

"We need a plan," I said. My mind raced through the options.

"The entrance is close to the stairwell. We could make a run for it," Rudder offered.

The guys talked through the options. I worked through the problem; what information did I know for sure? We were being hunted by a horde of insects, Ian was gone and presumed dead (by me), and Ian had said we couldn't leave.

"What's rule number one?" I asked, interrupting the guys' debating the plan.

Carlos blinked at me. "The customer is a liar."

"Right. So what do we know for sure?"

"I don't follow," Rudder said.

"Carlos's number one rule of troubleshooting. The customer is a liar. They don't always know they're lying. Either they forget something or don't know a detail is relevant to the problem. It's the number one rule to remind you to question what you know for sure and what you were told. We troubleshoot what we know if what we're told doesn't make sense."

"Now we're fucking talking," Carlos grinned.

"How is this relevant?" Rudder asked.

"We make a run for it." Carlos said with a nod. "Because we don't know if Ian lied or just thought he was telling us all the information. So, if we make a choice based on what we know instead of what he said, then we leave, right?"

"Yes. I know this isn't like the last time when there were enough of them to fill the courtyard. But then, I was able to get out and they didn't follow me."

Rudder looked at Carlos and then at me, shrugged, then opened the backpack. "We should be ready, in case." He took the paper cutter machete and gave a canister of canned air to Carlos.

"Good call," I said and pulled the padlock out of my pocket. I wrapped part of the cord around my hand till the padlock was hanging at my side but not hitting the ground, then tested swinging it to make sure I wouldn't give myself a concussion.

A flash of light and the heat of an open flame came from behind me. I spun around. A streak of flame disappeared. Carlos dropped his lighter and the canned air, shaking his arm with the binder taped to it. A blue flame crawled up his arm. He fell on the landing, smothering the arm until the flame went out.

"Stop, drop, and roll." He smiled as he pushed himself up off the ground, checking his arm for damage.

"What the hell?" I said.

"I had to test it," Carlos said. "Proof of concept. It needs some tweaking."

"You think?"

"Hey, the three-ring binder. We take the metal ring part out, duct tape it to the can and the lighter. Boom! No more flaming hands." Carlos began digging into the backpack for supplies to test his new design.

Rudder shouldered the backpack. "Ready?"

"One minute," Carlos said as he tore off duct tape with his teeth.

"You ready?" Rudder asked me.

"Yeah," I lied. Nothing could have made me ready.

"Okay, I'm good." Carlos gave the canister another test and didn't catch fire that time.

I rolled my eyes.

"After you, my evil little sister," Carlos said.

I swiped my badge, the reader beeped, and we ran for the door. It was twenty feet, another right turn, and then maybe another twenty until we were at the glass doors. Rudder got out in front; Carlos brought up the rear. I turned the corner. Unable to stop myself, I skidded into Rudder as he stood frozen, looking at the door.

All the lights went out; time slowed as my eyes struggled to adjust to the darkness. It was dead calm. The glass doors were opaque. Were the lights in the parking lot out too, I wondered, not understanding. In the darkness, the opaqueness of the door crawled. Insects covered the glass doors from floor to ceiling.

I went around Rudder and banged on the door to scare them away. If any moved, others took their place. I tried the door, thinking I'd run through them and at least we'd be out. But the doors wouldn't budge. I dropped to the ground and checked the locks at the bottom of the door; they were unlocked, but still the door wouldn't budge.

Ian had been right, sort of. He'd said I shouldn't leave, not that I couldn't leave. It was an important detail he'd either omitted or hadn't known.

An engine roared to life. I jumped back in surprise. "It's the generator. It's diesel," I said, catching my breath. It kept the datacenter running during loss of street power. The only light on in the building was the glow from the datacenter, three floors below.

"What's that buzzing?" I reached for my ears. Both guys covered their ears too. We turned toward the source of the sound, inching away from the glass doors and past the elevators. The swarm poured up from the courtyard and through the railing, swirling and gaining form, like mist becoming a cloud, gathering into something. My stomach lurched into my throat and I looked away before I threw up.

"We need to get down to the fourth floor," Rudder said.

"The badge reader on the stairwell is probably active since it had emergency lighting, but it was the last place I want to be." Carlos bent over, placing his hands on his thighs.

"Good point. By the time we get down there, who knows what we'll be walking into." No need to discuss the elevator; no power equals no elevator.

"Can we just pick a direction?" Rudder said, throwing his hands up while still holding the makeshift machete.

Something hit my neck. I jumped and swatted it away.

A grasshopper landed on Rudder. He brushed it off.

They were everywhere, blocking the path back to the stairwell and the walkway. The swarm started to move, not forward but around. As the moths, grasshoppers, and whatever else found its way into the swarm, it took an almost human shape. The main body moved and flickered like an image pixelating and redrawing itself. Its head was a hair's width from touching the ceiling. We had nowhere to go.

"The elevator." Carlos held out his hand and yelled, "Bag."

Rudder tossed it to him. The way out behind us would create an avalanche of insects which would slow us to the point that we might as well stay still. But the creature in front of us grew in stature and the light around it glowed brighter as it formed a single entity.

Scrape. I turned, hearing metal on metal. Rudder had forced a large flat-head screwdriver in between the elevator doors. The doors were half an inch apart. Carlos and I put our fingers in the gap from either side and pulled with everything we had. The door moved an inch.

"Faster," I said.

Rudder pushed as we pulled. The doors gave an inch at a time. "Stop," he yelled, then disappeared through the half-open doors.

"Hurry." Carlos's eyes went wide as the swarm stopped flickering and became solid, with six insect-like legs and four arms. With the body of caterpillar, fleshy and soft. The wings were composed of thousands of moths, its head a lump on its body with no neck to turn it. I looked away, closing my eyes tight, but tears spilled out. I wiped them away and sucked it up. Carlos investigated the elevator shaft.

"You're next," he said.

I nodded, went in, forced myself not to look down, and only focused on finding something to hold on to. I allowed myself to look down. The inside of the elevator was disorienting and I sucked in my breath. The elevator car was two flights down. Too far to jump.

"There's a ledge." Rudder pointed down at his feet. He stood on the rails of the door one floor down. "Get in."

I stepped onto the tiny ledge with only my toes. Carlos came in behind me. We pushed the doors together, but a dozen moths entered. One got caught in the doors, crunching as they closed on its body.

"Okay, you need to drop down," Rudder said.

"Um, how?" I asked. I tightened my grip on the edge of the door.

"There's a hand hold to your right."

"That is not a hand hold," I said, looking at the slick metal beam mounted on the wall to my right.

"It's what you got," he said. "Carlos, you're going to need to get right."

"With God?" Carlos asked.

"Jokes? Really?" I asked.

"Yes. Really." He smirked.

Inching my left foot over, I willed myself to bring my right foot next to it while refusing to relinquish my grasp on the door, tenuous as it might have been. The concrete walls of the shaft seemed to vibrate with the pulsing sound. No matter where we were, and no matter how many doors and walls were between us and it, it found us.

The next foothold was out of reach. I was going to have to let go of the door. I felt for a groove in the walls, anything to feel like my hands had purchase on something. I shifted my weight against the wall. I grabbed the cold metal and clung to it for dear life.

"Is it a ladder?" I asked, noticing that it had staggered footholds.

"No clue, but you can use it as one," Rudder said.

"Why isn't there one on this side?" Carlos said.

"You can make it," Rudder said. "Just lower yourself down. There is less than four feet between that rail and this one. Come on; Lara Croft could totally do that."

"Funny." Carlos jumped to the other side. As he fought for his balance, I braced my body on the metal beam and footholds and Rudder grabbed Carlos's leg. His hands flailed for anything to hold on to; he grabbed my shirt. I clasped his forearm and pulled him toward me. He let go of my shirt and pressed his face into the wall as if he'd been lost at sea and it was the first dry land he'd seen in months.

"I'm here for you, man, but maybe don't do that again," I panted.

He exhaled a hard and jagged breath.

"I'm going to die," he said weakly.

"You're fine," I told him, even though we were far from fine. We were dangling inside an elevator shaft.

"Maybe we'll all die," he said.

"You're panicking. Stop," I said.

Rudder held his hand out to Carlos and pulled him to the beam he was on and off me. "Okay, we're halfway there. The hard part is over. We just need to climb down to the elevator, climb in, and then pry the doors open."

"And then fight the creepy giant monster?" Carlos asked.

"Yes, and then that. One step at a time," I said. "Don't die in the scary shaft and then we fight the boss of this level. Or just run from it."

With Carlos steady, I started lowering myself down rung by rung. I could feel vibration through the metal on the makeshift ladder. It could be the generator.

I got to the elevator car first and opened the hatch on the top. "Just like the movies," I said.

193

"It's probably a safety feature," Carlos said.

"I know I feel safer," I replied. "Help me down?"

Rudder and Carlos lowered me down till I was two feet above the floor.

"Let go," I said.

I dropped the remaining two feet and moved out of the way while the guys lowered themselves down. Rudder landed first and I took the screwdriver out of his back pocket before he could object. I pried open the inner doors, revealing the outer doors, then paused.

"Do you think it knows where we are?" I asked.

"No clue," Rudder said.

"We still have to get to the fourth floor. If we have a clear path, we can take the stairs," I said.

"That's a big if," Carlos said, landing in the elevator.

"So, we run?" I asked.

Carlos nodded and shrugged. "I guess. We should probably play it by ear."

"Ready?"

Carlos and Rudder answered by grabbing the other side of the door and pulling it open. We pulled ourselves up and out of the shaft onto the third floor, and then the work cell phone rang.

37

Before

I'M IN THE DATACENTER alone. A swarm of moths envelops me in a murky puke-green glow. Their grotesque wings brush my skin, my face, my mouth. I'm weightless, held aloft by an unseen force. My hair floats around my head as if I'm underwater. A wing scrapes across my eye. I blink several times as my eye wells with tears, trying to expel the foreign object.

All at once, gravity yanks me out of the air. I land hard on the ground, my knees and elbows taking the brunt of my fall. My cheek is flat on the cool datacenter floor.

I'm in the past. This happened already, but I'm experiencing it like it's happening now. I'm shifting through space and time. The off-white floor tiles of the datacenter are superimposed onto the off-white linoleum of the floor in the hallway at the mental health hospital. Both are real: I can feel and smell both at the same time.

Holding two truths in my mind simultaneously is ripping me to pieces. I can't be in both places at once. I am on the floor, running my finger over the seams between the floor tiles in the datacenter and feeling the hard linoleum floor of the hospital room I share with Erin.

My wonder at this dual reality is pushed aside by the pain setting in from my fall. The badge reader on the datacenter door beeps. I hear it over the air conditioner, the servers, alarms, and the sound of Erin yelling. I need to run; they're coming for me.

Readying myself, I push myself up off the floor, crouch, and take in my surroundings. The walls fade in and out; one second, I'm surrounded by servers and the next it's the hallway outside my room. The EMTs and firefighters are in the hallway outside my room at the mental health hospital, and then I shift and orderlies cautiously approach me in the datacenter.

I panic because I know what happens next. It's the same as what happened before, when they brought me to this place. The EMTs approach. I'm wild. Babbling and throwing my arms, I rush at them. I'm not trying to go after them; I'm trying to get to the door. The orderlies find me inconsolable and ugly crying. I rush through them, trying to find the exit. Their fingers bite into my arms, pulling me down.

"Carlos," I scream. Lunging in the opposite direction, I break free and run to see if he's okay. He's not safe. I need to help him. I'm knocked to the ground.

"She's a runner," say the paramedics in the datacenter and the orderlies in unison. They're working together. The people who pulled me out of the datacenter, they put me here. They pull me by my ankles as I claw at the floor.

The words of the EMTs sound like traffic. It's the sound of screeching tires and honking horns. Fingers dig into the flesh of my arms.

"We need to sedate her," one of the EMTs says.

Then as if an echo, one of the orderlies says, "Get someone down here to sedate her."

"Just get her to seclusion," Darla says.

The shadow is moving closer. I expect it to be an EMT with a syringe of something that will sap my will and steal my fight. I cock my fist and throw it forward like I'm pitching a baseball. Instead of connecting, my fist goes through the figure and connects to something on the other side of it. Darla yelps in pain. "Bitch."

They lift me and drag me down the hallway. I buck and fight with everything I have, but it's pointless.

Light leaks in from in between the moths. The outline of a person grows closer.

"Rudder," I yell, finding my voice again. He walks forward and the moths don't part, they just disappear into him. He plants his hands on my shoulders. I shift

196

fully into the present; the datacenter walls and the hospital walls fade away, leaving me standing with Rudder. I can't see what's beyond the slow glow of light that envelops us.

"Danni, look at me."

The peace on his face gives me pause and allows my panic to recede a fraction. I take a breath.

"Danni, you aren't here. You're there," he says.

"Carlos," I say, breathless. "We need to find him. We should run."

"Danni, you aren't in the datacenter anymore."

He's right. This isn't the datacenter, but it's not the hospital.

"Where is here?" I ask. He's not making any sense. Maybe he's in the mental hospital too. I shake away the thought.

"It doesn't matter. There's no time for that. But it's important you know that you left. You're out. But you're also in and you need to get yourself out," he says.

The moths form a bubble around us. "What's going on? Rudder, please tell me." I'm desperate. If I'm going to die, at least tell me why and how.

"You're fractured. Your consciousness was shattered and part of you is here in this moment and there's another part of you still in there."

"Fractured?" I ask. The word feels like an accurate description of what I've been experiencing. I haven't felt like I'm all here or all anywhere.

"Where is there? The moths... They're..."

"They're another fractured thing. Carlos gave you a meaning and you latched onto it. You tied them to yourself and to this place. It used your fear and your mind against you."

"But they're not hurting us."

Rudder radiates warmth, and for the first time in months, I feel completely safe and at ease.

Rudder smiles. "You could also take the other names or meanings, that you'll go bald or win the lottery. Depends on where you're from. The Hawaiian folklore for it is beautiful. It makes sense that you would connect to it as a harbinger."

"Why?"

He shrugs. "I don't have all the answers. Reality is complex. It can be fractured. Seemingly competing truths can coexist and if we embrace them, we're better for it. Like the moth and like you—both things that seem in conflict with themselves but really aren't. Like a word can mean more than one thing, so can a person. So can a symbol."

His words register but I don't understand or know why it's important. It feels important. Or this is a sign I'm truly detached from reality? Is this a hallucination? Was it all just in my mind? His face goes slack, devoid of expression; his eyes become cloudy. He blinks and he's back.

"It's time to go." Rudder pushes my shoulders and I fly backward with hurricane force. My face lands hard against the linoleum. The pain is sudden and throbbing. People are yelling and the words are getting closer, like a freight train barreling down on top of me.

"She's restrained," Erin yells. "You're hurting her."

I gasp as if I've forgotten to breathe. The light fades and I struggle to stay awake. That's when I feel the needle.

"Rudder." I reach out to where he was. He pushed me away, back into this place. I want to be angry, but it's hard to be angry through the disorienting pain and with my consciousness slipping away. I'm trying to make sense of it all. And everything goes bla...

38

Before

"Shit." The building shook as I contemplated my ringing phone. Someone was calling the help desk; someone was searching for help. I laughed at the absurdity of it.

"Are you seriously answering that?" Carlos asked.

"I might still have a job after all this. If I'm not dead, I'd still like to eat," I said. "Help Desk; this is Danni."

Rudder and Carlos turned, and both stared at me. I shrugged. What was I going to do, not do my job? I waved a hand at them and started walking to the walkway. I looked down over the railing and then up.

"My computer isn't working," the user said.

"What's on your screen?" I asked.

"A whole bunch of crap. I was working on a spreadsheet, and it has a lot of rows, and I was trying to copy—" he said.

"Right, so the screen is locked up?" I cut him off. Maybe it's not good customer service, but exercising call control was life or death.

The horde of moths eclipsed the sky, circling above us.

"Uh-huh, okay. Have you tried rebooting the computer?" I asked. I put my hand over the microphone. "We should run."

"I did reboot. The issue happened after I rebooted. Now all I get is this blue screen."

The walkway flooded with large moths, each with ten-inch wingspans. Carlos grabbed my badge off my pocket and swiped it in front of the badge reader.

Nothing happened. I tried the door and it wouldn't budge. I took my badge back from him.

"What's the error?" The swarm filled the walkway surrounding us. As they grew in numbers, they formed a monstrosity. I stuffed my badge into my back pocket and pulled out the padlock on the power cord, wrapping it around my hand. I swung and contacted one of the moths; it fell to the ground and flapped one wing in futility. One down, a million to go. I ducked, leaning back with the phone held to my ear.

"It's a bunch of numbers," the user mumbled.

I spun, wielding the padlock into the swarm, which made a satisfying yet disgusting squishing noise as it collided with a moth. Carlos flanked my other side and Rudder came up next to him with the machete.

"*A problem has been detected and Windows has been shut down—*"

"That's a default message," I interrupted him. I didn't have time for him to read the entire screen. "Look just below that message, next to the numbers."

"Oh, it says *IRQ not less or equal. If this is the first time...*" I pulled the phone away from my ear while he read the text.

Carlos pulled the trigger on the canned air and shot a stream of fire into the swarm, taking out several of them. The horde was getting closer, and the moths drew in tighter formation as the creature took shape with legs, a large torso, and a head with no neck. It screamed, a sound that was somewhere between a baby's cry and a screeching bird. Insects increased in number and flocked together; it seemed to be calling them.

"Can you hold for one moment while I research that message?" I didn't wait for an answer and set the phone down.

"Penalty hold?" Carlos asked as he pulled the trigger on the canned air, releasing a stream of flame into the beast. It screamed again. I covered my ears, half expecting them to be bleeding. My inner ears rattled at the intensity and volume.

"Research break," I yelled back. He smiled and nodded.

Rudder swung the blade. He was taking them out more by blunt force than by cutting. I pulled back and was able to get a few more swings in as it reconstructed in front of us. It was like trying to chop down a redwood with a pocketknife. We downed them one and two at a time, but it wasn't making an impact. It flickered and lost shape like a pixelating picture, and then reformed again. It didn't seem to feel or care about our feeble efforts.

I picked up the phone. "Can you turn off the computer and turn it back on while tapping on the F8 key? It's one of the keys on the top row of your keyboard," I said.

Carlos's flamethrower ran out of juice and he discarded it, pulling a keyboard out of Rudder's backpack. He swung it into the mass. It hit something solid, and an explosion of keys rained down.

"I found the any key!" he shouted.

"Good one," Rudder said.

"Okay, I'm at a menu. What's that sound?" the caller asked.

"Coworker is watching a movie. Great; let's arrow down to Last Known Good Configuration and hit enter."

I swung again; Carlos blocked with the binders he'd taped to his forearms and used them to push back the moths as he worked his way closer to the body of the creature.

"Hey, I'm back at a login screen. Thanks." The user hung up before I could tell him to have a great day. Last Known Good Configuration for the win.

"Ahhhhhhhh," Carlos yelled and swung wildly, running at it. It stepped forward with six legs, flickered, and Carlos disappeared into it. A sick green glow came from inside the beast.

"No!" Rudder charged forward, left hand out, and the blade clanged to the ground as he disappeared into the beast. Carlos appeared, lunging forward, gasping and flailing. His eyes were glazed and wild.

"Its eyes. I saw its eyes. It's full of eyes inside. It saw me," he said.

"Rudder," I said.

Carlos's eyes went wide. A tear ran down his face. "It's looking at him." His face was etched with age and sorrow. He had aged a decade in the span of seconds. "We have to get him out."

"Get him. I'll cover you," I said. Carlos rushed forward using the bracers as shields. He scooped up the paper cutter machete. The exterior of the thing was impermeable. He swung at it, hitting it in the middle; the machete thudded against it without making a dent in its exoskeleton. I let out a length of the power cord as I swung the padlock in a figure eight in front of me.

The thing was more fragile than it looked. It was phasing in and out, its footing in this world uncertain and tenuous. I swung the lock, made contact, and shredded delicate wings; several moths dropped to the ground flapping one good wing and going nowhere.

It phased out and pixelated again. Carlos grabbed Rudder and yanked him forward. Rudder landed hard and unceremoniously. Carlos knelt over him, dropping the blade on the ground.

"You okay?" he asked, even though he knew the answer. His pupils dilated; his head jerked from side to side. His chin flapped up and down and he tried to talk, but at first only garbled noises came out, like a man with his tongue cut out.

"I've seen past the veil," he said. "I know what lies beyond and I don't want to, I can't... it's unbearable." Rudder stood up suddenly.

The thing phased in and out, screaming as it moved closer. It seemed to move and shrink according to the space available to it, fed by a constant source of incoming moths. We had to lure it in from out in the open. If it had the full breadth of the courtyard, we'd be fucked.

Carlos grabbed Rudder and we retreated down the walkway to the other side. "I've seen the walls of other worlds," Rudder muttered. "I've heard the terrible call."

"Rudder, look at me. You're going to be okay. It's going to be okay," Carlos repeated as he led Rudder away, one arm wrapped around his shoulders like a wounded warrior. I brought up the rear, swinging at anything that moved.

"She heard the call too. That's why she's here. Karathala comes for us!" Rudder's voice rose. It was nonsensical to the point where the words almost didn't sound like English.

"It's a she?" I asked, looking back at it.

"But no, this is a manifestation of her will, just a foot soldier. She is the creator and the ruination," Rudder said, grabbing the weapon at his side.

The foot soldier flapped its wings. Rudder flew off the ground and into the wall. Carlos and I were knocked to the ground. "Run," Rudder said at a volume that I almost didn't hear and barely understood. His eyes focused again and he pressed against the wall. "Go," he said, more urgently.

"No," Carlos said as Rudder ran full speed, screaming and swinging his machete.

Carlos lunged forward. Rudder tossed the backpack to him and disappeared into the creature. "I know what to do." Rudder's voice floated over us like a dandelion on the wind.

I grabbed Carlos and we ran. My mind raced faster than my feet, trying to figure out how to get away. If we used the stairwell, it would be waiting for us outside the door, in the open courtyard where it wouldn't be limited by the ceiling height. Rudder had bought us a very small window of time.

"The rope," Carlos yelled at me. Before I could ask what rope, he pulled the braided extension cord from the backpack and looped it over the handrail.

"Go," I yelled. He swung one leg and then the other over the barrier. With no time to secure it, Carlos held the ends in either hand as he slid down it.

The thing roared behind me and then fractured into a swarm. The wall behind Rudder was visible. His body was translucent and then dissipated into the wind. Unable to move or collapse into a crying heap, I watched in disbelief as the moths pursued us.

I couldn't wait for Carlos to reach the bottom; I climbed the railing and wrapped my legs around the cord, trying to let my jeans absorb the friction instead of my hands.

Carlos yelled from below and the line went slack. It swung out and then back against the railing and the concrete. My side exploded in pain. My grip loosened and I slid, hitting the ground, and crumpled.

"Ow," I cried out. "Motherfu—"

"No time! Gotta go!" Carlos pulled me up. I screamed in pain then stood and ran for the datacenter door. I swiped my card and the badge reader's steady red light turned green.

"Yes!" We ran in and slammed the door behind us. I searched to make sure nothing had gotten in. I wrapped my arms around myself.

I fell against the door and slid to the floor. Fresh blood from my reopened wound streamed down my hand. My hands were red from rope burn and blood. I pushed myself off the floor, put pressure on the wound, and looked for a clean cloth to use as a bandage.

"What do we do now?" Carlos asked.

39

Before

I FOUND A T-SHIRT from a vendor in the supply closet and wrapped my hand. Thank God for free swag. I considered Carlos's question: What do we do now? "Rest, regroup? Pray for morning?"

"We need to go back for Rudder," he said.

"He's gone," I sighed.

"What you mean he's gone?"

"He disappeared."

"Disappeared?"

"Yes. When that thing dispersed, he... evaporated."

"Evaporated?" he asked.

"I don't know, but— None of this makes sense." I walked back to the door and turned the light on. It was supposed to make me feel better, safer, as if it could chase away what was outside. The lights assaulted my senses. I went to the supply cabinet, looking for anything, unsure of what I needed.

"We're not safe in here," Carlos said. "It broke the glass in the other office."

"I know." My eyes went to the floor. I'd thought if we got to the datacenter, everything would be okay.

"I think it's broken." Carlos pointed at his ankle. All his weight was on his other foot. He lifted his pant leg. I cringed. His ankle had turned a purplish-blue color and swelled. The color was draining from his face.

"When?" I asked. We'd run into the datacenter.

"Probably when I hit the ground; I barely felt it till now. Something about adrenaline and running for your life." He shrugged as if it were normal.

"We're so fucked." I put my head in my hands. What could we do? Carlos wasn't running on that foot.

The air conditioning unit against the window at the front of the room kicked on and shook the glass. I jumped and held my breath, waiting for it to break. It held, for the moment.

The room filled with the sound of rushing air and fans. I wouldn't leave Carlos behind, so this room was either going to be our last stand or our salvation. But with nothing in sight that would deliver salvation, things were grim. The supply closet was full of blank discs, old floppies, office supplies, and server parts. No weapons.

"You still want to try the earplugs?" he asked.

"We'll have enough issues hearing each other over all this noise." I tossed him a packet of earplugs. "Put them in if the glass breaks." Carlos caught them and limped gingerly to a computer chair a few feet away. He pushed himself back over near me with his good foot.

"Any luck?" he asked.

I bit my lip; I was trying not to cry. Of all the ways I could have died, other-worldly insect invasion wasn't on the list of options. I didn't know if we were affecting it with our attacks. If we killed moths, did it summon more? Were we weakening it? Was it better to find a corner to hide in, try to wait it out till morning? Or maybe we'd just be waiting for our deaths.

"It's all just a bunch of shit." I wasn't sure if I was talking about the situation or all the stuff in the supply closet.

"Could any of it be useful shit?" he asked as he leaned in.

"No." I pulled the CDs out, swiping my arm across the shelf and spilling them out onto the floor. The plastic cases crashed and cracked as they hit the ground. DVDs spread across the floor like flat disco balls as light danced off them. I fell to the floor on top of them and slid, picked them up by the handful and threw them back at the supply cabinet. A pained sound came out of my open mouth, the sound of defeat; my death wail.

The glass shook, the air conditioning cut off, and I could hear what it was drowning out, the sound of thousands of moths and grasshoppers throwing themselves into the window repeatedly. They sounded like rocks. "We're going to die, or disappear, just like Rudder," I said.

"Stop," Carlos said in a clipped tone. "Rudder isn't dead."

"Yes, he is," I screamed from the floor like a toddler. I didn't know what had happened to him or where he was. The pit of my stomach had dropped out and I felt like the wind had been knocked out of me.

"He just walked into it. Why did he do that?" Carlos asked.

He wasn't looking for an answer but I supplied one anyhow. "I think he found a way to buy us enough time to get here."

"But can he find his way out? If there's a way in, there has to be an out, right? We can't sit here and do nothing. We should be out there, trying to get him back. We both got out the first time; there has to be a way."

"Nothing gets better. Can't you see that? Everything in the past few years, it only gets worse. All we wanted was jobs that paid enough to cover the rent, food, a few essentials. Even if those essentials were video games and a new KT7A-RAID motherboard. Is that too much to fucking ask for?" I kicked the metal cabinet; the door flung backward and sprang forward.

"I just wanted to survive. Instead, we've been running for our lives, and now we're trapped. It's all fucking bullshit and I'm so goddamn sick of all of it." I kicked it again.

"You don't need RAID anyhow." Carlos opened the backpack. "Do we have anything useful left in here?"

He reached into the backpack and froze.

"What is it?"

He gently pulled out a red notebook, Rudder's notebook. Carlos placed it on his lap and ran his hand over the cover.

I wanted to withdraw and give him a moment, but I couldn't move.

Carlos opened his mouth, exhaled, and then struggled to find his words. "It's more than that; it's his entire plan." He opened the book and flipped through pages of drawings. "He was saving money to do a tattoo apprenticeship; he'd been

207

saving for a long time. We talked about getting out of IT and doing other things. I hooked him up with my uncle who runs a shop down in Casa Grande."

"He never told me." I shook my head.

"He probably thought you'd laugh at him." Carlos gave me a sideways glance.

"Why would I laugh?"

"He didn't have any tattoos partially because he was saving his money to be able to afford the apprenticeship, but also, he wanted to draw it himself and hadn't found the perfect thing. I tried to tell him there is no perfect thing. Sometimes you just have to choose a direction and go. Otherwise, you spend your life in paralysis."

I looked away and rubbed my arm. He was right; I would have. What kind of friend am I that Rudder couldn't tell me? We sat in silence for a few minutes while he flipped through the book.

He stopped on a page and I leaned in. Rudder had drawn a near-perfect replica of the picture I'd taken of the moth. He'd only seen it a few times, yet it was so detailed and nuanced, and through his eyes, the moth was beautiful. Carlos closed the book with a light touch and carefully returned it to the backpack.

"We can look at it later," he said.

"Will there be a later?" I wasn't sure anymore. Part of me didn't want there to be a later. I was angry at everything, but especially myself. A pit of shame and regret grew in my stomach. Shame for things I'd said, left unsaid, and all the ways I'd let other people down, including myself.

"Danni, there's going to be a later," Carlos said as he fished through the backpack. "Hey, we still have duct tape. We can solve anything."

I laughed as I wiped my tears with the palm of my hand. "Thank God, duct tape. All of our problems are solved."

40

After

Ivy warned me I'd end up here if I was unmanageable.

I turn it over repeatedly in my head. The vague warning she gave me about Darla, which hadn't made sense at the time but became blisteringly clear.

The room is soft from the floor to ceiling. I've read about rooms where the sound is measured in negative decibels. A place so quiet that the only thing you'd hear was your own heartbeat, breath, and stomach acid churning on half-digested food. It drove people insane if they stayed too long. I understand that, sitting here with nothing but my thoughts. Erin is gone. I'm unmanageable. It's just another word for inconsolable.

This is the violent ward. A place where they leave me alone with myself; it's the most violent place they can think of. It makes sense to me; being in my head is horrifying. I have nothing but time to relive it in the violence of my imagination. There's always something worse, something I won't survive. And sometimes, surviving is the hardest part.

There's nothing to write with and no way to keep it all straight. Anything I hold in my mind becomes mush. What happened first? I was born into this room. No, this is not the beginning.

A vibration rattles through my chest and transforms into a flutter. I scratch at my sternum and on to my back. There's something under my shirt that isn't skin. It's not my bra. It's something else—a bandage? Was I injured? They tackled me hard.

My head hurts and my body aches with every movement. The real pain was having Erin ripped from my arms. It's a deep ache that might never go away. I pull the shirt down in the front. The texture of my skin is like paper or like dried leaves. My hand trembles. Oh God, what is this? What have I become? Thoughts race through my head as my stomach lurches in fear and revulsion.

I sit up and crab walk backward into the wall. My breath is jagged, ripping in and out of my lungs like a saw. I pull the front of my shirt down, exposing my sternum. I'm covered in a... no, not covered. My skin is delicate and textured but really, it's not skin at all. My fingers twitch and I drag them across my chest. It feels like any pressure could rip it apart. It's like the exterior of a cocoon. It *is* a cocoon.

Something moves inside me, fluttering in my chest. I push against the wall and stand up. The tremor in my hands spreads to my entire body. It moves again, like a thing in my chest, brushing me from the inside. It pulses.

My crepe paper skin rips. Bile burns the back of my throat. The rip widens without making a sound. Movement inside my body like a seam ripper tearing apart the things that hold me together. I double over, crying from the fear and pain. But I've come this far. I steel myself. I've seen such hideous things, but they've never been me before. I am pushed to the edge of my sanity; this is my breaking point. I'm shattering into pieces. Fractured, just like Rudder said. I look, despite everything in me telling me not to and instead find a nice roof to jump off. I must look. It's better to know.

The edge of the rip is raised, no blood, no guts. I'm not relieved. A wet velvet thing, iridescent brown and purple, emerges from the rip. My mouth gapes open, unable to scream. I know what I am. I am the monster. A breeze brushes against my back as the sound of hundreds of moth wings disturb the air.

"Help!" I scream. My body crumples to the floor. I'm not breathing; my eyes are open and still. I'm above my body watching. There's no time to process if this is a hallucination or if I'm dead.

The door bursts open. Five people file in. They count out loud to themselves, "One, two," and on *three* they raise my body up onto a gurney and push me out. They check my pulse, my breath. There's nothing.

41

Before

"WHAT TIME IS IT?" Carlos asked. I flipped open my phone. I couldn't hear him with the earplugs in, but I knew what he'd asked.

I flashed the numbers on my fingers to communicate that it was 2:33 in the morning. He'd asked the same question every two minutes for the last hour. He leaned back in his chair, banging his head into the metal cabinet. He had asked the same question two hundred and sixty-eight times exactly. Each time, the question echoed in my mind. His words slowed the rotation of the earth, making time stretch out into infinity. A flashing red countdown ticked down how many more times I could tolerate it until I snapped.

We'd lost the paper cutter blade. As much as I wished we had it, it was good that we didn't have it. If it had been in the room, I would've driven it into his skull.

Carlos sat in the chair with his foot elevated.

"How is the pain?" I pointed up at his leg from where I was sitting on the floor. He motioned back and forth with his hand to say *so-so*. But he cringed, sweat beading on his forehead in the sixty-eight-degree room. He lied; I was sure it hurt like hell. It wasn't sprained; it was broken. He didn't have a job or health insurance and I had dragged him into a dangerous situation. Ian was right: I had no idea what I'd done. If we got out alive, taking care of his medical bills would sap the last of his reserves and mine.

"Survival is pointless," I said, even though he couldn't hear me through the hum of the datacenter and his earplugs. I planted my hands on either side of myself and pushed up off the cold floor tiles. Standing, I brushed the dirt on my hands off on my jeans. "Sitting here is waiting for death."

Carlos shrugged at me. I checked the window like I'd done every ten minutes to see if it was holding. It was intact. But so was the swarm outside, the entirety of the glass covered in a moving, crawling, fluttering black mass. I walked to the back of the room where Carlos and I had set up camp.

"It's hot," he said as I approached, fanning himself. The thermometer on the wall read 68 degrees. Under it, the wall-mounted holder for the tile puller was empty. No one put anything back where it belonged.

I found it on the floor down one of the aisles between servers. I dropped it suction cup side down on the tile in front of Carlos and motioned for him to roll the chair backward. He pushed back, straining in pain at every movement. I pressed the suction cups down and pulled up on the handle, lifting the thirty-five-pound tile out of its spot on the frame that made up the raised floor. I slid it out of the way. Cold air blew up from the hole in the floor. Cables were strewn about in the crawl space no more than eighteen inches deep.

"I should put this back where it belongs," I said, more to myself than to Carlos. The tile puller rested back in its cradle on the wall. Walking back, I stopped dead in my tracks. On the wall, in plain view, was a clock. How did I forget there was a clock?

"There's been a fucking clock there the whole goddamned time?" I yelled.

Carlos shrugged and pointed at his ears.

I pointed at the face of the clock; the second hand shook so furiously, it became a blur, then ticked forward one second and back two seconds. "There's a clock," I accused Carlos. There'd been a clock the whole time, all two-hundred-and-sixty-eight times he'd asked the time and the five hundred times I'd heard the echo of it in my head. That's 134,000 times he asked, all the while a clock ticked on the wall. 134,000 times that have been an assault on my senses and I'd endured it because of his pain. It became stunningly clear; he had done it with intent. Was his leg even broken?

"Are you getting back at me?" Every word, every question an attempt to drive a nail into the coffin of my sanity. Maybe it wasn't revenge; maybe he was one of them. This could have been a plan all along; after all, he knew about the Mariposa De La Muerte.

"What?"

I wanted to rip the earplugs out of his ears and scream at him that I knew. I knew what he was doing.

"Why are you doing this?" I stood over him in the chair. He shook his head with laughter in his eyes. His denial fueled a rage inside me that moved like a flash flood through my veins. I closed my eyes. Images flashed through my mind of the things I could do to him. Including me pushing him in the chair out of the datacenter, over the railing. I envisioned curling my fingers around the handle of the paper cutter blade, and what I could do with my bare hands. The images thrilled and disgusted me. I grinned and laughed while a deep burning shame crept through my veins.

The wall crawled and pulsated. Everything in my peripheral vision slithered. The speckles in the walls opened like pores, maggot-like creatures squirmed their way in and out, first only a few and then a hundred. I turned slowly to face it, my mind fighting it, screaming at me not to look. The urge to turn away, to close my eyes, was overwhelming. I couldn't help myself. I turned to the wall. There was nothing there. Were they there in the first place? I squeezed my eyes closed and shook my head.

"Are you seeing this?" I yelled at Carlos. "These aren't working." I ripped the earplugs out of my ears.

"What?" Carlos took out one of his earplugs.

"These aren't working," I held out the orange foam earplugs, then threw them at the wall.

"What do you mean they aren't working?" he asked.

"The walls are crawling. I can feel them. But then they aren't. Looking at them makes them invisible, but I think they're still there," I said.

"The walls are invisible?"

"The insects. They're crawling through the walls."

"Mine are working." He shifted in his chair, his face twisted in pain, and he sucked in a breath. "The bugs are outside. We're safe in here."

The walls squirmed with life every time I looked away; my eyes were drawn back again and again. I looked at Carlos, and then shot glances to the left and to the right. I spun around. I patted the sides of my head to make sure the maggots weren't on my eyes instead of the walls.

"Why are you losing your shit?" He sounded alarmed. "Danni, look at me."

I locked my eyes on him, willing myself to see only him and shut out all the movement.

"You can do this."

"I can't." Tears welled in my eyes. How long could I live with insanity in my peripheral vision? How long could I live with the unreal being real? And how long would it take for it to overtake me to the point where the crawling wasn't just near me, it was inside me?

"The earplugs are working for me. Why aren't they working for you?"

I jumped to the side. Maybe it was only the air brushing my arm, but it felt like spiders crawling on my skin. I brushed my arm. Then I rubbed harder. I would have rubbed through my own skin if Carlos hadn't grabbed my injured hand and squeezed. I screamed in pain; my knees buckled beneath me and I crashed to the computer room floor.

"Holy fuck," I cried out. "Why did you do that?"

"It's the pain," he said.

"What?" The world wasn't pulsing or crawling after I caught my breath. The only sound was the hum of the air conditioning and the fans in the servers.

"The pain is real; it keeps you grounded. I realized that every time I moved, my foot throbbed and my head felt a little clearer."

"Can you warn a girl next time?" Blood dripped from my hand onto the datacenter floor. I cradled my injured hand against my chest, bleeding onto my shirt. "Wait, does that mean it won't hurt us? That it will just try to drive us crazy?"

"Maybe. If you think about it, did it ever hurt us? Or did we only get hurt from running and attacking it?"

"What does it want?" I asked him, knowing there wasn't an answer.

Carlos shrugged.

"Maybe that's what it feeds off? Our fear?" I imaged it out there, drinking in our terror.

"Or that's just a fringe benefit," Carlos laughed.

"So the plan is to hide until morning and poke at each other's wounds every few minutes? That sounds fun."

"Sounds like hanging out with you on a normal day."

"Ha ha." I looked back at the door. "I'm usually inside when the sun starts coming up. What time is sunrise?"

"Five-thirty, maybe six," he said.

"Is that the right time?" I squinted at the clock as if it would tell me if it was right. "That means we need to wait it out for two or three hours?"

"Assuming it'll go away when the sun comes up?"

"Oh god, don't say that. It has to, right?" I looked at him, begging him to tell me it couldn't be, to tell me something he couldn't possibly know for sure. "What if we're the only ones that see it?"

"I don't know what would be worse. If we're the only ones that see it, then maybe it's a group hallucination. If other people see it, there will be mass panic. If no one can stop it..." His eyes went wide.

I nudged his injured leg with my foot. He screamed, then inhaled deeply, gathering himself. "Thanks."

"Anytime," I said.

"Do we sit here poking at each other's wounds until it gets in, we die, or it goes away?"

"Sounds like a normal night hanging out with you." I smirked.

"We should come up with a plan." He glanced around the room.

"I'm open to ideas. But you can't really walk. I'm losing my shit, and the only thing we have left is duct tape and a tile puller." The steady hum of the servers and the fans was deafening. "I'm exhausted and trying to formulate an answer to the question *Why did you leave your last job?* for my next interview after I get fired."

"They had an insect infestation?" Carlos suggested.

"They ran me ragged?"

"You had to work with some unsavory characters?"

"It was a hostile work environment."

Carlos laughed. "You should probably just say you are looking for a better opportunity to utilize and enhance your current skill set."

"At a company that supports my goals, which include staying alive and mostly sane."

The work cell phone started ringing. "Shit," I said.

"Don't answer," he said.

I opened the flip phone, "Help desk; this is Danni."

"This is your alarm monitoring service. We're calling about the facility on Camelback. There has been a glass break alarm on the third floor. Would you like us to dispatch police to that location?"

"I..." My eyes went to the entrance, to the window behind the massive air conditioning unit. "I'm here now."

"Do you need us to dispatch police? Are you in danger?"

"I should check the window. Can you hold on?" She was saying something, but I didn't hear it. I put the phone down.

"What is it?"

"It's the alarm company. They received a glass break alarm on this floor."

"Don't. Don't go to the window."

"I have to check," I said. It wasn't out of a sense of duty to do my job or try to keep my job. I had to know.

"Danni," he called after me. The lights dimmed and brightened rhythmically to a song I couldn't hear, the beat of which was getting faster and more frantic. I moved, transfixed, as in a trance.

"Danni, no."

I glanced back as I turned the corner at the last row of servers and out of his line of sight. His voice strained to penetrate the white noise of the datacenter, but his words no longer made sense to me. The air conditioner vibrated with activity; the machinery inside lurched and stuttered. The massive unit almost eclipsed the window entirely. The blinds swayed away from the window and back, clanging against it. I pulled one of the slats down with one finger, bending it down an inch to look outside.

216

I stepped closer, bringing my face inches from the window, squinting, looking for any light outside and not understanding why there was none. Something moved on the glass. I pulled the blinds farther apart. Then I saw it. I was looking at the underside of a moth. The glass was still intact. I released the blinds and took hold of the string, yanking hard, raising it a few short motions.

The window was covered, blocking out all light from the courtyard outside. I couldn't tell if the creature was still there on the other side of them or waiting to take form again. A spiderweb crack slowly spread from the bottom right-hand corner. The window flexed and the moths moved toward it, sensing the weakness in the window. I jumped back.

"Oh god," I whispered, knowing that no god could help me. I spun on my heels and ran down the row of servers glowing with angry amber lights. "Carlos!"

I turned the corner, running to the back of the room. He tried to stand on one leg as our eyes met. "Get in," I said.

"Get in where?"

I passed him and went to the supply cabinet. I tossed the shelves and pushed aside the office supplies from the cabinet. "Here," I said, not looking up, making room for him.

"What? No," he argued.

"The window broke. They are coming in."

"No. I'm not hiding and leaving you with that thing."

"Yes, you are," I insisted.

"No." Carlos shook his head.

I took a deep breath. I knew what had to be done. Or at least I thought I did. "Carlos, it's coming. You can't fight it with a broken ankle. You can't run. It doesn't make sense for you to fight on one leg. And we're going to need someone fast to fight them."

"That's not you." He stood on his good leg and winced as he tried to put weight on his other foot.

"You're here because of me. I roped you into this. Rudder is gone, and I have no idea what happened to Ian. I did this."

"It's not your fault," he said.

"I mean it's not entirely my fault but maybe it's my hubris. But I can do this. I can make sure my only remaining friend can walk... or, limp, out of here alive. You can't save us and maybe I can't save us either. But I can try, and I can save you. Maybe I can save me too. But I need to know that you're safe. So please, just get the fuck in the cabinet."

"What are you going to do?"

A shard of glass hit the floor, barely audible over the hum of the datacenter.

"Please, trust me. I'm going to duct tape you in, so you have air but they can't get in. Wait twenty minutes or until the fire department shows up. Then you can kick the door open. It'll be safe by then."

"No. What about you?"

"Please, just get in and let me try to fix this."

"Not like this."

"The plenum," I said.

Carlos cocked his head.

"There's room under the raised floor. I can go under the raised floor. The air there is from the AC unit. It'll filter out the halon." I had no idea if was true. But it sounded like it could be.

"The halon?" His eyes went wide with understanding.

"You can't crawl under the floor with your ankle and I can't tape myself into a cabinet."

Carlos stepped into the cabinet. I picked up the duct tape. "It's going to be okay," I said as I closed the door. It was a lie. I taped over the space between the metal cabinet door and the frame. A moth landed on the cabinet. I went faster, careful not to overlap the tape too much so Carlos could easily kick the door open. Another moth flew by my head. I didn't bother trying to bat it away. The rest of the glass crashed to the floor. I picked up the tile puller and took a fighting stance, waiting for the creature to come in.

"Come on," I challenged it. "I'm right here. Come get me."

42

Before

I TIGHTENED MY PONYTAIL, then slammed the tile puller on the floor tile next to me as moths swarmed around my head. Then I hoisted the tile up, dropping it to the side. I got down on my stomach and put my head into the void. It was dark. The space was crowded with a rat's nest of cables from years of pulling new cable and abandoning old ones. Cutting cords when they weren't needed anymore.

I was going to die because of poor datacenter management. Awesome. If anyone figured it out, I would live forever in Information Technology lore. You know you should clean up your cable; that girl died because the plenum was too full of crap. I grunted as I moved the heavy tile back. There was no room for me, no safe place.

The only thing left to do was execute the rest of my plan, even if it meant dying. But I wasn't going to let it take Carlos. It took Rudder. No more.

The room dimmed as it flooded with a horde of Black Witch Moths. I closed my eyes and waited. New plan: Do what I can, kill it, and run for my life.

Breathe, wait for it, don't panic. Don't go off too fast. Let the bitch come in, let her get comfortable. Their wings brushed my face and arms. They landed on my head and walked across my face. I breathed. This was my domain.

When I could no longer feel them flying around me, I opened my eyes. The monster stood at least eight feet tall, its body one fluttering movement. Its head brushed the ceiling. Green light pulsed in between the flapping wings. Its jagged mouth opened, emitting a piercing sound.

I clasped my ears and fell to my knees. My stomach lurched; the sheer unnatural force of it made my guts churn and my skin crawl. Voices sang out, urging me forward. The words were unrecognizable. The walls melted, the clock laughed, and my reality, my life, was a joke.

My mind reeled. My body froze. In the milliseconds that spanned millennia, I considered staying on my knees, holding out my arms and waiting for the sickly-sweet embrace of the creature. I didn't care if it would mean death or an eternity in the cavernous reaches of my broken mind, forever swimming in my insanity, wishing for the respite of death.

I dug a finger into the wound in my palm. "Ahhhhhh." I gritted my teeth. Keep it together. I've got one job: Burn it to the ground. I pushed myself up from the floor, its breath behind me as I reached for the wall, grasped the halon release lever, and pulled.

Nothing happened.

I stared dumbly at the handle. A siren shrieked out its warning. Its shadow eclipsed the lights above me. A moth landed on the handle in my hand; it flapped its wings, then became still. Thoughts crept into my mind like worms through soil. Thoughts about what people were saying, what death would feel like, and what this monster was going to do to me. I wanted to shrink, to disappear, to stop existing. I turned toward it, clenched my fists. It stooped over me, screaming when the halon cloud shot into the room.

The exit was blocked. A sick green light illuminated the room. The moths expanded away from the core of the beast, and the only way out became clear. I jumped forward into the green light. Rudder and Carlos had disappeared into this green glow; one came out, one didn't. I rolled the dice; maybe I'd survive. Maybe not.

In the green light, a man's disembodied voice calls out, "She's coding."

43

I'm FLOATING. THE WORLD is made of green light and dandelion fluff.

I'm floating above the edge of a plateau overlooking a chasm. On the ledges of the canyon walls below is nothing but me, versions of me, experiences I've had, or that I almost had. A hundred thousand iterations, moving and living their lives without making a sound, unaware of their surroundings.

I'm dead on the datacenter floor, I'm in a hospital, I'm in an office with my boss. The images are layered on top of one another, superimposed images, memories of my life. Drifting up to my ears are my own words, stupid things I've said, lies, hurtful, awful things. It's a window into the worst parts of myself. The canyon walls are lined with the personification of my negative self-talk. Ten thousand versions of me, all self-obsessed, negative, flippant, and selfish that I fear are the truest versions of myself. I jump off the plateau into the abyss, expecting to fall out of the green mist and back into the datacenter. But instead, I float to the ground at the bottom of the canyon.

The canyon floor isn't carved by a river; there's no dirt or riverbed. It's rock, but smooth and level. Unnatural sounds erupt behind me. It sounds like a mix of falling trees, wails of the grieving, and chewing—if the teeth were the size of Volkswagen Beetles and they were eating a thousand dying cows.

"Don't turn around," I tell myself as I close my eyes. "No."

My mind is reeling and trying to discredit every image, sound, and smell as a hallucination. But I know it's real. I chose this reality. I take in a deep breath and remind myself what Rudder said to me. I'm fragmented. These versions of me, they're just pieces. I force myself to look into the distance. There's more than these awful versions of myself.

Off to the side is me taping Carlos into the cabinet, knowing that I might be going off to my death. He would have died at my side if I let him, if I'd been selfish like I'd been for so long.

It looks like the bottom of the ocean, minus the water. The ground and the walls of the canyon are composed of dark rocks, and the space between the walls opens into a vast plain.

A version of me in a wedding dress, smiling and laughing at someone who isn't there. Next to her is a version of me in expensive shoes and a nice outfit.

An army's worth of variants are spaced out as far as I can see. It's like walking into a store and seeing yourself as a life-sized doll, packaged and presented as every occupation. Next to Doctor Danni is Dancer Danni next to Dead Danni next to Desktop Tech Danni. It would take a million years to see all of them, everything I've ever been and everything I could have been. I could stay here forever, without hunger or physical needs. Time doesn't exist. The wailing, crunching noise becomes a weird kind of lullaby.

The canyon walls molt like snakeskin and small tears are visible. Time may not matter here, but it's still ticking away elsewhere. A green light pulses.

I approach a variation of myself; without looking at me, she swings a diaper bag over one shoulder and bounces an invisible baby on the other hip. As I get closer, the faint green glow from the datacenter glows around her. The closer I get to her, the brighter the light and the stronger the pull. Reaching out my hand, I graze her arm. The walls of the canyon melt away.

"Where the fuck is your daddy?" she asks the crying baby girl as she bounces her up and down. She looks at the time and picks up her phone, presumably to find out where the baby's father is.

I jerk my hand back and the walls are once again black rock and unidentifiable plants. The next me is sitting behind a desk, leaning toward the monitors with an intense look on her face. I stand behind her as she taps the side of her headset, a faint green glow behind her ear. "This is Danni," she said, then listens. "Yeah, I'm working on it. The log files filled up the drive and crashed the server. I'll let you know when it's back up."

A thousand lives available to me at the touch of a finger. It is an endless warehouse of windows into other worlds, other possibilities. I could window shop for millennia, sampling life and moving on when it suited me. I entertain this idea, a new type of existence. Words came to me: "Deal with the trauma first." Someone said that to me once. I heard the echoes of all of Carlos's life lessons.

The sirens from the datacenter break through the wailing cries and falling trees. I turn. Behind me is an open portal to the datacenter; moths fall to the datacenter floor. "They're dying," I say to myself.

The opening flickers and dims, then it disappears, and the doorway through which I'd entered this world closes. I'm gripped by a searing pain as if the skin is being ripped from my body. Rudder said I needed to get out. I'm doing a real bang-up job. The only door back to the datacenter closes and I just watch as my only exit disappears.

I turn back to the horde of me, every one of them a doorway into a life. I play with the idea of choosing a successful version of myself, or maybe a happy version. If I could live a better life, a more stable, happier life, what's the harm in that?

But what happens to her, I wonder. Are they empty vessels of possibility? Or are they real, full people living lives in alternate universes? In a split second, I know I don't want the possibilities. I want my shitty life, my friends, my problems, and Erin. I have to find the me, not some version of me that may or may not exist. If I stay any longer, I won't make it out. Rudder didn't make it out. The wailing, chewing sound I heard moments or maybe years before gets closer. How long have I been here?

I run, scanning every face I pass, looking for the right one, unsure of whether I'll even know it when I see it. In the darkness, out of the corner of my eye, my body is lying on the ground. My hair covers my face.

Sometimes you just have to jump. Carlos's words echo in my mind as I approach the crumpled body. Her eyes are fixed off into the distance, seeing nothing. I brush her/our hair back behind her ear. She's traumatized and broken but alive because she's a survivor.

I found the right iteration, the version of me that exists in the world I know and formed by all my choices. Flawed, imperfect, and struggling, but still breathing. A small light emanates from her like the others, but it's dim. I lie on the ground next to her and place my hands on either side of her head, pulling her into me.

A hot, humid gust of air hits my back. The shriek of Karathala's foot soldier is so loud, the inside of my ear rattles. Its shadow envelops me. I squeeze my eyes closed and hold my limp body on the ground, immobile and unresponsive. Pulling her faint glow to me, I say, "I'm here." The green gaseous smokey vapor; I breathe it in and the black rock walls of the abyss dissolve into green mist.

"She's coding," a disembodied voice says. A searing pain like a hot knife stabbing me in the chest rocks my body as I lose consciousness.

44

After

FOUR PEOPLE IN SCRUBS lift my body off the floor and then drop me on a gurney. I have an over-the-shoulder view from outside my body, like a video game. My head flops to one side as they push my body down a hallway.

"Where are you taking me?" I yell. No one turns or answers me. I follow, tethered to my body, panicking that I took too long to save myself but just long enough to watch myself die.

"She's coding," says the short guy in scrubs as we enter an exam room.

"Charging," the other says as they grab paddles from the crash cart. I've crashed like a server. I'm down.

"Awesome. They're going to reboot me," I joke.

The paddles go to my chest, my body lurches, nothing happens. They wait and watch.

"Do it again," I whisper. They repeat the process.

"Charging," a nurse says. "Clear."

Electricity jolts through my body, but there's no change on the monitor. I feel a tug at my core, a tingle. Ivy watches through the window.

I know who she is, I know what this place is. It comes rushing back.

I just got here, but the last few weeks play like flashcards. I need to get out. I need to be alive again. My memory clicks into place, and I remember the water, the ground shaking, shattering glass, the halon gas all around me. If I had muscles, they'd be tensed as I'm overcome by the intensity of emotion. Angry, morose, grief-stricken, and frustrated to the point where I just want to fall to the floor and stay down.

The smoke alarm blares into the chaotic room, the sprinkler system opens, and water rushes into the hallway and flows into the room. People chatter in surprise. Just like in the datacenter when the halon went off, except it was gas instead of water.

They shock me again, the floor shakes, the counters shake, the pictures on the wall shake and plants fall off the nurses' station, breaking onto the floor. Windows shatter. Smoke fills the room. The green glow is all around us.

Behind me are two open portals, the datacenter in one and the chasm in the other. In one, I'm suspended in the air, surrounded by the light as moths fall to the floor and the foot soldier crumbles with them. My body drops to the ground, where I stayed until the fire department and the EMTs arrived to assess my condition. Unable to wake me, one of them smirked at the other as he cracked open smelling salts and waved them under my nose. My nostrils burn, I inhale deeply, my chest rises off the ground, and my lungs ache. I lunge at him, eyes wide, and out of my mind. I bit him. "Karathala comes for us! Her foot soldier cannot be killed." The paramedics restrain and sedate me and the portal to the datacenter goes dark.

The lights go out. The room's emergency lighting and generator kicks on. The medical team is unfazed. Commotion erupts in an adjacent room as flames erupt from a laser printer. I laugh. "Fucking printer." I'm watching it unfold, momentarily distracted from my lifeless body.

The portals shrink as they begin to close. In the second portal, the foot soldier stands over my motionless body still lying on the canyon floor. It lingers, then crouches down next to me. When its mouth opens, I brace myself for its piecing shriek, but instead, it hums. Its forelegs reach up as if in prayer and it sways back and forth. The portal is the size of a dinner plate. It reaches into its body, produces a thick, fleshy caterpillar. He kneels and thrusts his foreleg down into my chest, burying the caterpillar there. My body rocks up off the ground and then the portals close.

"Again," one of the doctors says. My attention returns.

Light flickers above my body. A shimmer of green and the peak of a moth's wing unfurls from my back. I was the pupa in a cocoon and now I'm changed. I'm reborn from the void as an inhumane thing. The monster is a part of me and only one choice: stay dead or move forward. I don't take time to consider it.

"Clear," they say. The monitor beeps in a steady rhythm and I black out.

45

After

"Hɪ Dᴀɴɴɪ. Hᴏᴡ'ʀᴇ ʏᴏᴜ today?" The doctor smiles as he shuffles papers on his desk.

"I'm alright. Not great, but I'm working on it." This time, I can manage brief eye contact. The walls and floor are still.

"Last time we talked, it'd only been a few days since the medical emergency you had. Can you tell me about that?" He looks up from my file.

"I still don't remember everything." I choose my words carefully; it's not really a lie. I don't have all the answers, but I'm not going to find them in here.

"You've made an amazing recovery."

"Yeah, that's what they keep telling me." What he doesn't say is that I'm a medical mystery. The doctors can't find a cause for my heart stopping. If I told them the cause, they'd keep me here indefinitely. The change was a traumatic event for my mind and body. The moth larva that was planted in my chest transformed me. Into what? I don't know, but I'm grappling with the reality of what that means for my identity and my life.

"You submitted the release request a few days ago." He scans the page, looking for the date.

"Three days, as of this afternoon. I've gained a lot of clarity in the last few weeks."

"Can you tell me what clarity means to you?"

This is a trickier question. When I got here, I felt inhuman and detached from myself. Now, I know I'm something other, not fully human, and somehow, I'm more connected to myself than I've been in years. "I'm sleeping better. I don't wake up screaming."

"No nightmares?"

"Some, but different. They are... manageable." Every night, I'm back in the chasm. It looks different on each visit, but it's the same place. I'm learning to navigate it, to explore it.

"What else does it mean?"

"I'm fragmented. Everything that's happened in my life, all the trauma, it shattered me into pieces, and I learned how to survive in pieces. But for the longest time, they never fit together. I let other people tell me which pieces of me were acceptable and learned to hide the rest. Now, I know that all the pieces are okay, and they do belong together. I've got the rest of my life to figure out how."

"What's the biggest piece?"

I tilt my head, giving the question the consideration it deserves. "It's the common thread. I know how to survive, and I've used my brain, my body, and whatever I had available to me to survive. I don't know that I ever stopped to give myself credit for my successes because I was so busy trying to recover from my shortcomings and failures. I'm rambling. I guess the biggest piece, which the real question is *Do I know who I am?* The answer is that I'm a work in progress, but I have a foundation now. And it's that I'm capable of things I didn't know were possible."

"I like that answer."

I glance at my hands. They're clean; the wounds have closed. The only thing left is to see how bad the scars will be.

"Do you have plans for your living situation?"

"It's been a month; my rent is past due. They likely will start the eviction process soon. I'll have time to pack up my stuff and I'm going to see if my friend still has a spare room."

"You haven't talked to them about it?"

"His phone's been disconnected for a while. He's been between jobs. And I don't have email in here."

"Is there a backup plan if that falls through?"

"I'm going to take it as it comes and figure it out."

The doctor makes notes in my file. As he closes it, he looks up at me and smiles. "You've come a long way and I'm glad you're starting to give yourself credit for that. When you're discharged, they'll give you a prescription for a thirty-day supply of your medication, and a prescription for a refill. You'll need to find a new doctor before that runs out."

I nod, standing up to shake his hand.

"Bye, Danni. Take care."

"Thanks, Doc." I leave his office for the last time, shutting the door behind me without touching it.

"You got everything?" Ivy asks in a bubbly voice that sounds forced.

"Yeah." I reach into my pocket to check for the thirty-day supply of antianxiety medication they gave me and the prescription. If I don't have a job in a month, I won't be able to fill it. But that's a problem for next month. Calm falls over me knowing I can walk out the doors, find a new job, put my life back together, and find Erin.

"I still haven't been able to find anything out about Erin. Something about medical privacy laws, blah blah blah," she says almost as if she knew I was going to ask again.

"Thanks for trying to break the law for me." I give her a weak smile. The ache in my heart won't go away. She would've told me to take care of myself, get better, then come find her. So that's what I did.

"You sure you don't want to call anyone?" Ivy asks for the third time.

"No one to call. I'll be okay." My belongings include a few dollars, enough for bus fare to get home. I avoid eye contact, crossing my arms over my chest. It's not the room I shared with Erin, although it looks identical.

The orderly who body slammed me gives me a beaming smile as he opens the outside doors for me. I'd like to elbow him in the gut as I walk past; instead, I smile back. I blink as I walk into the blazing afternoon sun, then cover my eyes with my hand. A short bark comes from across the parking lot and a blur of fur runs toward me.

"Britters?" I call to my dog. As she reaches me, I crouch down on the sidewalk in front of the hospital to hold her. The unruly ball of excitement and fur licks my face and my hands as I try to wipe away tears.

"Hey, stranger." Carlos waves at me from the parking lot. His broken ankle is in a boot, and he leans his weight on a cane. I pick up Britters and walk to him.

"Hey, old man. They finally gave you a cane, huh?"

"Yeah, I could have gone without. But it's a good look, right?" He gestures at himself with his free hand.

"It is. I'm so happy to see you. Thanks for taking care of Britters and for coming to get me." Carlos hands me her leash. I set her down, clip it to her collar, then give him a big hug.

"We have a lot to catch up on." He glances back, then turns to me. I have at least two dozen questions for him and one of them is how long he had known where I was and why he didn't call. Then I see why Carlos checked behind him. A tall man, with raven black hair and storm blue eyes, walks from behind an SUV.

"What—" The sentence isn't fully formed, and I have many more questions for Carlos.

"Well, that's one way to do things," Carlos sighs and pulls out a cigarette.

"What is Ian doing here?" I don't bother to whisper as I don't care if he can hear me.

"Hi, Danni," he says.

"I thought you were dead." I furrow my brow and stare him down.

He shrugs and smiles. "You sound disappointed."

"Just hear him out," Carlos says.

"I'm not ready for this." I ignore Ian and talk to Carlos.

"Just hear their offer?" he says.

"Offer? Whose offer?"

"They offered me a job. The company that Ian works for."

"You're going to be a security guard?" I shake my head, not grasping what Carlos was trying to tell me.

"No, I don't do field work. That's part of the agreement." Carlos shakes his head furiously.

"The company I work for would like to extend an offer to you. I have a contract ready if you'd like to review it," Ian says, pulling a folder from the messenger bag on his shoulder.

"You left us to die after talking to your company." I gauge his reaction. He smiles in response. "Why would I work for a company that left us to die? Rudder died. What kind of people do you work for?"

"I think you'll find the benefits package rather enticing." Ian smiles as he pulls a stack of pages held together with a binder clip from his shoulder bag. "Also, the firm took care of your rent while you were recuperating."

"Is one of the benefits that they cover funeral expenses after they leave you to die?"

"We can reach out to Legal about adding an addendum," he says with a wide grin and I'm unsure if that's a joke or a serious response.

"No. Absolutely not." I throw my hands in the air.

"Hey, Danni, it's a good offer. Just hear him out," Carlos says.

"Carlos, I just want to go home. I'd like to spend a night in my bed and then not deal with this bullshit," I plead. "What about Rudder?" I say the last part in a whisper.

"Do you trust me?" Carlos asks. He gives Ian an apologetic look and a shrug.

"Good, so we're going?" I turn to leave.

"We're prepared to cover the cost of your medical treatment," Ian says.

I stop and do a half turn. "If?"

"Just sign the non-disclosure agreement." He shrugs as if it's no big deal. "And hear us out."

"If I keep my mouth shut, the company will pay? For everything?"

"And we can talk," Carlos looks at me and then Ian.

"Yeah. If you sign the NDA, we can talk and I can give you a check which will cover the balance owed plus a little."

"You tell me everything and they pay for everything?" I ask, insisting on clarity.

"'Everything' is a broad term. I can tell you what I know. I don't know everything."

"Show me the check," I say.

He pulls it from the outer pocket of his shoulder bag, removes it from an envelope, and holds it up. It's more zeros than I've ever seen on a check. I try to keep my eyes from getting as big as saucers.

I narrow my eyes at him, trying to decide if it's a trick and what he's holding back. "You signed this?" I ask Carlos.

"Yeah." He nods.

"And you read it?"

"Yes, I read it."

I reach out a hand. "Just the NDA."

Ian grins and hands it to me with a pen. I scribble my name at the bottom, content that if Carlos read it, it's okay. Especially if they're going to foot the bill for the hospital. As far as I was concerned, it was their bill as much as it was mine.

"Okay, tell me what you know."

"I work for the StellarWinds Firm as a monitor. We're a jack-of-all-trades security company, from physical security to things a little more... intangible. The site you were working at was my first solo field assignment. It was supposed to be a low activity location to ease newbies in. And it was, before..." He gives me an accusatory look.

"Before I got there."

"You called the creature to you. We don't know how you were able to do it. The site was dormant for a long time, and it shouldn't be possible."

"Creature? You don't know what it was?" I say to him. I know I'm pushing buttons, but I'm in a button-mashing kind of mood.

He exhales heavily. "No, not really. It's one we haven't seen before."

"It doesn't sound like you know a lot. And the door?" I watch his face for reactions.

"What door?" he says, drawing his eyebrows together.

There's comfort in that fact that there are things I know that he doesn't. I want to know everything he knows and keep a few things to myself.

"Why did they leave us to die? How were you able to just walk away?" I say, my fist clenching at my side.

"They weren't. What I said was true: They were sending in a team. I miscalculated, thinking I could get out because you'd moved to a different room. My timing was a bit off."

"Then how did you get out?"

"That's... complicated. I had to create an escape hatch," he says. "It's an opening, like if you could pull open the wall between dimensions. It's difficult to explain. Also, it's a very unpleasant way to travel. It feels like you're having your skin ripped off." He hesitates. "Can we have this conversation somewhere more private?"

"Why me?" I ask, ignoring his question. "Why do they want me to work for them? I'm the one that fucked everything up, let a creature loose, and got my friend killed!"

"You're also the one that took care of it. You're the one that made a plan, saving yourself and Carlos," Ian says, then looks to Carlos, who shrugs and nods at me.

"It's true," Carlos says. "It was your idea that saved us."

"You made it out and kept your sanity intact." Ian says.

"*Intact* is a generous word. It's been touch-and-go." I grasp the pill bottle in my pocket to reassure myself it is still there. "You knew I was here and your company left me, just like they left us at the datacenter?"

"Danni, you needed to be here. And we didn't know if you'd be okay after what you'd been through. Also, if we'd explained any of this to you, they wouldn't have released you because you'd have sounded even more insane."

"I don't think this is a good idea. Can I just have a few days to figure things out and sleep in my own bed?" I look at Carlos with pleading eyes. I also want to talk to Carlos without Ian listening.

"We can go over the benefits and retirement package before you sign," he offers.

"Look, I'm sure it's a good offer and the benefits are amazing." I walk away.

"We know where Erin is," Ian says. "Anderson is a pretty common last name, and if she's unlisted, you're going to need our help."

"Who's Erin?" Carlos squints at me.

I freeze in my tracks, pivot around to face him. "If you could find her, then I'm sure I can find her too." My face is hot. My heart pounds in my chest and a tingle creeps up my spine. A breeze blows through the parking lot. I steady myself and it dies down as quickly as it began. How does he know about Erin? What else do they know?

"Fine. Let's talk."

Acknowledgements

This book wouldn't have been possible without the constant support of my husband Damian. You are my anchor, my home, and my dearest friend. Your unwavering support, love, and belief in me have been the driving force behind this endeavor. You have always seen me as an equal, stood by me through my difficulties, and encouraged me to pursue my dreams. Your humor, understanding, and unconditional love have carried me through the toughest of times. You see the whole of me, even when I was in pieces, and love me anyway. I'm forever grateful for you.

To my incredible writing group friends, Amanda Morris, Tracy McBride, and Leslie Groeneveld, who have been with me every step of the way. Your patience, support, and willingness to listen to me talk endlessly about this book throughout its various stages have been invaluable. Your insightful feedback and encouragement have pushed me to grow as a writer. Thank you for being my sounding boards, my cheerleaders, and my friends.

There's always a teacher to thank, and this is no exception. This book wouldn't exist without the teachers who encouraged me along the way. Thank you to Ms. Faith Risolo-Umlauf. You believed I was capable of more than I thought possible and wouldn't let me give up on myself when I thought giving up was the only option. You encouraged my curiosity and valued my opinions on literature. We disagreed on whether Jay Gatsby was romantic (you for, I against), but something

I said about the *Scarlet Letter* you loved so much you wrote it down and said you were stealing it. While it may have been such a small thing, it made an impression on me and gave me a boost that maybe I had something worthwhile to say. You encouraged my love of the written word, and I will be forever grateful. And thank you to Mr. Leavenworth Wheeler who told me that I had a gift for writing in the eighth grade. Teachers are one of our greatest treasures, they invest in our future with their words, and rarely get to know the impact they've had.

Thank you to all my beta readers: Jason, Hilary, Robin, and others. Thanks to several editors I've worked with along the way and everything you've contributed to this book. I truly had a village of editors and beta readers. A big thanks to Susan Helene Gottfried and Olivia Batker Pritzker. Your feedback has been heard and appreciated. This book wouldn't be the same without them. There are too many people to name.

And to Ellen, you have my deep gratitude and love. You always listened patiently, provided invaluable insight, and taught me how to put all the pieces back together. I'm who I am today because of you.

To all those mentioned here and to everyone who has supported me on this journey, whether through kind words, encouragement, or a listening ear, thank you from the bottom of my heart. Your belief in me and your presence in my life have made all the difference.

K. S. Allred lives in the sprawling desert hellscape of Phoenix, Arizona with her husband and their neurotic, ever-entertaining dog, Freddie. As a fourth-generation native of the state, she has a deep connection to the unique landscapes and rich cultural heritage that Arizona has to offer. The desert holds a certain allure for her, providing a backdrop that is both harsh and mesmerizing. The vastness of the landscape mirrors her boundless imagination, and it serves as a constant reminder of the resilience and adaptability that is necessary in both the natural and creative worlds.

When she's not immersed in the world of writing, K. S. Allred works as a systems engineer in the field of Information Technology. As a mechanical keyboard enthusiast, she finds joy in the tactile experience of typing on these unique devices, appreciating the blend of technology and artistry that they embody. In her downtime, you can often find her lost in the click-clack symphony of her favorite keyboard, crafting new stories, or lurking in her favorite keyboard Subreddits.

Through her writing, K. S. Allred invites readers to embark on captivating journeys, where they can escape the ordinary and discover extraordinary worlds. Her unique blend of creativity, technical expertise, and a profound love for her desert home allows her to craft stories about healing from trauma with vulnerability, authenticity, and a deep understanding of the complexity of the human experience.

Did you enjoy this book?

You can help!

Reviews are one of the most powerful ways to get this book seen by people who like the same books you read. As a new author with only one book, it makes a huge impact. If you have a moment to provide feedback, no matter how brief, I'd really appreciate it. You can scan this QR code to go straight to the Goodreads page.

Want More?

The second book in The Plenum Chronicles is coming. If you want to be the first to know about it, or the opportunity to join the advance reader team, sign up for the newsletter. You'll get an exclusive sneak peak of upcoming books, bonus content, and pictures of my dog. I'll never sell your email address or send you spam. Scan the QR code to sign up!

The Plenum Chronicles Book 2

Coming Soon